BEARLY DEPARTED

BEARLY DEPARTED

MEG MACY

KENSINGTON BOOKS
www.kensingtonbooks.com

KENSINGTON BOOKS are published by

Kensington Publishing Corp.
119 West 40th Street
New York, NY 10018

All Kensington titles, imprints, and distributed lines are available at special quantity discounts for bulk purchases for sales promotion, premiums, fundraising, educational, or institutional use.

Special book excerpts or customized printings can also be created to fit specific needs. For details, write or phone the office of the Kensington Sales Manager: Kensington Publishing Corp., 119 West 40th Street, New York, NY 10018. Attn. Sales Department. Phone: 1-800-221-2647.

Kensington and the K logo Reg. U.S. Pat. & TM Off.

eISBN-13: 978-1-4967-0964-6
eISBN-10: 1-4967-0964-0
First Kensington Electronic Edition: June 2017

ISBN-13: 978-1-4967-0963-9
ISBN-10: 1-4967-0963-2
First Kensington Trade Paperback Printing: June 2017

10 9 8 7 6 5 4 3 2 1

Printed in the United States of America

To Mom,
with love and
a big bear hug

ACKNOWLEDGMENTS

Thanks to my wonderful editor, Wendy McCurdy, and her assistant, Norma Perez-Hernandez, for helping to make *Bearly Departed* as shamelessly adorable as possible. To my sister Kris, who suggested buying a Paddington Bear at Harrods on our trip to England, to my mom, who added to my teddy bear collection, and . . . to El and Nari. You know why.

Chapter 1

By this time in my life, at thirty-one, I had planned to be a happy suburban wife chauffeuring three kids and the dog in a van. That plan had not exactly panned out.

Instead I was single and channeling my love for children into managing my parents' teddy bear shop in Silver Hollow, Michigan. I consoled myself with the knowledge that I could make kids happy, helping them choose a best friend, and then send them home. No tears, no temper tantrums, only happy faces and squishy hugs for their new toys.

"Hey, lady? Catch!"

A little boy tossed a bear, which I grabbed before it bounced off the ceiling fan. "You can call me Ms. Sasha," I said, and placed the bear in a bin chock-full of other brown bears. "Let's not play catch, though."

He flashed a mischievous grin and grabbed a white bear. This time, I gave him an *I dare you* stare. The little rascal squinted at me, gauging if I was serious, and then settled for swinging the bear around by one ear. That didn't worry me.

Our bears were nearly indestructible—depending on the abuse, of course.

"Daniel John," his mother said, "put that back. We're trying to choose one for your sister Sarah's birthday."

"Actually, he may have chosen the perfect bear for her—it's a polar bear," I said, smiling at Daniel. "That size fits any of our clothing, like the purple floral dress with the matching sandals."

Three racks included a display of shoes and fun accessories such as skateboards, balls, and sports items, tea sets, tables, and chairs, to fit all sizes of our bears. I'd convinced my dad that last-minute urges to purchase an outfit or toy for a gift bear would boost sales. He was skeptical until the profit figures soared within three months.

"Yes, how sweet." The woman took the bear from her son, holding it up to stare into its eyes. "Sarah loves the polar bears at the zoo. Sarah would love the purple dress and the sandals. And that straw hat! She could decorate it with tiny flowers, too."

"Certainly. I can ring you up whenever you're ready."

Meanwhile her son had scampered up the wide stairs in the central round tower of the Silver Bear Shop. We called the tower the Rotunda. Customers always gasped in delight while they admired our Parade of Bears along the inner curved wall, displayed in special five-shelf acrylic boxes. The Bears Around the World each held a tiny flag, and the Branded Bears from Gund, Boyds, Steiff, and Lloyd ranged from oldest to newest.

"I'm so glad we stopped in." The woman glanced around for her son and checked her watch. "Daniel John! You have a dentist's appointment, and we have to get you new shoes for school. If you're not down here in three seconds . . ."

"I'll go up and see where he is," I offered, since my sister had wandered in from the office. Maddie could handle swiping the customer's credit card and packing up her purchases.

I figured the kid would be safe upstairs jumping on "Mr.

Silver." Not the biggest stuffed bear in the nation but, at eight feet, giant enough for children to crawl over his fluffy legs or have their photo taken sitting in his lap.

I took the shallow stairs two at a time. First I glanced into the side room with the array of "profession" bears dressed in costumes—doctor, nurse, lawyer, and teacher—which lined the wall display shelves. The boy wasn't there. In the loft playroom, the plastic tea set, table, and chairs, plus several well-loved crochet teddy bears, were scattered across the carpet. Daniel landed on poor Mr. Silver with an audible "oof."

"Your mom is calling you. Time to go, and thanks for visiting!"

He scrambled to his feet. "Who's that?" Daniel pointed to a framed photo on the wall.

"My grandfather, who inspired my dad to open this shop."

"He looks old."

Daniel ran for the stairs before I could laugh. Kids—rascals or angels—were always honest. In the photograph, eighty-year-old T. R. Silverman posed with the bears he sewed by hand for his children, nieces, nephews, and the local neighbors.

"Miss you, Gramps." I quickly tidied up before heading back down to my sister, who manned the counter. "That was a nice sale, wasn't it?"

"Polar bear, clothes, and a small bear for the brother. Best yet this week." Maddie squinted at the cell phone in hand. "When was the last time you talked to Mom or Dad?"

"Uh. It's been a while."

"I sent a text to Mom on Monday. Almost three days, and she hasn't answered yet."

I shrugged. "Maybe they're busy."

Madeline and I didn't look at all like siblings. I cleared five-ten, wore my blond hair pulled back, and forced myself to swim, walk, and pedal to counterbalance my true passion for cookies. At five-two, with her dark pixie-styled hair, pale skin, and brown eyes, she embodied Audrey Hepburn's waif-like sweetness. She could wear anything and look cute, stylish, or hot. Today she wore a red cardigan over a white tee, red capris with matching espadrille sandals, and dangling earrings that flashed a rainbow of tiny seed beads.

Fashion with flair. My silver metallic shirt was wrinkled, like I'd slept in it, over blue twill pants and sneakers. Maybe I needed a shopping intervention.

"Mom always texts me about what she's doing," Maddie said, clearly worried. "And I'm swamped, so I haven't paid that much attention like I should."

"We both have been swamped."

"And you still haven't found that file of invoices," she reminded me.

I groaned. Maddie, far more organized than me, was a stickler for filing everything that wasn't nailed down. By contrast, I was always misplacing things. My keys, my cell phone, the staff schedule—which didn't include Will Taylor, our company's salesman and PR expert, who kept his own hours. He gave me the willies. Pun intended. But Maddie kept track of his comings and goings for the most part.

I caught a glimpse of two large SUVs pulling into the parking lot. A gaggle of little girls, adorable in their Girl Scout Brownie vests, tumbled out into the sunshine and then lined up behind two leaders. I waved my sister back behind the counter.

"Better stay put, Mads. The tour's here."

"I've got a ton of work, and a half-finished post for Facebook about the teddy bear picnic on Monday. See this adorable photo?"

She held up her cell phone. Two teddy bears sat on a red-checkered cloth, a teapot between them, with china cups and plates, and a tiny bear peeping out of the wicker hamper. My sister was a whiz on social media, posting photos, drawings she made, memes with bears—toys and real animals—on the shop's Web site, Twitter feed, Facebook page, Pinterest, you name it. Über-talented with pen and ink, watercolor, whatever she put her mind to do.

"Shamelessly adorable. I gotta run, though. I'm starting to wonder if we need to hire a full-time sales assistant."

"That would get Will's blood boiling." Maddie frowned. "He wants all our sales reports in time for the meeting tonight. He's already moaning and groaning again about staff—"

"Wait—what meeting?"

"Didn't you get his e-mail? Or his text message?"

I retrieved my phone and swiped it, but the screen didn't light up. Dead battery. Again. Maddie grinned while I scrabbled under the counter for the charger and plugged it in. Then I texted an order to Fresh Grounds, the local coffee shop and small bakery. Will had been gone for three weeks back east, doing who knows what. I loathed his frequent complaints whenever he returned to the office. The peace and quiet during his absence had been heavenly.

"He better not spring another stupid idea on us," I said.

"Let's hope he didn't convince Dad to cut jobs. You know he's been wanting that."

"Over my dead body."

Chapter 2

I rushed outside to greet the tour guests. Warm rays of sun bathed my face, although the early September heat would soon overtake the day. This weekend, the Labor Day holiday meant a parade through the village, our teddy bear picnic event, and extra hours at the shop. I breathed fresh air deep into my lungs. That braced me for my other job as tour guide, showing off my parents' dream-come-true business to seniors, children, or a range of ages.

"Welcome to the Silver Bear Shop and Factory." I flashed my brightest smile at the two dozen giggling, squirming Brownies. "Looks like you're ready to have fun, ladies! Stay on the painted paw prints—see the stones set in the path? Follow me."

Luckily, the troop leaders kept the eager young girls under control. We strolled beneath the covered walkway between the shop and factory, where purple clematis entwined the white posts supporting the roof. The lush green lawn against the garden's colorful flowers made for a pretty setting. The building interior wouldn't offer visitors that same serenity, however, given its rough wooden walls and beamed ceiling.

"Gather around in a half circle. Eyes on me! One, two, three," I counted slowly, and then pushed a stray blond hair out of my eyes. The troop quieted down after the last two girls stopped poking each other. "Before we head into the factory, listen to the story of my grandfather, T. R. Silverman. Can anyone tell me his first name? I'll give you a hint."

When I held up a brown bear, all the girls shouted, "Teddy!"

"Yes. He was named after President Theodore Roosevelt. Grandpa T. R. loved to sew stuffed bears for his family and the neighbors' children. Times were hard during the Depression. Many people didn't have jobs, and some didn't have enough to eat. They couldn't afford toys for birthdays or Christmas. So Grandpa T. R. cut the teddy bears' fabric from old feed sacks and sewed the pieces together. Then he stuffed them with cotton and gave them as gifts. Just inside the door, we'll see three original bears."

With that, I opened the factory door wide. The troop leaders kept the girls in two half circles so they could view the display case. I pointed to the closest bear.

"That patched one was my dad's, and he passed it to me. My younger sister didn't get a chance to play with Patches, though. His head had come loose. Over here in this display box—remember, follow the tracks!" I pointed to the painted paw prints. "These are my grandpa's tools. Scissors, needles, and all the thread, plus a sample of the burlap feed sacks he used. Can anyone guess how he used the corduroy fabric?"

One girl's hand shot up. "For the nose?"

"Good guess! That and the paw pads. Today we use a sturdy felt."

"What did your grandpa use for stuffing?" one girl asked.

"His very first bears had straw or corn husks, but they tended to get wet and moldy. Then he switched to cotton. Let me tell you how he started working at twelve years old. You've all seen the Quick Mix factory, right?"

Several piped up with, "It's near our school," and, "Behind our playground!"

"The girls wrote letters to Quick Mix asking for a tour, like we did here," one leader said. "We also visited the city offices and took part in a flag-raising ceremony. After marching in the parade on Monday, the girls will earn their community badge."

"And they earned money to buy a large teddy bear for our elementary school auction," the second leader said. "The profits will go to help the Wags and Whiskers pet shelter."

"Our company would love to donate a second bear for the auction." I ignored the fact that Will would rant against that idea, since he'd shot down the last chance we had to participate in a charity function. "Let's begin the tour, but please stay behind the railing at all times. We want you to stay safe at all times, girls. Each section shows the production process, assembling, stuffing, and then selling them in our shop next door."

"My mom says they're expensive," one girl said.

I smiled. Our teddy bears lasted three times longer than cheaper stuffed animals due to quality controls and a careful manufacturing process. Mentioning that fact seemed pointless, however. The troop came for a tour, not to hear a sales pitch.

We stopped at the fabric storage area, where the long rolls of fur in various colors were stacked on shelves. "We prefer realistic colors for our bears," I said. "White for polar bears, black, silver, and brown ranging from light tan to the darkest brown."

"Why are there silver bears?" The girl pushed up her glasses with a squint. A leader shot her a warning look for speaking up a second time, but I smiled.

"The Mexican grizzly bear had a grayish-white coat, although they're now thought to be extinct. Because of Grandpa T. R. Silverman, we used 'Silver' for our business name." I led them along the path until we stopped at the cutting machine.

"This is where our staff cuts the fabric. We stack the fur in alternating layers, fuzzy side up against fuzzy side down, and so on. The dies are like cookie cutters in the shape of arms, legs, torsos, and heads."

"What kind of fur are the bears made from?" one leader asked.

"Our most expensive bears are mohair, which is shorn from long-haired goats and woven into cloth before it's dyed, and also alpaca pelts. But we use synthetic fur for most of our bears. The hydraulic press machine cuts through all of the layers at tremendous pressure." I pointed to the cutting machine. "That's my uncle. He runs the factory side of the business founded by my father."

I didn't mention the dangers of operating the cutting press. Uncle Ross, who was busy stacking layers, lost part of two fingers five years ago, but refused to admit his carelessness. He resembled a sailing captain with grizzled gray hair, a bushy beard, and the navy corduroy cap he always wore. Tall and thin, almost skeletal at sixty-three, he favored Hawaiian shirts and khaki pants with plenty of pockets; he wore dock shoes without socks, summer and winter, as if he'd just stepped off a sailboat. Uncle Ross deliberately ignored the kids. I couldn't remember a time when he didn't act gruff, like an ornery bear woken from hibernation.

"From here, two of our staff work as a team on bears throughout the stations, trading them to check quality," I said, and drew the girls forward to the next area. Sewing machines lined up in several rows. "Say hello to Deon and Pete."

The girls chimed a greeting in unison. Pete waved, slouched as usual, hair half in his face. Deon didn't notice; he worked fast, wearing earbuds and tapping his foot in rhythm to his rap music, so focused on packing an order into a big box. I drew the girls to the next team, where Harriet and Joan sat at their sewing machines—one sewing ears on a white bear's head, the other sewing limbs on a silver bear. Lois and Flora were hand-sewing the eyes of their tan bears.

"Standards in the United States are very strict. The bears' eyes have to be secure to avoid any choking hazard—"

"Ach–choo!" A leader sneezed into her elbow. "I'm sorry."

"Tiny bits of fur, threads, or fluff always float around in the air," I said, half in apology, "although we try to keep it down with an air filtration system."

"How many bears do you make?" one girl asked.

"Around sixty to seventy each week." If things didn't break down, I thought to myself, since one of the sewing machines had gone haywire last week. "Each team takes their finished pieces to the stuffing machine. Our tiniest bears are soft, with-out the pin and lock washers on our larger bears. That's what allows a bear's arms and legs to move."

"But how would a washer make them move?" several girls asked at once.

I pointed to the joint of my index finger. "Everyone hold up their hand and then wiggle your fingertip. Pin and lock washers are sort of like the 'bones' inside your finger. We can't put them into our tiniest bears, since there's not much room. But our larger bears can lift their arms to hug you back," I said with a smile. "Now, the torso is the last part to finish. Here's the stuffing machine, but please stay behind the ropes."

Two girls wrinkled their noses. "It stinks!" The troop all convulsed into loud laughter, and I joined them.

"It's been oiled recently. Once a worker places the unstuffed bear on the nozzle, they press that pedal near the floor—it fills the toy at a fast rate, faster than a speeding car. They have to make sure the bear is stuffed the same throughout, which is tricky. The seams might burst if the bear is too full, or it might feel limp and squishy with too little fiber filling."

Lois, Flora, Harriet, and Joan waved at the girls. "Why can't each of them sew the same thing? Like one all the arms, and the other all legs," one leader asked.

"Too boring," Flora said with a hearty laugh.

I nodded. "It also ensures a quality product. They check and recheck each other's work, though. The very last parts the team sews are the tags, using a ladder stitch, right under the tail." Many of the girls giggled, and I heard a few whispered "bear butts" before the leader hushed them. "Then we attach the Silverman Bear Factory cardstock tag to the left ear with a plastic tab."

Another girl's hand shot into the air. "Will you let us stuff a bear?"

"No, I'm sorry." I fought a frown. Although one of our competitors allowed kids to stuff their toys and made three times the profits we did, we couldn't afford the extra insurance. "Let's go see our hospital and surgery center. Follow the bear tracks!"

The girls eagerly surged forward. Everyone oohed and aahed over the "hospital" corner. Two wooden shelving units with scalloped red and white awnings each held bears in soft paper gowns lying on padded beds. An adorable bear dressed in green scrubs and a mask stood ready to operate on one bear lying on a table for surgery.

"How sweet," a leader said. "Poor things!"

"We guarantee our toys' health," I said. "For a nominal fee plus shipping, we make any necessary repairs and return the bears to their owners. This bear had to be retrieved from a Florida swamp. Unfortunately, the alligator thought it was real."

Several girls gasped. "Oh no!"

"We sewed a new leg on without any trouble, so he's like new again." I herded the girls and leaders into the largest part of the building, where hundreds of plastic bins marched in rows holding bears from the largest to smallest sizes. "Guess how many bears are kept here."

The troop seemed awed by the various bears all wearing silver satin bows. "A hundred bears," one girl guessed. "Ten thousand," another said.

I smiled, wishing we could sell ten thousand in a year. "There's about three thousand. We take orders online besides what's in the shop, pack them, and ship them to anywhere in the world. How about this bear to sell at the auction for the pet shelter?" The girls squealed when I plucked a large twenty-four-inch silver bear from a bin.

"Thank you so much." The troop leader selected a light brown bear from the eighteen-inch-size bin. "We'll buy this one as a second bear for the auction."

The leaders shooed the troop out the door, back under the walkway, to our shop. "Girls, you need to be on your best behavior. It's time to choose your own bear. Pick out the five-dollar size, any color you like."

I followed the last straggler into the shop. "Do you make really teeny tiny bears?" a girl asked. "I'd like one for my doll-house."

"We only take special orders for miniature versions," I said gravely. "They have to be made entirely by hand. That's why they're quite expensive."

"Like ten dollars?"

"More like seventy-five to a hundred dollars or more. How about asking someone in your family, like a grandma or aunt, to sew one for your dollhouse?"

The kid's face brightened at that. Better to raise a little hope than disappoint. She joined the other girls near the bins holding the smallest bears in white, silver, black, brown, pink, purple, mint green, and yellow. My parents had decided when they first opened the shop that only the smallest would be nonrealistic shades.

Maddie calculated the sale in a receipt book, added tax, noted our donation, and accepted the leader's check for the other bears. The girls seemed pleased and happy when I led the troop out to the parking lot. Eighteen of our smallest bears plus a larger one made a nice sale. Especially for a Thursday. Only Will Taylor would complain. He was convinced these tours were useless.

Speak of the devil.

Will stood outside the door and watched the troop leaders herd the girls, each carrying a silver bag clutched tight, to the SUVs. While his ego was as big as Robert Downey Jr.'s and Matthew McConaughey's combined, he was nowhere near as handsome as either film star. His dark gelled hair, silvered at his temples, and an untrimmed goatee clashed with his dapper suit and tie; burnished-gold cuff links winked in the sunshine. His citrus cologne hit me like a tidal wave.

"Let's hope they didn't leave sticky fingerprints all over the merchandise," he said, walking into the shop. "I'm surprised you started tours before the school year."

"Welcome back." My voice dripped with sarcasm. "This tour was a reschedule from last spring. Learn anything useful in New York?"

Will stuck a hand in his pocket. "My trip was profitable, as usual. New Jersey, not New York. Met your dad, too. He flew up from Tampa to see the toy show."

I met Will's sharp gaze in surprise. "Really."

"I hope the tour group paid for that very large bear. Hmm?"

Ignoring him, I figured Maddie was itching to know when I'd return and let her get back to the office. Will's cell phone beeped. Coins jangled in his pocket when he dug out his phone and then answered the call. His tranquil tone immediately changed to one of annoyance.

"—told you to send my shirts out to the cleaners. See you later."

No doubt a call from his wife, Carolyn, who owned the Holly Jolly Christmas shop across the street. She often kept an

eagle eye out for his car and called whenever she saw him.
Everyone knew she didn't trust him out of her sight. I didn't
care. Maddie did, since Carolyn often called the office if Will
didn't answer his phone. That drove Maddie crazy. My sister
wasn't responsible for keeping track of a wayward husband,
though.

I unlocked the back door that led to our residence and
whistled for my dog. A mix of Bichon Frise and Lhasa Apso,
Rosie's short brown and white curly hair and shaped ears resembled the teddy bears we produced—she looked adorable.
My ex had named her after Eleanor Roosevelt when we rescued her; her hangdog look fueled our sympathy. During the
divorce proceedings, I claimed her as my baby. Flynn couldn't
argue, since he'd never paid that much attention to her during
our marriage. Rosie was the only thing I'd taken of signifi-
cance besides my clothes. I was glad he didn't claim shared cus-
tody.

My sweet dog bounded toward me now, leash in her
mouth, sheer joy in her eyes. She barked, letting the leash fall at
her feet. I clipped it to her collar and strolled out to the garden
once more. I'd meant to fetch her earlier, so she was ready to
do her business.

Rosie sniffed around, squatted, and then led the way back
to the air-conditioned house. Mom had insisted on installing
two units, one for the shop and one for the living quarters, plus
ceiling fans, during renovations. Summer days above ninety
weren't my favorite, unless we visited the beach.

The cat swatted Rosie on her way to the kitchen's window
seat. Rosie barked sharply at Onyx, who backed away with a
hiss. I sighed.

"Be nice, you two. Why can't you share?" I asked them. They
ignored me, although Rosie's tail wagged when she jumped onto
the window seat. Onyx lay down in the bright sunshine, her back
to the dog, defiant. Rosie curled up, indifferent. "Behave."

I took the shortcut through the house to the shop in front, making sure the double doors were securely locked behind me. The last thing I needed was a customer strolling around our private quarters, picking up a few knickknacks or valuables. Unfortunately, I ran into Will Taylor, who blocked the door near the clothing racks. The flier for this weekend's teddy bear picnic hid his face. Maddie darted toward the office with a grin and a wave. Traitor.

"So." Will lowered the flier and raised his eyebrows. "I hear you didn't get my message about the meeting tonight."

I noted his tone's steely edge. "No, but I will be there."

"Your dad and I had an interesting conversation about sales."

"Save it for the meeting." I nodded to the front door, where two women had entered and set off the tinkling of tiny bells on a string. "Customers."

Chapter 3

Will stalked to the shop's farthest room, muttering under his breath. I greeted the two older women and then gave them space. They quickly chose small tan teddy bears, one with a blue ribbon, one with pink, and brought them to the counter.

"Twins," one woman said with pride. She patted the bears. "My first grandchildren, too. Jaclyn hasn't chosen a nursery theme yet. I suggested blue and pink, but she might want a neutral color like yellow or green. Or Winnie the Pooh. Do you carry them?"

"Pooh is with Disney, while all our bears are unique."

"That's why we wanted these," the other lady said. "My daughter Natalie said everyone has Winnie the Pooh or even Paddington. Jaclyn's twins will love these bears."

I smiled. "Congratulations, and best wishes for an easy delivery."

"I hope Jaclyn makes it to the baby shower. Natalie had her last baby in record time."

"It's possible they'll take the babies early. . . ."

The women discussed the possibilities while I processed the sale. Will paced between the rooms, his impatience distracting. Did he expect me to rush customers? They both admired the clothing and accessories while I wrapped the bears in tissue, stamped the receipt with a *Thank You!* and then placed them in our largest silver bag. I'd hoped Will would leave when another customer arrived, but no. He watched, arms crossed over his chest, as if supervising.

Once the last customer departed, I locked the front door. During the lunch hour, we closed to give our staff a chance to regroup and relax. Not that customers paraded through the door all day long. But closing the shop and factory meant visitors could head to one of the lunch spots in Silver Hollow, which helped other local businesses. Will blocked the double doors to the back, however, and stopped me cold. Ignoring my displeasure, he held up a flier.

"Another teddy bear picnic? I told you before tours and events like this are a big waste of time. Your dad hasn't been around to run them anymore."

"So? We have more than twenty families signed up to attend."

"And half of them probably won't show. People go to the bigger parks for the holiday, or else have big family barbecues at home instead."

"Silver Hollow's parade is on Monday, remember," I said, and suppressed my smug tone. Something about Will Taylor burned me, but I wasn't going to allow him to play the "Dad" card without a fight. "The teddy bear picnic afterward is tradition ever since Dad first started it. And Maddie will cover at the store on Monday."

"What? We're open on Labor Day?"

"We always get customers after the parade for our annual sale."

"Another sale?" Will tapped a finger against his jaw. "I hope you realize that our profits are declining. They've been declining all year, in fact."

"The sales figures I've seen tell a different story. Check with Maddie."

"I had her make a report for the meeting."

His sly smile annoyed me. "Like Maddie doesn't have anything better to do."

"One thing is certain. We need to sell more than just teddy bears," Will said. "Bunnies, dogs, cats, foxes, you name it. And your dad is on board with cutting staff."

"Oh, sure. Let's produce more toys with less staff. That makes a lot of sense." I snatched the flier out of his hand. "I'm starving. Now there's only forty-five minutes before we open again and Rosie needs a walk. Thanks for wasting my time."

I turned my back on his murderous glare, pushed past, and locked doors behind me. Once out of earshot, I breathed a sigh of relief. "Come on, Rosie!"

I whistled. Her claws scrabbled across the kitchen's tile floor to meet me at the back door, tail wagging and leash ready in her mouth. I grabbed from the fridge the sandwich I'd slapped together this morning, crammed a floppy cotton hat on my head, and then raced ahead of Rosie outside. The day was a scorcher, as predicted. We kept to the shade. Given the meeting tonight, I had no choice but to exercise my dog on a midday walk.

Rosie didn't mind the sun beating down, though. She kept straying back and forth, almost tripping me a few times, and snuffled trash left on the grassy meadow bordering Silver Lake. Grabbing the potato chip bag that scuttled across Theodore Lane, I marched to the closest bin under the stand of birch trees near Main Street and deposited it along with my sandwich Baggie.

"If only the copsh would catch the littering jerksh," I

mumbled, my mouth full from the last bite of peanut butter and bread. Rosie jerked the leash nearly out of my hand, trying to chase a squirrel. "Hey! Cut that out. You nearly caught a baby yesterday."

The twin to our Victorian house-turned-shop, Barbara and Richard Davison's home, looked romantic with its black shutters, wraparound veranda, central tower, and stone steps. They had a far better views of the lake, since trees blocked most of the shimmering blue expanse from our windows. Richard Davison, a retired CEO from one of the Big Three automobile companies, and his wife must be out of town given the lack of cars in the long driveway.

The former one-story carriage house opposite the Davison's house had been converted into an upscale restaurant, Flambé, with floor-to-ceiling windows. Tyler and Mary Walsh, owners of Ham Heaven in the village, lived in a small cottage next door surrounded by a white picket fence. Past that, around the lane's curve, a brick Queen Anne–style house boasting several gables and blue trim nestled among a stand of trees. Owned by Glen and Jenny Woodley, the Silver Leaf Bed and Breakfast looked empty with only one car in the lot. That was surprising given the upcoming Labor Day holiday.

Both of them waved to me when I walked Rosie down the street. Jenny weeded in the garden while Glen painted a fresh coat of white on their mailbox. Perhaps their guests wouldn't arrive until tomorrow. It seemed too hot to be working outside, but to each his own.

I race-walked to the end of Theodore Lane and Kermit Street, where the Holly Jolly Christmas shop stood on the corner. Rosie nosed the huge green ceramic pots of red geraniums in front of the narrow white-painted Italianate building. Lush ferns drooped from hooks hung along the veranda. Carolyn Taylor kept her red and green door propped open, showing off sparkling Christmas trees in every corner and window. Even the letters "Holly Jolly" above the door sparkled, and twinkling lights lined the eaves. She never closed for lunch. Inside, she stood chatting with customers and pointing out Santa Claus figurines.

I had no idea how Carolyn tolerated Will's conceit. His arrogance grated my nerves to pieces. She looked fashionable, dressed in black as usual, wearing an overly large flashy red necklace over a sleeveless maxi dress, plus beaded sandals. A black and red bracelet clunked against the counter when she processed a sale. She wore bright red lipstick, and her boisterous laugh was infectious. Carolyn's bouncy blond curls also made me envious.

Some people had all the luck. Sigh.

Customers to her shop breathed in tantalizing scents of pine, balsam, peppermint, plus gingerbread—from the dozen cookies she baked for customers. Once in a while I stopped in to grab one; not that I was proud of it, but why waste an opportunity for a good cookie? Carolyn had Marilyn Monroe–worthy curves. I had the Silverman gene for thunder thighs, a trait I could live without. Walking Rosie every day helped. My sister could eat anything but never gained an ounce. Maddie had a notorious sweet tooth but rarely indulged or thought about food. Ever. Me, I had to fight sugar cravings with a whip and chair.

Rosie and I quickly headed down Kermit Street. A few pedestrians exchanged waves with me, including Ben Blake, the village pharmacist who had the best smile in Silver Hollow. He soon disappeared inside the corner café. Rosie and I hurried past Fresh Grounds, run by two good friends, up the sloping hill toward the village green. The courthouse, an imposing three-story stone building with Ionic columns between the tall windows, looked huge compared to the rows of brick shops in the village.

The green swath of lawn behind the courthouse was Rosie's favorite spot. She sniffed around, cocked her head at a few odd smells, and then headed toward a tree. I tied the "doggie doo" bag, trashed it, then led her back to Main Street. My great-grandfather had somehow talked the town's original surveyor into naming Silver Hollow's streets for President Theodore Roosevelt's family: second wife Edith, daughters Alice and Ethel in the historic home district, plus Archibald, Kermit, and Roosevelt in the main shopping district.

Grandpa T. R. Silverman had resented leaving school in eighth grade to work. He learned every job from the ground up at the Quick Mix factory, taking over management when his father died, but passed on his love of toys to my father. Dad had chosen law school but after two decades of a punishing schedule quit to open the Silver Bear Shop & Factory. He'd hired Uncle Ross to supervise the factory production. Once Dad retired seven years ago, I took over as manager—although he and Mom still attended toy fairs. Was Will Taylor privy to information Dad had kept from me? I doubted it. My sister would be worried sick if sales had taken a turn for the worse. Mads hadn't said a word to me about our shop nose-diving into the red.

Rosie halted at the door of our favorite shop, Fresh Grounds. Mmm. The scent of sweet cinnamon rolls wafted toward my nose; the coffee-and-bakery, run by Mary Kate and Garrett Thompson, was a popular place all day long. A line of customers wound out the door. I'd kept in touch with Mary Kate since high school, along with Elle Cooper, who owned Cat's Cradle Books with her husband—my cousin Matt. Both Elle and Mary Kate had succeeded in finding a decent husband and having kids.

Was I jealous? Maybe a little, but I was glad for them.

I'd ordered Mary Kate's lemon blueberry scones and half a

dozen orange muffins the minute I heard about the meeting, hoping to alleviate any bad news Taylor brought to the table. That would take the edge off of a late supper. I knocked on the side window.

"Hi, Sasha! Here ya go." Mary Kate handed me the box. "How's business?"

"Decent," I said. "Labor Day should be a whirlwind, we hope."

"I'm glad we'll have extra help. By the way, I popped in a sample of the cookie you might want to serve at the teddy bear picnic."

"Great. The June picnic was so popular, we had to promise an encore."

She laughed. "I'll be there with my baby. You can bet on that."

I nodded. "I'm thinking of another event for early October. We'll kick off the annual village Oktobear Fest with a tea party and include the kids with their teddy bears. There aren't many events this fall that do, given the microbrewery with its beer tasting."

Mary Kate squealed in delight. "I love the idea! I'll ask Garrett if we'd have enough room to hold it here. My mom would love to help out, too. Gotta run, Sasha."

"Hey, how much do I—"

"You're good for it. Pay me whenever you stop by next time."

She rushed back. Rosie sniffed against my leg, definitely aware of the fragrant scones wafting from the box. My face warmed with pleasure from Mary Kate's words, although I'd expected her to gush with enthusiasm. Providing baked goods for a tea party would boost her business as well. Rosie nosed the blue door of The Cat's Cradle Books. My cousin Matt Cooper had opened it as The Bookworm fifteen years ago, but the name hadn't gone over well. After he married Elle, she convinced him to change due to the cats roaming the shop.

I caught sight of Elle ringing up a customer. But I hurried on without knocking on the glass. I'd be late getting back to my shop, plus I didn't want to distract her.

Yellow and orange chrysanthemums, a sure sign of early autumn, bloomed in the round island planter on the corner where we halted for the light. Several seniors stood near the sidewalk tables at Dottie's Deli & Diner across the street—Gil Thompson, Victor Blake, who had retired from directing the funeral home, and Uncle Ross. My gaze lingered on them. I almost ran into the former neighbor who'd come out of nowhere and blocked the sidewalk.

Jack Cullen glared down at Rosie, an unlit cigar dangling from his clenched teeth. "Keep that mutt away from me or I'll sue."

"Rosie's never bitten anyone." I mustered a cheerful tone, despite his churlishness. "It's such a nice summer day."

"What's so nice about it?" Cullen took out his cigar stub and stood eye to eye with me. "Your dad robbed me, pure and simple. Figures. All lawyers are crooks."

His white mustache twitching, he stalked past. I wanted to defend Dad, although I didn't bother. Jack Cullen wouldn't change his mind. The stubborn old coot refused to be reasonable. Dad had argued for years with him, to no avail, trying to convince him that the Silver Hollow city council meant business. Cullen's dilapidated house—with a rotting staircase, broken windows, missing floorboards—was labeled a blight. The city council offered the property for sale to recover back taxes. Dad had paid up, demolished the house, and paved a parking lot. It wasn't our fault that Cullen neglected to act. But he refused to admit it.

I watched the old man's uneven gait, wondering if he was half-drunk. I hadn't smelled any liquor on his breath. A baseball cap covered his mostly bald head. Despite his venom, I felt sorry for him. His droopy jeans, held up by a worn leather belt, hung on his skeletal frame.

"He must not eat much," I said aloud. From what I heard, the old man lived in a rented apartment near the library, across from the gas station. "Maybe he's ill."

Whatever the case, Jack Cullen held tight to his grudge.

Chapter 4

Rosie pulled me toward home along Theodore Lane. I adored every inch of the Silver Bear Shop & Factory, surrounded by colorful flower beds that set off the Victorian house. The corner turret rose above the covered front porch like a giant raised thumb, and a brick chimney flanked the second-floor windows. The bedroom suites upstairs for Maddie and me had private baths. We kept the third bedroom suite intact for Mom and Dad, but two other guest bedrooms—or storage rooms depending on our needs—shared a bath. The bookshelf-lined library opened to a small screened sunroom above the back porch. Quite cozy.

Lucky us.

Will Taylor's silver Camry with its vanity plate, 1MRIGHT, had disappeared from the parking lot. "I'm right, my foot," I grumbled.

He was so full of himself. He and Carolyn had been married for at least fifteen years, give or take. No children, though. She poured herself into the Christmas shop instead.

Deon Walsh's motorcycle was in its usual spot, right next

to Uncle Ross's blue and white 1956 Thunderbird. He kept his pride and joy in perfect running condition. If any mark or smudge showed on the peacock blue leather interior, he acted as if Armageddon had rained fire and brimstone. Dad called it The Rattle Trap as a joke. My uncle ribbed him right back, calling his Chevy a pretend "Fur-rarri" and not worth a plugged nickel.

I let Rosie in the house and laughed when she rushed to the water dish. Onyx flashed a look of disdain at the dog, stretched her sleek black body over the sunny window seat, and resumed her nap. Rosie whined, but I shrugged.

"Sorry, Rosie. You know she's not gonna share all the time."

I scratched Rosie behind her ears before she headed to her "happy corner" where her teddy bear toy sat. She loved it like her baby. Rosie stretched her paws out with a contented sigh, head on Barry Bear, and closed her eyes.

The bakery box I'd set on the kitchen island tempted me to peek inside. I caught my breath at the peanut butter cookie in the shape of a teddy bear head, with a chocolate Kiss for a nose and two tiny blue candy eyes. Adorable! I'd already unwrapped the package before I stopped myself with a flash of guilt. Maddie hadn't seen it yet. Reluctant, I set the cookie back into the box. Stared at it, closed the lid. Grabbed tape from below the counter and sealed it shut. Mary Kate had such great ideas, and the kids would gobble the cookies up in no time.

Shadowy figures passed by the kitchen window—the sewing ladies were returning from lunch. Flora, Lois, Joan, and Harriet hurried to the factory. The hall clock had already chimed one five minutes ago, so I rushed to the front door. Two customers stood waiting.

"Wow, it's warm out there," I said. "No breeze, either."

"Much cooler in here." The man swatted the string of

bells aside, mopped his face, and then shoved his handkerchief into a back pocket. "What a relief."

"Could be worse if we were home in Florida," the woman said.

I checked the outside thermometer—eighty-nine, in the shade. Summer was my least favorite season. I preferred autumn with its crisp, cool mornings, the changing colors of the oaks, maples, elms, and other trees, plus the apple orchard events and Halloween fun. Three boxes had been delivered on the front porch, light enough for me to carry inside without the rolling cart.

While the couple wandered together around the shop, I unpacked the boxes. One held spools of thread. Another overflowed with packages of plastic eye studs. The third had our custom round tags printed with our logo. I set them below the counter, figuring I could walk the boxes over to the factory later. I couldn't leave customers alone, and we hadn't run out of anything yet.

"Look at these adorable bears!"

The customer's words, music to my ears, usually led to the sound of our old-fashioned cashier's happy ring. So much for Will's predictions about declining sales.

Once the couple left, the rest of the afternoon dragged. Dread settled in my stomach. What kind of trouble would Will Taylor bring? Between worrying and taking care of customers, I was busy restocking bins and clothing racks for the next day. I even rearranged accessories. Some days I wanted to switch jobs with Maddie. Bookkeeping and answering phones, filling online orders, keeping Will Taylor at bay, and doing whatever else she did, though, would drive me batty. At last I closed and locked the door at six o'clock and walked to the back of the house. I always relaxed after work, grateful another day was over. But not today.

The inviting country kitchen formed the center of our

domain shared with my parents and sister. Mom had designed it. Golden-brown oak cabinets lent an earthy tone compared to the painted rectangular island in distressed moss green, which was topped with granite. The extra sink below the window and its swan neck faucet came in handy when we cooked. Two brass fixtures hanging above added a warm glow, although the bay window seat also allowed in plenty of sunshine. Mom's iron-work bakery rack served as a display shelf for houseplants, cookbooks, and a wide green ceramic bowl filled with fake oranges and lemons.

"Whew. I hope this meeting won't take long." Maddie carried a stack of papers into the kitchen. "Poor Rosie. How long has she been whining like that?"

"I took her for a walk at lunch, but I bet she wants fresh air. Come on, girl."

I clipped the dog's harness to the rope stretching from one of the back porch's posts. She'd be fine, chasing squirrels away from the bird feeders and sniffing around the various bushes and trees until the meeting ended. I dumped her outside water dish and then refilled it. Back inside the house, I fetched the tea basket, filled the electric kettle, and plugged it in. Then I placed the scones on a cut-glass plate and surveyed the buffet table. Mom would be so proud of my hostess skills. Ha. At the very least she'd put a doily under the treats.

With its extended mahogany table and padded chairs, the former dining room now served as a large staff meeting area. I wished Dad were here, so I could question him about what Will Taylor actually did as our sales representative besides attending trade shows. Maybe we could cut his job and be better off.

Maddie arrived, set a stack of papers at the table's head, and handed me a pile of letters. "You ought to check for the mail whenever you take Rosie out for a walk."

"I keep forgetting. Hey, what's this?" I opened a large envelope on the bundle's bottom. "Ooh, look! It's an order from that South Dakota museum shop for the Teddy Roosevelt bear. Do we have enough wire-rimmed glasses? And uniform buttons?"

"We have an unopened box of spectacles from February of last year, I think. I'm not sure about the buttons." Maddie did a pirouette, still graceful from her ballerina days. "So much for sales slipping. Let's hope Will finds find something else to do tonight and skips his own meeting."

"I doubt that. It's his chance to complain about the same old things." I steeped a cup of mint and lemongrass tea. "Unless he's come up with new things."

"Like how Uncle Ross comes in late, and doesn't keep the staff on track. Oh, wait. How about your crazy ideas, like the Largest Teddy Bear Fourth of July flag—"

"Just missed the Guinness book for the world record," I said with a sigh.

"And the Teddy Bear Cub Run," Maddie sailed on, "plus the Take Your Teddy to the Zoo. Now I bet he'll complain about the picnic and how the tea party will cost us too much money." Maddie laughed at my sour look. "What?"

"Don't ruin the suspense. But look at this." I grabbed the bakery box, minus the scones, and pointed inside. "Isn't this the most adorable cookie ever?"

Maddie eyed it with a squint. "I expected a little fancier design. With icing around the edges, maybe sunglasses or something suggesting a picnic."

"Mmmfph," I mumbled, since I'd bitten off the bear's ear. "Peanuf buffer."

"Would she be hurt if you told her to make a sugar cookie instead?"

"I shuppose I could ashk." After polishing off the rest of the cookie, I wiped my mouth. "Get ready."

Uncle Ross tramped in, his deck shoes thudding. He made a beeline for the scone plate and sank into the plush leather armchair in a far corner. "I'm starving. Six o'clock is time for suds and a burger, not a meeting. What the devil does Taylor want now?"

"Wish I knew." Deon had followed him into the room and now checked his watch. "We gotta be at Quinn's Pub by seven thirty, remember."

The slender young man still wore his earbuds draped over his shoulders. He kept his dark curly hair cropped short; handsome, with a light coffee-hued complexion, Deon was striving for a business degree at the local community college. Pete Fox sauntered into the room. He had the same lean build, but was a head taller, with lank dark hair and a permanent slouch. He never said two words if he could use one. Grabbed a scone from the platter, pulled out a chair, and then plopped down with his feet draped over one side. Harriet Amato, Flora Zimmerman, Joan Kendall, and Lois Nichols all rushed to make a cup of tea and fill their plates with a scone or two.

"So where is Will?" I peered through the window blinds at the parking lot and checked my watch. "He's late."

"Ha. Remember that when he gripes about us," Deon said.

"He's so full of himself," I grumbled. "Wanting a meeting and—dang."

Before I could finish my sentence, his silver Camry pulled into his spot. I watched him emerge from the car, adjust his suit coat and sunglasses, and then stalk toward the back porch. Will didn't see his wife waving from her shop across the street. Or else he deliberately ignored Carolyn. I pushed the blinds back into place, hoping he hadn't noticed. Then again, he always seemed aware of people watching his movements.

"Is it true some of us will be laid off?" Lois sounded worried.

"Where did you hear that?" I asked. They all exchanged

furtive glances. "There won't be any jobs cut. Trust me." And I meant it, too.

"Mr. Taylor told me that business is falling off," Flora said.

"And that production will be moved to China," Joan added. "Is he serious?"

"We're keeping our bears American made. That's important for our toy business, and my dad would never agree to such a crazy idea."

My cheery tone didn't seem to relieve their fears. Uncle Ross tugged his cap as if to signal me, his eyebrows raised. I twisted around. Will stood in the doorway, one hand in his pocket, a smirk on his face. The ladies slipped into chairs around the table without speaking. I stood my ground when Will spoke.

"Crazy idea, huh?"

"Yes," I said. "We're an American company."

"We all want to get this meeting over with and go home," Maddie said.

"I agree."

Will sauntered toward the stack of papers, but my sister grabbed them and shuffled them like a deck of cards to the staff around the table. I sat at the table's head, where Dad would be if he were here. Will flipped through a copy of the report Maddie had prepared, rustling the pages in the silent room. Someone's teacup rattled against the saucer. Lois cleared her throat.

"Get this meeting started, Taylor." Uncle Ross chomped into a lemon blueberry pastry and spoke around a mouthful. "No muffin can replace a burger."

"That's a scone," I said.

"Whatever."

"All right." Still standing, Will eyed everyone in the room except me. "I met with Mr. Silverman in New Jersey during last weekend's toy fair. We agreed that action is necessary to

avoid losing the factory. That means sending production overseas—"

"No. Dad would never have agreed to that," I cut in.

"Are you calling me a liar?" This time he faced me squarely.

I narrowed my eyes, uncertain, and turned to my sister.
"Mads. Call Dad right now and find out what he said exactly,
and if he agreed without talking to us first."

She rushed out of the room, cell phone in hand. Will
looked surprised at our quick reaction, and Uncle Ross scrambled from his chair. "I see the handwriting on the wall, Taylor.
Why don't you admit you're trying to get rid of me? You want
me out as factory supervisor so you can control everything."

"I want to streamline production. Sales have taken a down-
turn, and Mr. Silverman saw the numbers. That's why he
agreed with my ideas."

"Our sales numbers are fine," I said. "Look at Maddie's report."

"Then you haven't read it."

I snatched the stapled sheets and scanned the first page.
Puzzled, I flipped to the second. The numbers weren't horrible, but they did show a decrease. If my sister wasn't all that
concerned, however, I refused to believe we needed such drastic change.

"We just received a large order from South Dakota today."
I tossed the report back on the table. "That will raise our sales,
enough to keep production right here. Dad always said being
based in Silver Hollow is the best thing about us. He's not
going to throw away the fact that our products are American
made."

"Um, Sash?" Maddie stood in the doorway, biting her
upper lip. "Mom said Dad was considering Will's ideas. That
otherwise, we might lose everything."

I stared at her in shock. What was going on? How could
Dad cave on such an important decision and then not call and

warn us? Will looked triumphant, but I wasn't about to back down. Not without a fight.

Uncle Ross rose to his feet, hands shaking. "You've had it in for me from the minute you stepped in the door five years ago," he said, his voice low but menacing. "You want me outta here. And now you're influencing my brother. Taking over my job is the first step to taking over the whole business."

"I'm not—"

"Don't try and deny it." My uncle shook a fist. "I heard a rumor that our biggest rival, Bears of the Heart, has a copy of our teddy bear pattern. Got an explanation, Taylor? Did you sell it to them and pull a fast one over my brother?"

Will stared him down. "That's a damned lie."

My uncle's cruder curse in reply elicited a gasp from all four sewing ladies, plus Maddie. He didn't apologize, either. "If I find out it's true, bucko, you'll be sorry," he retorted. "I'll have your head on a platter, wait and see!"

"Uncle Ross, please. This is getting out of hand," I said firmly. "We don't know for certain if Bears of the Heart has our bear pattern."

He ignored me. "Taylor wants me out of here, Sasha. That's the only way he can control my brother and put these changes into place!"

Will held up both hands in surrender. "I'm doing the job Alex Silverman hired me to do, watching the market trends and scoping out the competition. Plus boosting sales. I'm telling you here and now that if we send production overseas, we'll triple our profits. That's a guarantee."

"Maybe we need a new sales representative." Uncle Ross barked a laugh. "How much you wanna bet our numbers will improve after that?"

"Maybe we need a supervisor who shows up on time, and doesn't go off for long lunch hours with his buddies," Will shot back. "Time to retire, *bucko*."

I stepped between them, afraid they'd come to blows. Deon pushed Uncle Ross toward his corner chair. "You'll be sorry for that wisecrack, Taylor," my uncle muttered. "I may be close to retirement, but I get the job done. The whole job."

"Ease up, man. It ain't worth it," Deon said. "Take it easy."

"Uncle Ross does his job perfectly well," I said in his defense. "He's not ready to retire anytime soon, and keeps things under control at the factory. No one's job will be cut. You've got my word on that."

"You tell him, Sasha." Uncle Ross sank into the soft leather chair. "Alex will have to pry my cold, dead fingers off the cutting press or the stuffing machine before I take a hike."

I was thankful Will didn't take a crack at my uncle's missing fingers. He sounded bitter when he replied. "Obviously you won't face facts. The commercials on TV around the holidays, the stuff-your-own-toy places at the mall. Can we afford to do that? No. Cute posts on Twitter or Facebook don't sell bears. Wait and see. We'll keep on losing money if we don't expand our product line and manufacture in China."

Lois struggled to her feet. "Mr. Taylor, I can't afford to lose my job. I can't," she said in desperation. Her eyes glistened with tears. "My husband needs long-term care and treatment for cancer. Paying for private insurance will break us."

Will ignored her. "We could add bunnies, dogs, cats, and all kinds of zoo animals. Maybe we could let the kids stuff them if that's what it takes to compete."

"So instead of being unique, we'll end up just like every other run-of-the-mill company," I said. "Your big idea sounds more like business suicide."

"It's a sidestep, Sasha. Our prices will beat the competitors after production costs go down. It's the only way to do it."

Lois shook a fist at him. "I can't lose my job! I'll kill you first—"

"Whoa," Uncle Ross said. "I'll be the first one to gut him like a fish."

"No more threats, please." I held up my hands. Maddie inched her way to stand beside me, and I was relieved that we made a united front. "Grandpa T. R. must be rolling over in his grave. Nothing will change until Mom and Dad come home and discuss the issue. In person."

"Don't worry," Maddie said to Lois, who hadn't sat again. "I'm looking into a different medical plan. The premiums are almost equal with more benefits."

Lois looked ready to hyperventilate. "They'll never take him in his condition."

"There's a new law that prevents discrimination against people with preexisting conditions," my sister reassured her. "So that won't be the case."

Will cleared his throat. "Can we get back to the real issue of staff cuts, please?"

Lois wailed at that. "We can barely afford the deductible now—"

"*No one* is losing their job at this factory!" I matched Will's venomous stare.

Uncle Ross jumped to his feet again. "I can't wait till my brother gets home from that toy fair. I'll find out exactly what he said, you thieving son of a—"

"Please, stop!" Maddie looked close to tears. "This isn't doing anyone any good."

"If I ever find out Bears of the Heart did get a copy of our pattern, my brother and I will both boot you to Main Street." Uncle Ross looked triumphant.

"Try and prove I had anything to do with it." With that, Will stormed out.

Chapter 5

"How else could Teddy Hartman get our pattern?" Uncle Ross grumbled. "I'll prove Taylor is behind it. No matter what it takes."

My uncle headed out, followed by Deon. Pete Fox moseyed after them in silence. I figured they'd both keep an eye on Uncle Ross and make sure he didn't do anything foolish. Then I drew a deep breath and turned to the others.

"Well, that's the end of this meeting," I said. "Go home, everyone. Rest up. The weekend is going to be busy with the picnic and our annual sale. We'll have to start that big order next week for the Teddy Roosevelt bear."

Flora, Harriet, and Joan fled. Lois Nichols hung back, her eyes brimming with tears, but my sister whispered something to her. The older woman slowly walked out, although she didn't look happy. Even Rosie looked sad outside, waiting near the back porch steps. No one had stooped to scratch behind her ears or acknowledge her wagging tail. Cicadas thrummed loudly in the trees overhead, adding to the sense of misery. I held out a hand to my dog.

"Poor thing. Nobody loves you? We do, baby."

I knew Rosie ate up the lovey-dovey stuff, so I piled it on. After she trotted inside and stretched out on the kitchen tile, I rubbed her belly; tongue lolling, her fuzzy paws begged for more whenever I pretended to stop. Maddie tiptoed around us, the empty scone plate in hand. Apparently she'd snitched the last one. I heard her sigh with pleasure at the last bite.

Finally I stood and faced my sister. "Okay, spill. Did Dad really agree with Will about sending production overseas?"

Maddie set the dirty plate in the dishwasher, delaying the inevitable until I repeated my question. "Okay, already! I didn't actually talk to him. Mom texted me, that's all. He did meet with Will during the show in New Jersey. It's true our sales are down, a little. Not to a dire point, but probably enough to worry them. I'm sure Dad will explain when he calls."

"And when is that going to be?"

"I don't know, Sash. Maybe this will all blow over."

"Not if Will did sell our bear pattern to a rival."

Maddie massaged the bridge of her nose. "Uncle Ross didn't say he had proof."

"That's what it'll take, I suppose."

I stood at the bay window, watching the parking lot. Everyone had left except for Will Taylor, who chatted with his wife in the middle of Theodore Lane. Or were they arguing, the way Carolyn waved her arms around? Then again, she always did that. Will pecked her cheek and headed to his car. Carolyn stalked to her store, clearly miffed.

"I thought Uncle Ross would have a heart attack," Maddie said, and checked the fridge. "How about we go to Ham Heaven for dinner and then a movie?"

"Sounds good." I flexed my shoulders, but the tension didn't drain from my muscles one bit. "Could it be true about the bear pattern? I thought we kept that locked up. So how could Will Taylor have gotten a copy?"

"No idea."

"I take it Mom didn't say anything about when they'll be home." My sister shook her head, and that worried me. "I don't trust what Will said. Dad always wanted to keep our bears American made, so why would he change his mind? It doesn't make sense."

"I haven't gotten a straight answer from Dad on anything. You know how he gets when his mind is elsewhere." Maddie plopped on a tall stool at the kitchen island and dragged the cat into her lap. She buried her face for a moment in Onyx's silky fur. "Oh, Nyxie, Nyx. Tell her that Dad only trusts Sash when it comes to shop business."

"It's not that he doesn't trust you—"

"He treats me like I'm ten years old."

I had to admit she was right. On the other hand, whenever Mom couldn't attend fairs and trade shows, Dad dragged me along. I'd accompanied him to New York, Sacramento, Las Vegas, and other cities, living out of a battered suitcase, but grew weary of seeing the same vendors and a horde of strangers at every turn. But it did give me the foundation for understanding and managing the business, and how to deal with people. With one exception.

"I wish Dad would fire Will. What can we do to make him quit?" I surprised myself by saying that thought out loud. Maddie laughed. "He's so arrogant."

"Dad? Or Will Taylor?"

"You know very well who I mean."

"I was teasing." She set Onyx aside and rose to her feet. "One thing I thought of—Wendy Clark works at the Pretty in Pink bakery. I bet Mary Kate could get her to help with a fancier cookie for the picnic. She decorates those fancy 'lace' designs."

"I wonder if Vivian Grant would allow that," I said. "She's a stickler."

Mary Kate's delicious scones, muffins, croissants, and breads had eaten into Pretty in Pink's sales—no joke. Vivian's bakery produced cakes of all kind, plus a variety of cupcakes and petit fours, packaging them in pink-and-white-striped boxes tied with pink satin ribbons. Their prices were far higher than any baked goods Garrett and Mary Kate Thompson offered at Fresh Grounds.

"I'm starved." Maddie said. "Nyx, time for your supper."

The cat meowed while my sister tore a package of wet food, dumped it into a plastic bowl, and set it mid-level on the climbing tower by the window. Onyx only lapped the gravy like water and left the food for later. That is, if Rosie didn't somehow get to it while Maddie and I were gone.

After donning a light sweater, I brushed my hair and tied it back into a ponytail before adding a baseball cap. Maddie grabbed a sweatshirt, tied it around her waist, and followed me outside. Glorious streaks of yellow, gold, orange, and red painted the sky above the horizon even though the sun wouldn't set for another hour or two. My sister snapped a few photos with her cell.

Carolyn Taylor locked the Holly Jolly Christmas shop and headed to her car in the corner lot. I waved back at her. She was a good neighbor, always directing customers to our shop and displaying an array of our bears tucked under her orna-mented trees, on rocking chairs, or inside gift boxes. We re-turned the favor with a display of Santa Claus figurines holding teddy bears—with the Holly Jolly shop tags intact. If interested, customers could pop across the street to purchase copies.

Carolyn's small two-door sedan turned onto Kermit Street. I wondered if she knew smoke trailed from the tailpipe. At least my car didn't burn oil. We followed, although Carolyn pulled into the parking lot beside Quinn's Pub.

"Maybe she needs a burger and beer, too. There's Uncle Ross's car."

"I hope Will Taylor doesn't join her there." Maddie sounded worried.

"Yeah. I'd hate to hear about Will and Uncle Ross shooting off more fireworks."

We parked in the small lot behind Ham Heaven down the block. Owned by Deon Walsh's parents, the small diner opened at six in the morning. They served breakfast and early lunch, then closed from two until five. From five until eight, they served light sandwiches and soups. We chose tall stools at the counter, even though a few tables were free. My sister ordered her usual, a crispy fish sandwich, while I chose the brisket. We always split an order of sweet potato fries piled in a huge plastic basket lined with paper, fresh, hot, and lightly salted.

I loved this place, with its black-and-white-checkered tile floor, pink and turquoise 1950s-style interior, plus stuffed pink pigs everywhere—hanging from the light fixtures, mounted over the Ladies and Gents signs on the restrooms, resting in every corner or on the windowsills. The toys wore pink feather boas, poodle skirts, sunglasses, or held a skateboard, a football, even a baseball bat and glove. Kitschy, but cute.

Mary Walsh carried our plates from the kitchen, curls bouncing, and dabbed at her damp face. "Whew, it's smokin' hot in there. I'm ready to crash for the night, and maybe even the weekend. We need a vacation!"

"We do, darlin'," Tyler called out from the back. "Let's go!"

Maddie and I grinned, digging into our food, knowing they always said that near the end of the week. Deon often urged them to get away from Silver Hollow for a week or two, but they never did. They sure loved to cook and were popular in the village.

We wolfed our sandwiches down before Tyler flipped the Closed sign. I licked savory barbecue sauce from my fingers. "No one can beat your grub."

"Music to our ears," he said. "Mary, you ready? Honey, I'm bushed to the max."

"Soon as I restock the fridge for the morning rush, Sugar Pie."

Ham Heaven was better known for their ham, of course, melt in your mouth, sweet in flavor, with a hint of smoky mesquite. Their breakfast omelets were to die for, especially the ham-spinach-feta-and-onion. And the tomato, bacon, and Swiss. Oh, and the asparagus and goat cheese. They baked their own sourdough bread, too. Buttery and crisped in the oven, their sandwiches were loaded with meat, dripping with sauce, and tasted delicious.

Mary paused near us, arms loaded with clean bowls. "What's this I heard about cutting jobs at the factory? Deon called me about ten minutes ago."

I slid off the stool with the bill. "No one is losing their job. I promise."

"Good. That boy of ours is a work in progress." She heaved a deep sigh. "Finally got him focused on getting a decent education, although he skips class too much. The last thing Deon needs is to go job hunting."

"And he refuses to work for us." Tyler relieved Mary of the bowls. "Neither will our girls. We'll have to close down when we retire."

"You? Retire?" Mary gave him a playful slap. "Go on, sweetie, finish up. I need some wine!"

"Show starts at eight fifteen," my sister said. "Come on."

"Night, Mary." I left a big tip, paid at the cash register, and followed Maddie out the door. "I hope you chose a film that isn't too gory."

"Nah. You'll love it."

We drove to the closest cinema near Ann Arbor via Baker Road. I loved seeing the tall green cornfields, oaks, and other trees, all lining the country roads that curved over hills past silos and farmhouses. We passed swayback decaying barns, feed and supply stores, and squat grain elevators; a few repair shops already had stacks of wood for the coming winter. Large and small vegetable stands were loaded with the baskets and bushels of beans, peas, cucumbers, sweet corn, peppers, and tomatoes.

Southeastern Michigan in all its glory, with autumn on the doorstep, meant the trees' foliage would swiftly change to brilliant hues of yellow, orange, and red once chillier weather arrived. Apples of all kinds, cider and donuts, mazes, and hayrides added to the fun. But summer had a tendency to linger through September with humidity and hot weather.

Maddie parked in the lot. "How can I be hungry already? I'm dying for popcorn."

"Me, too."

Inside the busy cinema, I added a dash of salt over my small bag. Mads poured a river of butter over her bucket, shook it, and then pushed the button to soak it a second time. I'd also picked out a box of chocolate-covered raisins, more in line with my mood. If cinemas ever offered chocolate-covered popcorn, I'd be first in line.

"Hey. Isn't that Vivian Grant?"

I pointed out the bakery owner's tall, leggy figure, pale skin, frizzy black hair, plus the bright pink top and matching capris she wore. Her purse and sandals were also pink with loads of bling. Wendy Clark, petite and thin, her light brown hair cut and styled in short spikes, accompanied her boss. I nudged Maddie with a questioning glance.

"I didn't know they'd be here," my sister whispered. "And I'm shocked Wendy's hair isn't purple and green. She's always coloring it."

"By the way, I called Mary Kate. She said no problem about a fancier cookie."

"I hope she's not charging us more."

"Nope. Out of the goodness of her heart, she'll keep you happy."

Maddie stuck out her tongue. We followed the duo at a distance down the long hall and into the same theater. Vivian and Wendy sat near the front, while we found seats up the stairs at the back. The movie was based on a Marvel comic. I lost track of the plot, since my thoughts wandered despite the noisy action. Maybe I should have called Dad after the meeting ended. Then again, he might have sensed my panic. The last thing I wanted was for him to think Will was right, that our business needed drastic changes. Besides, I still wasn't convinced. Even after seeing my sister's sales report, I knew in my gut the Silver Bear Shop & Factory was solid.

Summer sales might not be as strong as other years, but once school began other groups would sign up for tours. Despite Will's displeasure, senior citizens loved seeing our factory and trooped in by the busload. They always bought bears as keepsakes or as presents. And Christmas shopping would also boost any sales figures. We could easily recover before Black Friday, when the online sales poured in. Both Maddie and I never had a free minute that entire weekend. Our own holiday shopping had to wait.

"Hey. Did you fall asleep?"

My arm throbbed from Maddie's sharp elbow. "No. Got an extra napkin?"

She handed me the last one while the credits rolled. "All right, what gives? Did you even watch the movie? You didn't laugh at any of the funny parts."

"I was thinking." I crumpled my popcorn bag, unaware of when I'd finished the snack, and stretched my back and shoulders. "It's too late to call Mom and Dad, I bet."

"Oh, leave it alone. Don't let Will Taylor get to you."

"I wish I could."

"I'll drive, or we'll end up going the wrong way." Maddie snatched the keys from my hand. "You're not usually a worrier, Sash. We'll survive. Dad was probably humoring Will. You know how he gets all diplomatic."

"No, I don't."

"He hates conflict. Maybe Dad pacified Will for the time being, and that's why the jerk came back acting like he'd been given the go-ahead."

I shrugged. "I hope so. But I'd still like to hear Dad's version of the story. In a conversation, not by text message."

"Hey, Wendy," Maddie said to the petite woman on our way out of the theater. "Didn't you come here with Vivian Grant?"

"Oh, she got a text from her son and had to leave. Good thing we both drove. I'm opening the bakery tomorrow at five, so I'd better go. Great movie, though."

Wendy walked off with a brief wave. Maddie and I hit the restroom first and then headed home. I was glad my sister chose to drive; I yawned so wide and often, my jaw popped. Silver Hollow's brick rows of buildings were darkened, the only light from the ironwork street lamps puddling along Main Street to guide us. Cars crammed the lot beside Quinn's Pub. Lively music rose when two couples emerged, and then faded when the door slammed shut behind them. We turned left onto Kermit and passed Church Street, opposite the imposing First Presbyterian edifice with its towering steeple. We stopped at the light.

"We should have caught a movie tomorrow night instead."

"Like that matters. I'm planning to sleep in until noon on Saturday," Maddie said, "so you can cover the shop. When I'm ready, I'll do the afternoon shift."

"When it slows down, right." I didn't mind, though. I'd

rather be busy. "Did you make reservations for our annual trip up north? I love seeing the fall colors."

"You bet. Sisters weekend, Mackinac Island!" Maddie turned onto Theodore Lane, dark as usual with so many trees. We both saw a car in our lot beside the house, the parking lights aglow. "Wonder whose car that is?"

I saw two cars, actually. Will's Camry sat beneath the light at the factory's door. The other car's headlamps flashed bright, right into our eyes. I squinted, holding a hand up, and heard tires squeal past us toward the street. Followed by a crash—I blinked fast, my eyes adjusting slowly. Maddie yelled in my ear.

"Hey, they hit our mailbox!"

We both jumped out of the car and ran to assess the damage. The banged-up mailbox remained attached to the broken wooden post, lying on the blacktop. For the second time this year, we'd have to replace the whole thing.

"Teens and their stupid pranks," I grumbled aloud. "I told you we should have let Uncle Ross build a brick post around the whole mailbox."

"Okay, you were right." Maddie pointed toward the other car. "So who's still here? And why? What were they doing this late?"

"That's Will Taylor's car, and I have no idea."

I yawned again, couldn't help it. Slowly the usual night sounds returned: the chirp of crickets, a dog's loud barking in the distance, a train's warning whistle that faded. I marched over to the Camry while I groped in my purse. Definitely his car, since my narrow penlight confirmed the vanity license plate. Too bad I didn't have any mud right now. Oh well. I didn't like the idea of him having a key and snooping around this late at almost midnight. What could he be doing? And why. That was more important.

Maddie followed me to the door. When I turned the handle, she grabbed my arm. "Wait. Maybe we should call the cops."

"He's gotta be inside." I listened for a minute. Nothing. No voices inside or footsteps. That was odd. "Hey, Will! Are you in there?"

"I'm calling 9-1-1, Sasha." Maddie punched the numbers into her cell. "We don't know who was driving that other car, and they sure left in a hurry. . . . Yes, we'd like a patrol car. We think there may have been a robbery."

A robbery? I wasn't sure about that. Curious, I opened the door wider. *Creak.* Uncle Ross hadn't oiled that hinge yet. No shadows danced beyond the light I switched on. I tiptoed farther inside. When Maddie touched my shoulder, I jumped.

"Gaah!" I clutched my chest, heart hammering beneath my fingers, my ears filled with a *rat-a-tat* pounding. "You scared me to death."

"The dispatcher said to wait in the parking lot."

"Looks like no one's here. Maybe Will couldn't start his car and left it here."

"Sasha, don't go looking around," Maddie hissed, but I ignored her.

Creeping past the first few stations, the sewing machines, and the supply shelves, we both tiptoed toward the looming hulk of the cutting press. A dim light streamed from the high window above, not enough to clearly see. Maddie found the switch on the wall.

"Hello? Will, are you in here? Will Taylor?"

Long shadows stretched to the corners beyond. My foot kicked a soft object. I groped around until I found a teddy bear—with a seam ripped open. That was odd. None of our workers had ever mentioned losing track of an unfinished toy.

The fiber machine tube had bits of fluff clinging to it. "Hey. Doesn't Uncle Ross clean this up before he leaves?"

Maddie nodded. "Look at all the fluff on the floor."

I'd missed noticing the drifts of white. We both knew the floor was always swept clean at the end of the day. A faint whine of sirens grew louder. Maddie grabbed my arm and pointed behind the stuffing machine. I rushed around it and knelt beside Will Taylor, stretched full length on his back. He didn't move. My stomach knotted at the sight of his staring eyes. His skin looked gray in the factory's dim light.

Worse, his cheeks and throat bulged with white fiber.

Chapter 6

My eyes ached from the constant flash of blue and red lights. Three police cars blocked the parking lot, and a Dexter County Sheriff's Department SUV sat on Theodore Lane in front of our shop. I blinked, still numb, unable to process what we'd found. I pinched myself. Hard. Ouch! So this wasn't a nightmare after all. I wanted to burrow under the covers in bed and hide from reality. Finding Will Taylor dead—it just didn't seem possible.

I'd never seen a dead body like this before. His face looked gray, his skin waxy. All the other people I'd seen after death looked sort of a pale version of themselves, lying in a plush and polished wood coffin. Grandpa T. R. seemed at peace after such a hard life. Aunt Marie, the life of every family party, had looked nothing like herself in thick makeup and with every hair in place, wearing a silk dress and pearls. She would have laughed that boisterous laugh, tickled pink, and then closed the casket with a wink. I smiled, remembering her casual velour jogging suits and scuffed tennis shoes.

But what about poor Carolyn? I didn't want to think how she'd take the news of her murdered husband.

Shivering in the chill air that rustled the leaves overhead, I wished I'd worn a jacket or hoodie. Maddie paced unevenly in the shadows under the covered walkway, snuggled in her warm sweatshirt, cell phone in her shaking hand. My frozen brain remained numb. My sister reacted to stress with frantic energy. She'd been calling our parents in Florida nonstop, refusing to leave a message. Mads clicked her phone off again in frustration.

"It's gone straight to voice mail every time! Why aren't they answering? The least they could do is text me."

"It's late. Maybe they're sleeping."

"You'd think they would wake up. Should we be worried?"

"I don't know."

She punched numbers again. "Hey, Mom, please call us," Maddie pleaded into the phone. "It's an emergency. Really, really, important. Call us." She turned to me again. "Aren't you wondering what's going on?"

Stung by her words, I exploded. "Of course I am! I'm trying to process what happened, for heaven's sake. Cut me some slack, okay?"

"Okay, okay. I'm sorry."

"Will Taylor obviously didn't kill himself. So guess what that means."

She looked stunned for a few seconds, then drew in a shaky breath. "Yeah. I get it. It's all so unreal, though! Like on a TV show, or in a mystery novel."

"Yeah." I swallowed hard. "Murder. There, I said it."

"It's horrible." Maddie shivered. "So what do we do?"

"Ms. Silverman?"

Hearing the husky masculine voice behind us, we both

turned around. Maddie's eyes widened. I could tell she hadn't recognized the man either. "Yes?"

"Detective Mason, Homicide."

He looked like any pedestrian on the street of a Midwest town. I had to admit the man resembled our Teddy Roosevelt bear with his wavy short brown hair, rosy plump cheeks in a round face, and wire-rimmed glasses. He wore a dark blue shirt with a sheriff's badge on the front and a light jacket over it, sort of a uniform except for the jeans and scuffed loafers. Juggling a Moleskine notebook and pen in one hand, he fished out a small leather wallet, flashing it open for a moment before stashing it under his coat again. I caught a glimpse of a holstered gun, too.

"Mind if I ask you a few questions?"

"Let me see your badge again. Please." As if the shirt didn't convince me, but I had to be sure. "Silver Hollow doesn't have a homicide detective, as far as we know."

Mason looked amused, retrieved his credentials again, and handed the wallet over for me to examine. "I'm from the Dexter County Detective Bureau, working under Sheriff Vanderbeek. You've heard of him, right?"

"Sort of," Maddie said. "I read about him in the *Ann Arbor News*. He's cracking down to arrest online predators of children."

"Yes, it's a big problem everywhere."

"Our village newspaper doesn't have much beyond ads for the shops and some school news. Although once the editor gets wind of this . . ." My voice trailed off and my hands still shook. I dreaded the idea of our toy factory being front and center in the gossip mill, the local newspapers, or around the county. I'd squinted long enough at Detective Mason's badge, so I handed the leather folder back. "Thanks. What do you need from us?"

"First, I'd like to review Officer Sykes's notes—something wrong?"

He turned to Maddie, who'd doubled over and snorted with laughter. She looked guilty at Mason's odd look. I suspected she was overcompensating from the shock of finding Will dead.

"Um. Officer Sykes—we call him Digger Sykes. Doug is a friend," my sister said, and gulped hard. "I went to high school with him."

"Digger, huh." Mason had raised an eyebrow and then opened his notebook. "Sounds like a good story. He identified the victim as William Taylor, who resides here in the village and works as a sales representative for the Silver Bear Shop and Factory."

"That's true."

"What else can you tell me about Mr. Taylor?"

Maddie and I exchanged glances. "He recently attended a trade show," I said, "in New Jersey. He met with vendors and suppliers. We didn't expect him back this week at all. Suddenly he showed up this morning. Er, yesterday morning."

"I see. And you both found the deceased inside the factory building at eleven fifty-five p.m.? Or is that the time the call was registered?"

"We called right after midnight," Maddie said. "I checked my watch before we went inside. We usually don't leave a light on at the factory door. And Will never comes to work late at night, so we wanted to know what he was doing inside."

"Were the lights on inside?"

"No, we had to switch them on."

"Right after we found . . . Will. Stuffed," I added. "That was quite a shock. Is that how he died? From all the fiber?"

"The medical examiner will determine that."

Maddie shuddered. "There wasn't any other way? Like being hit on the head?"

"I'm sorry, I couldn't tell—"

"He must have been," I said, and hugged my sister. She squeezed me back. "I can't see Will letting someone do that to him otherwise."

Mason didn't seem aware of our fragile emotions. "Did you touch anything besides the light switches and the door handles?"

"No. Well, I don't think so."

"Meaning you may have." He frowned. "All right, the crime scene is secure, but the evidence techs won't be able to arrive until morning. They're busy somewhere else right now. I'll return tomorrow at nine and make sure they get your prints and eliminate them from any others they find at the factory. Most fingerprints are too smudged to be of any use, though."

"Not like NCIS on television, I take it."

"Afraid not. You found the deceased lying on his back?"

I had to think about it, my head was so fuzzy. "I'm not sure—"

Maddie cut me off. "Yes. And we found a toy teddy bear. Ripped open."

"Well, the back seam was open," I added. "Very strange, because any unfinished bears are kept in the sewing machine area."

He looked skeptical. "So you think someone moved it? Deliberately."

"No idea. Some of the stuffing had been taken out. I can show you—"

"Officer Sykes already bagged and tagged the item as evidence." Mason looked up from his notebook straight at me. "How about we go inside and talk? You look cold."

"Sure, thanks."

I'd been shivering the whole time he questioned us. Maddie sprinted ahead to the back door and unlocked it. Rosie bounded out; I caught her mid-woof. I hadn't even thought about her waiting to go out, poor thing. Fighting to get free of my tight hug, she kept barking her fool head off at Detective Mason. He backed away. I'd never have expected him to be fearful of a small dog, although he looked more surprised than afraid. Maddie attached Rosie's harness and leash and then dragged her past us.

"Hush, you silly girl," Maddie said, and headed to the lawn's far side.

Inside, I perched on a tall stool at the island's counter and slid Maddie's cell phone back and forth across the wood. My nose tingled. The scent of stale popcorn wafting from my sweater mingled with the detective's musky aftershave. Should I ask him to sit? I'd never spoken with a homicide detective before. Mom would be offering him coffee or scrambled eggs and toast, insisting on something, ever the good hostess.

Good thing Mom wasn't here.

Detective Mason remained standing, oblivious to my discomfort, scribbling on a fresh page in the folder. He finally resumed without waiting for Maddie's return.

"So you're sisters, from what Officer Sykes reports. Alexandra and Madeline Silverman, and your parents own this business. Have you contacted them yet?"

"We've tried." The fact that my parents hadn't yet returned our frantic calls bothered me more than I cared to admit. I changed the subject and explained our stop at Ham Heaven and the movie afterward, then our return home. "We both thought it odd to see two cars in the lot. We recognized Will's Camry."

"So he doesn't usually come in after hours."

Unnerved by Mason's apparent indifference, the way he focused on writing notes instead of meeting my eyes, I stammered a little. "N-not that I've ever known. I go to bed pretty early, but Maddie might have noticed if he ever came after hours. She stays up later. Sometimes after midnight. Comes and goes more often, too, with her friends."

"But Mr. Taylor does have a key to the factory."

"I'm not sure. Uncle Ross would know, since he keeps track of keys."

Mason had raised an eyebrow at my hesitation and then jotted that answer down. "So you saw another car?"

"Yes, but the driver sped off in a hurry. There's two ways to get in and out of the lot, and he took the one closest to the house. Clipped the mailbox post and broke it off halfway from the ground. Bent the metal box all up, too."

Maddie barged through the door, lugging the thirty-pound Rosie past the detective. Despite her growling, my sister shoved the dog into her wire crate and latched the door. Rosie whined. "It's okay, baby. Be good for a little while and then it'll be time for breakfast. Uh, sorry it took so long—"

"I won't keep either of you much longer," Mason cut in. He flipped to a new page in his book. "Your sister said you might have noticed cars or visitors in the parking lot at various times. Before tonight, that is. Did you ever see Mr. Taylor or anyone else enter the factory after hours?"

Maddie didn't hesitate. "Not that I remember. Although one time, I did see a car in the lot near the trees out back. Uncle Ross said the next morning he found cigarette butts on the ground, and a . . . Other stuff. But you'd have to ask him." Her cheeks flushed deep pink.

"I will. Can you describe the car you saw tonight?"

I answered first. "A dark car, sort of sporty—"

"Like those old Gran Torino muscle cars, only smaller," Maddie said. "But I think it was bright red. Definitely red."

"Brown. Or maybe maroon," I mused aloud. "It's gotta have some big dent to the grille and front bumper, if it has one."

"Did either of you recognize the driver?"

My sister and I blinked at each other. "No," I said. "It was dark."

"It happened so fast," Maddie said. "All I remember is hearing the tires squeal, and like wham! It hit the mailbox, turned into the street, and took off."

"Man or woman?"

"Pretty sure it was a guy. In a hat?"

"Young," my sister said firmly. "No hat."

"He did too wear a hat," I said.

Mason frowned. "Okay, thanks. If you remember anything else, here's my contact info." He dug out a worn business card and handed it over. "Better get some rest."

"We have to get up early and open the shop—"

"You'll be closed over the weekend." His voice sounded flat. "Shop and factory. Like I said before, the forensic techs will be here as soon as possible. The coroner's on vacation, so the techs will transport the body to the county morgue later this morning. It will take time to process the scene. But first, I'll need to interview the staff."

My mouth hung open until I realized how foolish I must look. "But we're having a big sale! We have to be open this weekend. And our teddy bear picnic is at the park on Monday. People have paid money to attend. We can't cancel."

"Besides, the shop and the factory are separate," Maddie said.

"I'm sorry. You're closed."

"Detective Mason, we can't possibly suspend production. We have orders to fill. A big one came in today for our Teddy Roosevelt bear—"

"You're closed until further notice." He refused to listen to further protests. "I'll talk to the sheriff about the picnic, but until we're done here, the public is off-limits. Don't remove the crime scene tape, and make sure your employees come in by nine o'clock for interviews. I'm sure you'll be happy to co-operate with the authorities."

With that, Detective Mason departed. Rosie had been scrab-bling at her cage with her claws, whining in her throat, despite our attempts to quiet her. Maddie suddenly laughed.

"You'd think Rosie suspects him of the murder."

"Ha. Maybe we should have watched what Digger was doing inside the factory."

"He booted us out so fast, my head spun. I tried calling Uncle Ross, but he didn't answer his phone. Should I call him again?"

I glanced up at the wooden clock above the kitchen sink and sighed. "At half past two in the morning? He'd bite our heads off. Then again, if he doesn't find out till tomorrow morning he'll be worse mad. I don't know. I can't think straight."

"I'm calling him again."

Maddie waited, cell near her ear, and then hit the speaker button. "Uncle Ross? Hello? I'm sorry to wake you, but there's been trouble at the factory—"

He mumbled something like "whaaa the hell" before his voice barked over my sister's reply. "In the factory? It's not even morning yet, for God's sake. Wait—was there a fire? I've been worried about the electrical panel for a while now."

"No. Nothing like that."

"Then what?"

"Will Taylor," I blurted out. "We found him. Dead. Inside the factory."

Uncle Ross didn't answer for several seconds, but his tone softened. "Oh, God. Are you girls all right? Did you call the cops?"

"Yeah, they just left."

"What was Taylor doing there at night?"

"We don't know. And we can't get through to Mom and Dad," Maddie said.

"Wait, let me get dressed. I'll be right there."

"No," she said wearily. "We need some sleep. But the homicide detective is coming back early to interview everyone. We figured you'd better know ahead of time and herd them away from the factory. There's crime tape all over."

"How about we talk things over at breakfast. Fresh Grounds," I said.

"What's wrong with the Sunshine Café? Oh. Better not," my uncle said. "The chief of police owns it and his wife is in charge. Not that I don't trust Lenore—"

"I'd rather talk things over at a neutral spot. Unless you'd rather come here?"

"Nah. See you two in the morning."

Uncle Ross ended the call before we could reply. "I wonder if the police have called Carolyn and told her. I feel horrible about this," I said.

"Yeah. That's gonna hit hard. Even if they've been having marital problems."

Maddie plugged in her charger and headed upstairs. Onyx padded after her and slipped into my sister's bedroom. Good idea. Cat hair on the pillow, ugh. I liked our cat, but no bones about it—I preferred the dog as a sleep partner.

Rolling over, I faced the wall. Nearly a decade ago, while getting my business degree at the University of Michigan, I'd reveled in a whirlwind courtship with a charming and handsome lawyer. Flynn Hanson was charming, sweet, attentive—so like my dad, I thought he was perfect. An expensive wedding and exotic honeymoon fulfilled my dreams. Until I learned that Flynn—named after Errol Flynn of classic movies—also had a womanizing nature. Despite him begging for forgiveness, I gave my husband a bouncing baby divorce before our first anniversary.

I still hadn't gotten over the deep hurt and betrayal. Maybe that's why I didn't trust Will Taylor. He reminded me too much of Flynn. Rosie stretched out, head on the other pillow, her nose touching my hand. I scratched behind her ears, grateful for her loyalty.

Unlike my ex, Rosie never chose someone else's bed.

Chapter 7

I woke the next morning, groggy, from a hard shake. "Come on, Sash," Maddie said. "It's almost time to meet Uncle Ross at Fresh Grounds. Up and at 'em, madam! Move!"

"Gaah."

I stretched, yearning to return to the odd dream I'd had, some elusive thread about a missing teddy bear with broken spectacles. Rosie wasn't on the bed. I heard birds trilling outside the open window, and the lace curtains rustling in the breeze. I disliked mornings. Spending a little time after the alarm went off was something to savor. But Maddie snatched the light coverlet away and yelled in my ear.

"Get up! Now. We're supposed to meet Uncle Ross for breakfast."

"Ugh. I can't think of food after what happened a few hours ago." I staggered to the bathroom, stood under the shower, and finally opened my eyes. Maddie hollered from the stairs. "I'm coming," I shouted back, and brushed out my hair. "Some of us can't bounce out of bed like a jack-in-the-box. Not naming any names!"

I checked the clock. Ten minutes till seven. That made around four hours of sleep. I'd need a few triple espressos to stay awake for the family powwow. With the shop closed, I pulled on my rattiest jeans and a navy-and-white-striped T-shirt. Jammed a favorite straw hat on my wet hair and slipped bare feet into sandals before I ran downstairs. Maddie had already taken care of Rosie, who wagged her tail from the kitchen's window perch. Onyx gave me a cold stare. My sister always cleaned the cat litter and fed her, while I got the stank eye.

The car's honking horn drew me outside. While I fastened my seat belt, Maddie tore out of the lot toward Fresh Grounds. Given the early hour, she passed traffic heading to the freeway and jobs in Ann Arbor or elsewhere. I rubbed my eyes, wishing I had time for a quick nap.

"You're wearing two different shoes, Sash."

"I am?" I sighed. "Why didn't you tell me before we left?"

"Nobody will notice except me. By the way, I put up a sign on the factory door, and on our back door in case anyone didn't get the text message. Uncle Ross called Deon, who texted everyone. I've gotten three phone calls already. Mary Kate called when you didn't answer your phone. Both Abby Pozniak and Jodie Watson called me. Word's getting around fast."

I dug in my purse and came up empty. "Dang. Didn't I put it on the charger?"

"Yesterday. It's still on the kitchen counter."

"I'm sure Mary Kate told Elle, if it's true gossip's going around."

Maddie shrugged. "I've heard plenty—Will was shot, stabbed, strangled, but no matter what, he's dead. And we found him. Jodie heard he'd gotten in a car accident along with Carolyn, who wasn't hurt. Abby wondered if it was true we stumbled over his corpse in the garden."

"Oh, brother."

We parked on the street before Fresh Grounds, which looked empty. I figured we had half an hour before the usual crowd started lining up at the counter and out the door. We all loved this shop with its tall windows, the long counter painted mint green, and its butcher-block top; it matched the polished oak floor. White beadboard walls marched around the room, with built-in benches attached. Slabs of wood served as tables, and short metal stools provided seats on the other side. A few framed photographs of lush green coffee fields marched in a row toward the French doors that led to The Cat's Cradle, closed this early in the day.

The chalkboard greeting today had a huge heart with *Welcome to Caffeine Heaven!* written in swirling cursive letters. "Morning," Garrett Thompson said with a nod. "Sorry to hear about Will Taylor."

I nodded my thanks. We headed toward Uncle Ross and Deon in the bay window's alcove. Formerly a milliner's shop from the early 1900s, Fresh Grounds still had the original wood plank floor. Garrett's uncle Gil opened the shop forty years ago; now he manned the counter with his nephew in the mornings. A short, pudgy old-timer with a huge schnozzle and a bigger infectious laugh, Gil made everyone smile.

"Hey, girls. Good to see you two," he called out before banging out used espresso beans. "Got your order coming right up."

Garrett capped one drink and started another. Tall and lean, dark-haired, with black-rimmed glasses—he'd given up on his contacts—he was quiet compared to outgoing Mary Kate. Her reddish-blond hair caught in a ponytail that flipped around while she dished up baked goods and cashed out orders. But she looked worried when she approached our small table in the window's alcove, smoothing down her black apron over her white blouse and black capris.

"Sasha, Maddie—gosh, how horrible." She hugged us both. "Are you okay?"

"Sort of." I blinked, still fuzzy. "I think."

Mary Kate signaled her husband. "Coffee is coming right up."

Uncle Ross looked haggard. He wore the usual Hawaiian shirt, khakis, and boating shoes along with his hat. "Still nothing from Mom and Dad," Maddie said, glancing up from her phone. "Have you heard anything from them, Uncle Ross? Did you try to call them this morning?"

"Plenty of times. Damned if I know what's going on, or where they are. I left at least half a dozen messages." He scratched his gray beard and grabbed the coffeepot Garrett brought over along with two china cups. "Got more cream?"

"Yessir." Garrett set down a small jug before him, then passed around the specialty coffees. "Triple-shot Mint Mocha for Sash. Teddy Bear for Mads. Back to the grinder for me, but I'll catch the details later."

"The real story," Maddie said, "not the silly rumors running around town."

"Like Will hanging himself from the rafters in the factory?" Mary Kate asked. "I'll be right back with some muffins and toasted bagels."

"Hanging himself? Now I've heard everything." I sipped my espresso, wondering if a little brandy in it would calm my nerves. "What will they think of next?"

My sister shrugged. "That a ghost knocked him off, I suppose."

Maddie looked fresh and energetic, in a white-and-blue-patterned dress that reminded me of Delft china. As if losing sleep after finding a dead body didn't bother her at all—maybe that was unfair. But I truly resented her bubbly morning persona. Until I had at least two cups of morning coffee to fortify myself. How had I missed noticing her outfit in the car? I glanced down at my mismatched shoes. At least I remembered to wear pants. And underwear.

"I bet Will let his killer inside. Does he have a key, Uncle Ross?"

"Not that I know."

"He must have gotten one, then."

"Tone it down, Mads." I waved a hand. "Really. I can barely see, much less think."

Mary Kate returned with a big platter of bagels and muffins. "Sunshine lemon for Uncle Ross," she said, and perched on an extra stool. "Your favorite. Maddie gets the blueberry, and Sasha's is the streusel cinnamon."

"Thanks! I'll take one of the toasted bagels, too."

I spread a thick layer of cream cheese on the warm, crunchy halves. My stomach grumbled before my first bite of muffin. Mm. Brown sugar and cinnamon crumbles, cakey goodness. Twenty minutes ago, I couldn't think of food. Now I was starving. Go figure. I polished off the muffin and started on the bagel.

"So what really happened?" Mary Kate asked. "Spill."

Maddie dove into the story, since my mouth was full. I filled in the gaps whenever I could get a word in between bites. Uncle Ross didn't say anything, only sipped coffee. I studied him, pondering about his perspective on the situation.

"I can't remember if there ever was a murder in Silver Hollow before—"

"Yes, there was."

When I twisted around, I almost slid to the floor. Dave Fox poked the wire-rimmed glasses on his nose with a huge grin. He joined us, dragging another stool over and setting his iPad on a small space not filled by plates and cups. Dave jotted notes constantly with his stylus while he talked.

"This is the second, in fact. After three decades of peace and quiet," he said. "Domestic violence gone bad. Not at all like Taylor's murder."

Uncle Ross glared at him. "What happened thirty years ago?"

"Wife beater got shot. Damn shame he bled out so fast."

"Are you implying Will Taylor's a saint? Because he isn't. I've heard and seen plenty of arguments between him and his wife."

"But Carolyn couldn't have killed him. There's photos to prove it." Maddie brought out her cell and booted up Facebook. "Her friend posted a selfie last night."

I peered close at the screen, which showed a blurry picture of several ladies laughing, holding drinks in hand, cleavage showing, arms around one another's necks. I recognized Carolyn in the center. "Where is that?"

"Quinn's Pub," Uncle Ross said, although he hadn't glanced at the photo.

"How do you know?"

"I was there. They were the loudest group in the whole place."

"Here's another one," Maddie said. "Carolyn's half falling off her chair."

"Not surprised, she was so drunk," my uncle said.

Dave Fox cleared his throat. "So what about Taylor?"

"What about him?"

"Getting whatever details I can from the horse's mouth."

Pete's dad kept his dark hair in a short ponytail, Paul Revere–style, favored blue denim button-down shirts and navy chinos, but always wore beat-up sneakers. They looked ready to fall apart any day, with rips and holes, although he laced them well. His *Silver Hollow Herald* only came out once a month—twice if there was any special news—so we all knew what he wanted. A camera was looped around his neck in case he had to snap something without preparation.

Uncle Ross snorted. "No comment."

"Come on, what happened?" Dave glanced at us one by

one. "Pete told me about the fireworks at the staff meeting you had after work. How you threatened Taylor—"

"Better check with Detective Mason," Maddie interrupted. "He might not be happy if you repeat certain rumors and make his job harder."

"Fine."

Dave stalked out with his iPad. My sister breathed a sigh of relief. "So what are we going to do about Mom and Dad? Maybe they were in a car accident!"

"Don't blow this out of proportion," Uncle Ross said. "They'll call."

"I talked to the Hilton desk clerk in Hasbrouck Heights, the one where the trade show was being held. Mom and Dad checked out after Will Taylor left. So they must be traveling between New Jersey and Sarasota."

"Did you try the condo complex?"

She shook her head. "The manager wasn't in."

"Maybe Mom and Dad decided to travel. Out of the country, or on a cruise." I wanted to believe that, since Mom had talked Dad into spontaneous trips in the past. "If only we had the phone number of a neighbor for emergencies like this."

Maddie suddenly poked me. "Hey. Flynn moved to Clearwater Beach, or was it Tampa? Why don't you call him?"

"Why don't I stab myself with a fork instead."

Mary Kate handed me a dirty spoon. "This will have to do," she teased. "Really, Maddie, leave Sasha's ex out of this. She's had enough grief—"

When Uncle Ross slammed a fist on the table, I jumped. "Augh. What now?"

"Maybe something bad did happen," he said.

"You said not to blow this out of proportion."

"Well, how else are we gonna find out if we can't get hold

of them? So call that miserable son of a gun. It's the only option we have right now."

"But—"

Uncle Ross cut me off. "He owes you, Sasha, big time. Call all the hospitals within fifty or a hundred miles of their condo. But first see if he'll check out their place. He can go pound on their door, see if they're hiding. It's the least he can do."

I closed my eyes. My world had gone berserk.

Chapter 8

Joan, Flora, and Harriet crowded around the moment we arrived back at the Silver Bear Shop & Factory. "Ms. Silverman! What happened last night?" I climbed out of the car to a flurry of questions. "Is it true Mr. Taylor was murdered?"

"Give us a little room to breathe," Maddie said.

"Oh, sorry."

Still bleary-eyed, I noticed the sewing crew dressed in their usual black pants and silver logo T-shirts. "We're the ones who are sorry. The police have closed us down to continue their investigation. No idea if we'll open tomorrow, either."

"But what happened?" Flora demanded. "How did he die?"

"We found him under the stuffing machine." I avoided their gazes. "It was either the fiber in his throat or—Where's Lois?"

I knew someone was missing from the group, although Pete wasn't anywhere in sight, either. The ladies shrugged. Deon's motorcycle roared into the parking lot, followed by Uncle Ross's Thunderbird. Both men stalked toward the factory but kept clear of the yellow tape swaying in the warm breeze. Clouds scudded across the sky. Today wouldn't nearly be as warm as yesterday. Maybe. Michigan weather could change in an instant. I wished now I'd brought a second triple Mint Mocha espresso from Fresh Grounds. My head pounded.

"Let's all go inside."

The ladies followed me. I should have brought a box of muffins, too, and kicked myself for not thinking of it sooner. Maddie carried in two large bags, however, filled with bagels, plus a cardboard tray of coffee cups she'd stashed in the backseat. God bless my sister. Maybe being an early bird wasn't so bad.

Especially on days like today.

"What time is it?" I grabbed my cell phone, which read 8:02 a.m. "Okay, so we have nearly an hour before this detective arrives to interview us—"

"Uh, Sash? He's already here."

Maddie placed the tray and bags on the kitchen island. Rosie started barking before we heard a hard rap on the door. I caught her by the collar before she could jump Detective Mason. This time he extended an elbow for her to sniff, which surprised her. Today Mason wore a navy blazer, striped tie, and slacks, but still resembled a grumpy bear, with dark circles under his eyes that pointed to lost sleep. Rosie's barks had settled into a plaintive whine while she struggled to get free of my hold. Mason raised an eyebrow and glanced around.

"I'll need to talk to you all individually. Somewhere private."

"Yes, this way."

Maddie led him to the former study, which was my favorite room downstairs. Glass-paned French doors had kept Rosie and Onyx out of trouble since the day they'd knocked Mom's expensive pottery collection to the floor. Her collection of rare Madame Alexander dolls were safe inside a locked curio cabinet as well.

My sister returned alone. "He wants to start with Uncle Ross. Where is he?"

"Probably standing outside the factory, watching the evidence technicians' every move. I'll go tell him."

First I attached Rosie's harness and leash. Outside, Deon paced the parking lot with my uncle, who was indeed arguing with several young techs in orange vests with "Dexter County" in black letters. My frantic waving caught their attention. Uncle Ross and Deon both stalked toward me. I braced myself for worse fireworks.

"They're bound to make a huge mess in the factory! It'll take hours to clean it before we can get back to work. And we have that big order. . . ."

I let him ramble on, since it was futile to interrupt. "We'll deal with it later. You're up first with Detective Mason, though. He's waiting in the study."

"Oh, brother. I don't suppose your dad ever called or texted?"

"Nothing yet."

"Then call Flynn, for God's sake. We need Alex. It's his damned factory. He needs to explain why the hell Taylor thought he could push us around with his big plans for sending production to China."

Uncle Ross stomped inside. I headed to the back garden, dreading this. Then I pulled my cell phone from a pocket. The time had come to bite the bullet. Flynn Edward Hanson, a lawyer specializing in personal injury, medical malpractice, and breaking hearts. My hands shook so badly, I nearly dropped the phone. Disappointment hit me when I saw no messages waiting, and no missed calls. At least the battery showed full.

I stared at Flynn's profile photo. I should have deleted it long ago. I could do this. Really, I could—no big deal. I kept telling myself that while booting up Facebook via the Internet. Maybe Flynn was on vacation. Off to Europe on business. He always posted selfies. Photos of himself on the beach in Florida. Showing off plates of food in fancy restaurants before meals.

"Oh, brother. Look at that."

I scanned over the latest on his timeline—Flynn taking a bite from a shrimp cocktail while holding a forkful of linguini toward a gorgeous brunette. Her cleavage showed more flesh than a baby's bottom. Another at the beach, arms outstretched, grinning beside the woman who was draped over him like a shawl. Clearly he didn't lack for company.

Over the past seven years, I'd progressed slowly from sheer loathing to an uneasy truce. Had I forgiven him? Maybe, but I'd never forget how I'd been a fool to fall for his infectious charm. We'd first bonded over a similar sense of humor. But it wasn't funny discovering his cheating ways. Mere months after our spring wedding, despite a blissful honeymoon in Jamaica, feeling so in love and sharing every moment of our days, even exchanging delightful gifts over the Christmas holidays. Until New Year's Eve, when everything had crashed around me.

Flynn's betrayal hurt. Still. I dialed anyway.

He actually answered my call, despite the early hour. "Sasha? Is that you? Hey, you caught me on the way into court, but I have a few minutes. What's up?"

"Uh, yeah. Ow! Sorry—Rosie, get back here."

"How's she doing?"

"Fine."

"Good to know," Flynn said with a laugh. "So is something wrong?"

Hearing his sexy baritone sent a shiver up my spine. I kicked myself for being vulnerable to his voice. "I guess you'd call it that. Mads and I . . . We need a favor. Kind of a big favor. Rosie, stop. Ow, quit stepping on my toes."

"What's the favor?"

"Well, it's important. Really."

"You sound like one of my clients. Quit dithering, dammit, and spit it out."

"Give me a second."

My dog's extra-long leash was tangled around my legs. I almost fell straightening it out. The phone clattered to the ground at one point. If the call had dropped, I would have claimed it as karma and let it go. Unfortunately, Flynn remained on the line.

"You there? Hey, Sasha! I'll be late for court if you don't make it snappy."

"I'm here." I took a deep breath. "We haven't heard from my parents since last week. We have an emergency here. At the factory."

"Uncle Ross cut off another finger?"

"That's not funny!"

"Oh, come on, I was kidding." Flynn's chuckle burned me worse than his sick joke. "You would have laughed years ago."

"Someone was killed—Augh." Rosie had circled me for the second time. I twisted and staggered to free myself and finally sat on the porch's top step. "One of our employees— Maddie and I found him last night."

"How was he killed?"

"I don't have time to explain, and you don't have time to listen to the whole story. We're so afraid Mom and Dad got into a car accident on the way home from New Jersey. We sent a bazillion texts and voice-mail messages on their phones. Is there any way you could visit their condo? See if something happened, or if they've gone somewhere else. Whatever. To make sure they're all right."

"Sure. Hope they aren't skinny-dipping in the club's pool."

"My parents? Yeah, right."

"Gotta run."

"I'm calling the hospitals—"

Flynn hung up before I could finish my sentence. Oh well.

That was pretty normal for him. I was shocked he'd agreed to help.

A car door slammed across the street. I stood on tiptoes and squinted between the trees. Debbie Davison rushed up the steps of the Holly Jolly Christmas shop. After unlocking the door, she swept inside. Odd. I pulled Rosie along, tugging her leash when she sniffed a bush, and crossed Theodore Lane. Perhaps Debbie could tell me how Carolyn had taken the news about Will's death. Murder. I shook my head. Ugh.

Debbie and her sister, Cissy, grew up in the Victorian house that matched ours—on the exterior, of course. Barbara Davison was my mom's best friend. Cissy rented an apartment, while Debbie owned a small house and land beyond Richardson's Farms; she kept between twenty and fifty beehives and processed honey with two other friends. Cissy and Debbie's parents owned the row of buildings on Main Street, including the Time Turner, a quaint boutique managed by Cissy, along with the Holly Jolly shop.

Debbie often covered for her sister, but I'd never seen anyone cover for Carolyn before today. I led Rosie up the porch steps and knocked on the open door. "Hello?"

Smoothing her dark hair behind an ear, Debbie reminded me of Mia Farrow, with a sharp chin and cheekbones, plus huge blue eyes. "Morning! We're not open yet—Oh, Sasha! Thank goodness. I need to use the bathroom. Can you watch for customers? Too much coffee."

Without waiting for an answer, Debbie dashed through the red and green beads hanging over the back doorway. I stood in the doorway, admiring the shop's graceful interior even though everything was too orderly to my taste. I'd have chosen a charming eclectic mix instead of the Santa Claus figurines shelved on one side of the shop, the handmade crafts and painted tables or chairs in one corner, and the themed trees lined against the other wall. One had all animal ornaments, another cartoon characters, and so on. Thankfully Debbie had not turned on all the lights yet. My headache hadn't subsided, and my caffeine level was fading fast.

I winced when Christmas music blared from a nearby speaker. Thankfully the volume decreased before Debbie popped through the beaded curtain. She'd tied a red and green apron over her black dress and donned a headband with antlers. A bit much, but perhaps she thought the cuteness factor would make up for Carolyn's absence.

"So. You're holding down the fort for a while?" I wondered how much Debbie knew. If anything. She was closer to my sister's age, and Cissy was a year older than me.

"She's a mess," Debbie said with a laugh. "We all went out last night—me and Cissy, Nickie Richardson, and Carolyn. Oh, and Kristen Bloom came later. We had sort of a 'pity party' at Quinn's Pub. Carolyn's been so down since finding out about her husband's affair, we wanted to cheer her up. She got totally smashed! So we left her car at the pub and drove her home last night. I told her I'd open the shop until she could drag herself in today."

"A pity party?"

"Carolyn wasn't happy when Will refused to go with her for marriage counseling. Sure, he helped boost sales when Carolyn opened the shop after she divorced her first husband. Will really was great back then. Carolyn said he wouldn't give her advice lately or do anything she needed. And then he showed up yesterday, after some business trip, and wanted her to drop everything for him!"

I wondered how much Debbie knew, if anything, about Will's death. "I bet the pub must have been crowded even for a Thursday night."

"Packed. They had that trio playing Irish music," Debbie

added. "Plus George French was doing his magic tricks, and he's almost as popular. I saw your uncle there. The one who drives that swanky vintage car."

"Uncle Ross?"

"He didn't stay long, though."

"I heard Deon Walsh was with him."

"Yeah, and his sister Devonna. They left before your uncle." She lowered her voice. "He said out loud, to everyone all around his table, how Will Taylor would be toast if he cut jobs at your factory. That he'd gut him like a fish."

Great. Bad enough Uncle Ross said it at the meeting, and then he blabbed it in public. And why was Deon's sister there? Apparently Debbie hadn't heard the news about Will's death from anyone in town or from Carolyn, either.

"What did Will ask Carolyn to do instead of going to Quinn's Pub?"

"Cook him a fancy dinner, can you believe it?" She rolled her eyes heavenward. "He'd gotten his way at last and wanted to celebrate. But Carolyn refused to cancel our party."

I squinted. "Gotten his way—what did he mean by that?"

Debbie blinked. "Don't you know? Will finally talked your dad into sending production overseas and cutting jobs. I don't blame your uncle for being so mad. And Carolyn thought it was a dirty, lowdown trick. Your factory workers depend on their jobs. So she told him to go celebrate by himself."

"I bet Will wasn't happy."

"Carolyn didn't say, but you can bet he hightailed it over to his latest honey."

"Honey?"

"You haven't heard? It's not just rumor that he's got a girl-friend, but I'm not gonna spill her name. Carolyn would be mad." Debbie fluffed up her dark hair. "I'm usually the designated driver, only I was useless by midnight."

"Oh. So who was?"

"Cissy. Nickie had so many martinis, her husband had to collect her. Carolyn was so bad, we all had to help carry her to the car. I threw up in the backseat. My sister was so mad! She made me clean it up this morning, and that was no fun."

I was surprised any of them made it home without crashing. I hated losing control. I'd never gotten drunk in my life and never intended to, for that fact alone. One drink, if that, was my limit. Seeing others smashed out of their minds wasn't a pretty sight.

"So Carolyn didn't tell you anything this morning."

"Like what?"

"About Will."

"She said he never made it home, if that's what you mean." Debbie snorted. "I wouldn't be surprised. Carolyn didn't get a chance to tell me much, because she said a cop car was pulling into her driveway and she had to answer the door. She said she felt like a truck hit her. I felt the same way, but here I am. I hope she comes in soon. I'm supposed to treat the beehives for mites."

I imagined Carolyn would never get her act together after hearing about Will's murder. "Well, I hate to be the bearer of bad news—"

"What?" Debbie had leaned down to retrieve her purse.

"Her husband is dead."

Debbie clutched her chest, genuinely shocked. "You— you're kidding, right?"

I shook my head. "No."

"What happened?"

When the cordless phone trilled on its holder, we both jumped. Debbie snatched it and answered. "Hello? Hi, Mom . . . Oh my God, I just found out! . . . From Sasha Silverman! Right here—yeah." She turned to me, receiver held out. "My mom wants to talk to you."

Reluctant, I took the phone. Rosie had been sniffing

around while I was distracted. I grabbed a stuffed elf out of her mouth and wiped the slobber off the felt. Debbie waved me on to answer, brown eyes wide, and then scrabbled for her cell phone inside her purse.

"Um, hello?"

"I heard about Will Taylor! What in the world? I can hardly believe——"

I listened, unable to get a word in edgewise while Barbara Davison listed the various sources she'd heard from about the murder. Rumors around the village had multiple versions of ways he'd been killed, even more colorful than this morning. Then she demanded I tell her what I knew, asked how could a murder happen right next door to her own house, whether the police could save the village from such violent killers, and so on. I figured she was too much in shock to ask for the real details. Then again, Debbie didn't know I'd found Will's body. Good thing, or she might have fainted on the Holly Jolly Christmas shop floor.

"I know, Cissy," Debbie said. "I just heard from Sasha. She's right here, talking to mom on the shop phone. Yes, last night! At the factory."

She stuck a finger in her ear, talking faster, quickly hung up, and then dialed someone else. I realized Mrs. Davison had asked me a question. The second time louder.

"What's that? I'm sorry——"

"Who would possibly want to kill Will Taylor?"

"I don't know. I'd better get back."

Without listening to her protest, I hung up and led Rosie outside.

Chapter 9

Despite my constant commands to stop, Rosie barked and barked at the parade of cars cruising narrow Theodore Lane. Drivers had to turn around and drive back once they discovered the dead end. Everyone craned their necks at the crime scene tape stretched across the factory entrance. Rosie and I waited for a break before we squeezed between cars and crossed the street.

I felt horrible. Poor Carolyn, who'd fought to save her marriage to that sleazeball. Took our side against her husband over his nasty plans and now had to deal with the scandal of a small-town murder. I couldn't help feeling sorry for her.

We'd always traded stories about the hard work we did promoting our shops, holding sales, and hosting special events. While the tough economy had slowly improved, our products were considered "extras" rather than necessities. So I wasn't about to let Detective Mason cancel the picnic on Labor Day, after I'd planned so carefully and already paid Mary Kate to bake and decorate the special cookies.

"Sasha!"

I twisted around, wishing I hadn't spent so much time talking to Debbie Davison. Jenny Woodley, co-owner of the brick Silver Leaf Bed and Breakfast, waved frantically from the porch. The Queen Anne structure with its multiple gables and one turret was shaded by multiple silver maples. Many of its unique features were hidden from the street due to the trees. Jenny rushed to join me, her brunette hair flowing behind her, her warm brown eyes full of concern. Over her black capris and striped T-shirt, she wore a yellow apron with daisy appliqués and printed with "True Love Is Breakfast in Bed" below their leaf-shaped logo.

"Glen and I were wondering what happened last night. We saw all the flashing lights, and the police cars."

"Yes. We found a body."

"A dead body?" Jenny's high intake of breath reminded me of a baby pig's squeal—not that I was an expert in farm animals, but it sounded odd. "Who was it?"

"Will Taylor."

She gaped at me, eyebrows slowly rising. "Will Taylor? Your sales rep?"

"Yes," I said, tired of having to draw this out. "The police are investigating."

She wrung her hands. "Glen told me he saw you and your family at Fresh Grounds early this morning. But when he asked Garrett Thompson what happened, he couldn't get a straight answer."

I blinked. We hadn't asked Mary Kate and Garrett to keep the information under wraps, but I was grateful. Gossip always spread through Silver Hollow like a burst water pipe flooding everywhere. I was shocked Jenny hadn't gotten a phone call from Debbie or Barbara Davison. Then again, she might soon enough.

"So what happened?" she asked. "A heart attack?"

"Uh, no. He was killed."

"Murdered?" Jenny squawked again. "Like, stabbed or shot?"

"I can't say, really. Like I said, the police will find out what happened."

"No wonder so many cars have been driving past!"

Rosie had tangled my legs again. I unwound the leash and nearly dropped it. Lucky for me I didn't, because Glen Woodley jogged around the house at that moment. Rosie would have chomped his leg, for certain; she had a thing against men, probably from past abuse, and I had to be careful whenever strangers came near. Jenny and Glen both had the same oval-shaped face and light brown hair, but Glen's hazel eyes had thick lashes that no woman could achieve without two or three fake layers. I knew they both worked hard to run their bed-and-breakfast business. The Woodleys' three daughters served as maids and bakers, helped with gardening, and even mowed the lawn.

"Will Taylor's dead," Jenny said to Glen. He looked startled at first, eyes wide, and then shook his head in either regret or sympathy. "Sasha found him in the factory. Isn't that horrible?"

"I can think of a few people who'd have it in for Will Taylor," Glen said, hands on his hips. "I asked him for business advice last month. Wish I hadn't, because it's been a disaster for us. Everyone knows your uncle hated him—"

"He's not a killer, though," I interrupted, and then changed the subject. "Your place always looks so neat and orderly. I hope business is good."

"We're fully booked this weekend," Jenny said quickly with a smile.

Glen looked sour. "After telling us about a murder in your factory last night, you're hoping business is good?"

I bit my lip. Maybe that had sounded a little stupid. "I didn't mean it that way—"

"She gave us a nice compliment," Jenny cut in, and shot a warning look at Glen.

He ignored her. "How much do you want to bet more than a few guests will cancel? This murder's going to affect everyone around here, not just *your* shop. Look at the traffic— gawkers wanting a front-row seat to watch the cops."

"Is that my fault?" I resented his sarcastic tone.

"Glen, please." Jenny gripped his arm. "I'm sorry, Sasha, for you and Maddie."

"I saw your uncle at Quinn's Pub last night." He loosened his wife's grip with a flash of anger. "Heard him loud and clear. So did a bunch of others. Ross was steamed over Taylor's threat to cut his job. He even said he'd kill Will if the jerk sent production overseas."

"Then I suggest you tell Detective Mason that informa- tion." I shouldered my way past him. "Uncle Ross didn't have anything to do with Will's death and I'll prove it. No matter what he said last night at the pub."

Rosie jumped and twirled, excited to be heading home. Together we loped around the house to the garden, where I waited while she sniffed the lawn and flower beds. Rosie cir- cled the yard once more, trying my patience.

"Come on, girl. I'm sure I'll be up next on the hot seat."

At last we headed inside. I changed the water dish in her crate, ignored her whines, and hooked the door shut. I didn't need Rosie taking a bite out of crime—er, a Detective Mason. Uncle Ross's loud voice echoed from the library. Maddie paced the floor, clearly worried, while the other ladies ner- vously ate bagels and drank coffee in silence. Almost as if Will's ghost hovered over us all. Deon sat on the window seat study- ing a book on business management. Where were Pete and Lois? They usually called in by now.

I sidled over to my sister and asked her in a whisper, but she shrugged. Great. That meant I had to track them down and find out why they hadn't called. I used the phone in the dining room and punched in Lois's number.

She answered in a rush, out of breath, with an apology. "My husband—he's taken a turn for the worse. I need to keep an eye on him. Sorry I didn't call sooner."

"Okay then. Let me know if you can help Sunday in the shop."

"Sure."

Lois hung up quickly. I dialed Pete Fox's cell next, but he didn't answer. I left a message and then retrieved my laptop from upstairs. I looked up all the local hospitals in Sarasota and near my parents' condo on Siesta Key, then started dialing. Once a staffer confirmed there'd been no record of Alex or Judith Silverman coming into the emergency room or being admitted, I crossed that name off my list. Uncle Ross's voice rose from the hallway outside the study.

"Why the hell would I kill Will Taylor? That's a crock of—"

"You threatened him at the pub last night." Mason trailed behind my uncle when he stormed into the kitchen. "Several witnesses heard you."

"What about that wife of his?"

"We're investigating Mrs. Taylor's alibi as well."

"But I'm your prime suspect? Totally ridiculous. Even if he did steal our company's bear pattern, I wouldn't kill him over that. Take a punch or two, yeah. But I never got a chance."

Mason jotted that information down. "How about over eliminating your job?"

"He wanted to cut a bunch of jobs and send production overseas!"

"But you're the only one who threatened him at the pub. I believe your exact words were 'I'm gonna kill Will.' And something about serving his head on a platter." He flipped over a few notebook pages. "Several people also heard you say you'd gut him like a fish."

"Uncle Ross would never hurt anyone," Maddie said.

The detective shrugged. "I've heard that a million times about cold-blooded killers. 'He lived right next door. He was a great neighbor, so quiet.' Sorry, but it doesn't mean squat."

"I saw Will and Carolyn arguing last night in the parking lot." I leaned against the door's frame. "It looked that way to me. According to Debbie Davison, Will wanted her to cancel plans with her friends at the pub."

"Yeah, I saw the ladies there," Uncle Ross said. "They made so much noise, laughing and drinking, that I left early. Right, Deon?"

"Yeah. We couldn't even hear the music, they were so loud."

"You can tell me all about it in the study." Detective Mason hooked a thumb at the young man. "You're next. And don't get any ideas, Mr. Silverman, about leaving the village. Without informing me first, that is."

My uncle scowled while Deon followed Mason down the hall. I bit my lip hard. None of us had been prepared for Will's return from the East Coast, his sudden announcement about changes at the factory, or seeing his glee at our dismay. Yes, glee. He'd been downright elated about convincing my dad to agree with his plans. And without hearing from either of my parents, I couldn't help wondering if Will had succeeded.

I could only hope not.

"So how are you going to prove that Will stole the bear pattern?" I asked Uncle Ross. "Or whether or not he actually sold it to Bears of the Heart?"

"The only ones who have access to that pattern are me and your parents. Who else could have done it? Not you or Mads."

"I didn't even know we had a specialized pattern until Dad showed me last year." I snagged a bottle of water from the refrigerator and twisted off the cap. "And he kept it locked in the office safe. How could Will have gotten it out? Tell me that much, unless he asked Dad to see it."

Joan Kendall raised a hand. "Actually, I know how."

We both turned to look at her in surprise. She tucked a strand of her long red hair behind an ear, a little nervous. Her usual pale, freckled complexion looked whiter than usual in contrast to her blue eyes, except for two dark pink spots on both cheeks. Joan wore silver tennis shoes to match her shirt and, of all the sewing ladies, was the fittest. Her slender frame looked almost bony, in fact, compared to Flora's plumpness; the older woman had a frosted bob, plus turquoise earrings and necklace. Harriet reminded me of my grandmother with her bluish-silver cap of curls and a pair of magnifying eyeglasses on a silver and gold beaded chain. Joan was the youngest and the quietest of all our staff.

"Well?" Uncle Ross barked.

"I suggested making an optional change in the pattern a few months ago. I had an idea for sewing a pouch or pocket in some of the bears. A child could put her tooth inside, and the parents could take it out and put in a quarter or a dollar. Your dad thought it was a great idea."

"That *is* a great idea," I said. "Was Will involved?"

"Oh, he was. In fact—"

Maddie waved her phone. "Look, a text from Mom! She says she's too busy to call."

"That's all she said?" I stared at Maddie. "Didn't you tell her what happened in all your messages? How can they possibly be too busy?"

My sister nodded, just as frustrated. "I don't know. Every time I texted, I said it was an emergency. I asked her where they are, and if everything's all right, but Mom didn't answer. Have you heard from Flynn yet? You did call him, right?"

"Yes, but I have no idea if he can help us at all."

Maddie groaned, but I had to think this through instead of worrying about my ex. What in the world would keep Mom so busy she couldn't explain via a simple text or call us for a few minutes? She'd always been the stable influence through childhood. We barely saw Dad. He worked long hours at the law office and missed most school or summer activities. Holiday events revolved around Mom taking us to visit her parents, and Dad would sometimes join us.

We'd lived in an upscale neighborhood east of downtown Ann Arbor, close to Barton Park, during my elementary school years until Mom and Dad decided to return to Silver Hollow. My grandparents had been thrilled, of course. And I'd kept track of Maddie and her circle of friends while Mom worked. Maddie and I often complained, but we had a privileged childhood compared to most kids.

I'd been shocked that after Dad worked so hard for years to make partner in a law firm, he quit like a snap of his fingers. Somehow he convinced Mom that starting a toy shop and factory was his dream come true. Dad once told me that seeing Grandpa T. R.'s teddy bears on a shelf jogged him into action; he realized, at last, that investing in family was more important. Opening the teddy bear factory—plus renovating the house into a shop with living quarters—was the right move. Quick success paid off all the risk.

But why were my parents being so secretive? Maybe Maddie was right about being treated like a kid. Maybe I was fooling myself about how they saw me; after seven years, they had yet to treat me with the same level of respect as Will Taylor. My edginess ratcheted up a few notches. Were Mom and Dad gearing up for another radical shift? Planning to sell out? Was that why Will acted so self-assured? So happy, as Carolyn put it. Ready to take over. Gaah.

"Did you actually text Mom or Dad that Will was murdered?" I asked Maddie.

"I figured I'd tell them on the phone. In person would be better yet."

"It's time to spell it out in a text. We have no choice."

I sent a new text to both of my parents' cell phones. *Emergency due to murder at the factory. CALL ASAP!!* That ought to do the trick.

If that didn't rattle them, nothing would.

Chapter 10

"Okay, let's see how busy they are after hearing the grim news," I said. "Now, back to the teddy bear pattern issue."

Flora and Harriet backed up Joan's story about the "tooth" pocket. Joan even sketched out what they'd come up with, which was quite clever. When I said as much, she beamed.

"So Dad got the bear pattern from the safe for Maddie to copy?" I asked.

"Actually, your dad wasn't here. He asked Will to fetch it from the safe and copy it," Harriet said. "Maddie was out that day with a cold."

I thought back to the week, almost a month ago, when my sister was sick. Maddie never missed work; she'd dragged around the office for days, sneezing and coughing, until I sent her upstairs to bed. I juggled customer calls along with sales in the shop while Flora covered for Maddie in the office. Flora had once worked as a receptionist and took care of things until my sister recovered from bronchitis the following week. I'd been so frazzled with other needs at that time—Rosie had been sick, too.

No wonder we hadn't heard anything about the bear pattern. Dad probably thought it wasn't important enough to tell us. Clearly he trusted Will. Instead, our sales rep had taken advantage of the situation. What a jerk.

Uncle Ross walked outside to the back porch for a smoke. I joined him, sitting on the swing and squinting at the midday sun. Dark clouds amassed in the west, threatening rain, and the humid air was thick. I couldn't complain, because the grass did look brown in spots and our flowers needed rain beyond the automatic sprinklers. The chains creaked when I rocked. I'd forgotten to oil them the last time Maddie asked me.

"So Bears of the Heart might have our bear pattern. Why would they want it?" I asked. "Anyone could buy a bear and take it apart. They could make a pattern of their own that way."

"Teddy Hartman is our biggest rival. I know Taylor wanted to get rid of me, and then take over production." My uncle sounded sullen. "Maybe get rid of the jointed pins. That would make the bears too much like every other product on the market."

"I still don't see why Hartman would care."

"Deon told me something that he hasn't told Detective Mason. At least not yet, unless he's telling him now. He saw Hartman meeting with Taylor, a week ago, before the trip to New Jersey. They were sitting in that Camry of his, at the edge of town."

"But how did Deon see them?"

"Deon was filling up at the gas station and followed them on his motorcycle."

"To where?"

"Weber's Inn near Ann Arbor. Will Taylor dropped Hartman off and then headed to the airport. I'd say that was pretty suspicious. And right after their meeting, Taylor goes off to convince my brother about sending production overseas. Hmph."

"Ms. Silverman?"

I whirled at the sound of Detective Mason's voice from the doorway. He crooked his finger. Deon had collected his textbook from the kitchen's window seat and now rushed out the door past us. Uncle Ross leaned close to my ear.

"Don't let him rattle you, Sasha. Give him hell."

I choked back a laugh and headed inside. Flora, Harriet, and Joan all gave me a thumbs-up signal when I followed Mason to the study. The roar of Deon's motorcycle muffled Detective Mason's voice; I figured he'd asked me to sit given his gesture. I breathed deep, waiting for him first. I wasn't going to let him dominate me from above. He settled in Dad's comfortable chair, behind the massive carved-edge mahogany desk dominating the room; shelves above held leather-bound classics and African animal statues collected during a Kenya trip. Mason leaned back and spread out, arms akimbo.

I chose Mom's classic Chippendale chair, so I could keep my back straight and even bend forward a little. Sending him a message—I viewed him as an equal and even invaded his personal space. Mason's smile faded. He sat up and opened his notebook.

"So, Ms. Silverman. May I call you Sasha?"

"Uncle Ross didn't kill Will Taylor," I said flatly. "He's threatened people who touched his car, the blue and white Thunderbird outside, if they bumped it by accident. He once promised to skin me alive for spilling peanuts on the seat. But it's all talk."

"It's natural you'd come to your uncle's defense. Commendable, too. But Ross Silverman is only one suspect on my list, Sasha. If you knew me better, you'd realize I keep everyone in mind. This is only day one of the investigation."

"So who else would murder Will? Or maybe it was an accident?" My curiosity always led me to blurt out things, although I didn't feel any shame in doing so. I did want to know, if only to add a few people to his list. "Maybe someone followed him—"

"Enough with the maybes. Guesswork isn't part of my job," Mason said.

"Are you like Columbo, knowing who did it right away?" I asked, half-joking, and then realized that might not be a good thing to bring up given his suspicion of Uncle Ross. My nerves didn't help matters.

"No. Stop being a Jessica Fletcher on *Murder, She Wrote.* Stick to selling teddy bears and leave the investigation to the police." He flipped to a fresh page. "So you and your sister were together last night, the entire time?"

"Yes." That annoyed me. "You don't think we—"

"You mentioned seeing the Taylors arguing in the parking lot. What time was that? As close as you can recall."

I thought back to when the meeting ended. "Maybe seven or seven thirty. Our meeting started shortly after six, I think."

"Did you see either of them later than that?"

"When Maddie drove to Ham Heaven for supper, we saw Carolyn driving to Quinn's Pub. If that's what you mean."

Mason jotted all that down. He'd already heard our story last night about going to see a movie. How many notebooks did he use for one case, given the size that could fit into a jacket pocket? How small did he write on the pages? I squinted, leaning farther, until he glanced in my direction with a frown. From what little I did see, his printing resembled tiny block letters. Hmm. That indicated a tight focus. Maybe the budget only covered a certain number of notebooks.

I cleared my throat. "Did you hear the Taylors had marital problems?"

"Sounds like gossip."

Despite Mason's skepticism, I related what I'd learned from

Debbie Davison. He didn't react with any hint of surprise. "I don't know who this girlfriend might be—"

"Why would she have a compelling reason to murder Mr. Taylor?"

"Maybe she wanted him to divorce Carolyn. Maybe Will refused."

"More maybes. Can you confirm whether it's just rumor?"

"No. Not yet." I shrugged. "Carolyn wanted to keep the marriage alive, from what I understand, since she attended counseling."

Mason's pencil was poised over his notebook, and he gave me a searching glance before he flipped to a fresh page. "More speculation, which I will confirm if possible. I know talk goes around in small towns like Silver Hollow, but save it for the coffee shop. Now, about the meeting Taylor called for after work yesterday. What can you tell me about that?"

Reluctance must have shown on my face, the way his eyebrows rose. "Well, it wasn't pretty. But I suppose you know that already."

"I do. Mr. Taylor wanted to cut jobs, and people were not happy."

"I don't blame them. I insisted that no one would lose their jobs until we could discuss things with my parents. I wasn't going to jump to any decisions without their input. That reminds me." I steepled my fingers, Sherlock Holmes style, and cocked my head. "Why was there a teddy bear on the floor? With a side seam ripped open?"

"No idea. So who is Jack Cullen?"

"He used to own the house next door. The village council condemned it," I said, and then explained the situation of our parking lot. "Why?"

"You might want to ask your uncle about Mr. Cullen." The detective stood and produced a box. Mason set out an ink pad, a sheet of paper with a template printed on it, and then gestured to the materials. "I'd like to take your fingerprints. With your permission, of course."

I shrugged. "Doesn't the county have digital scanners?"

"Not in the field." He handed me an alcohol wipe to clean the ink once he'd pressed each of my fingertips and thumbs on the sheet in the specific boxes. A few had smudged. "Thank you for cooperating. And like I said, leave investigating to us."

I slowly rose to my feet, not as ready to end our discussion. "But I want to know how Will got into the factory last night, and what he was doing there. Besides meeting who knows who and for what reason. Why the factory, instead of the park, or his own house, or anywhere else? He didn't have a key."

"We found a key on him and entered it as evidence."

"How did he—"

"I have other members of your staff to interview. If you'll excuse me."

Mason herded me out, his hand firm on my elbow, signaling the end of the interview. Clearly he wanted me out of his hair. How annoying. I was tempted to give him a piece of my mind, but saw Maddie's pleading look; my sister knew too well how my impulsive nature got me into trouble. I kept my mouth shut and watched her follow Detective Mason back to the study. The sewing ladies returned to their murmured conversation around the table in the dining room. I'd have to stick to getting information from Uncle Ross.

First I retrieved Rosie from her crate. She looked offended that I'd left her so long in it, but I fastened her harness and leash. Her claws clicked on the floor before she settled by my uncle's feet near the island. The kitchen felt warm from the blast of late-summer sun. I checked the wall thermostat, retrieved a fan from the lower cabinet, and plugged it in. That helped. So did adjusting the window blinds.

I drew a stool close to Uncle Ross, wincing at the loud scraping noise on the tile. "So how did Will get a key to the factory?"

"Same way Taylor got a copy of the bear pattern." He jangled his ring of keys in front of my face. "I keep these on a hook, remember? Right near the light switch, because I've lost 'em so many times. I bet at some point, Taylor swiped the factory's front door key. Made a copy at a local hardware store, then put the original back on the ring."

"I wonder how we can find out—"

"If he paid cash, I doubt they'd have any record of it. He could have gone to a store in Ann Arbor for all we know. Lots of places make duplicates cheap."

"Huh," I muttered. "Mason said to ask you about Jack Cullen."

Uncle Ross grinned. "I found the bugger sniffing around here a few weeks ago. Claimed he was heading to the lake, but our hedges block any access. Saw him last Sunday nosing behind the factory, cigar in his mouth. He ran off when I yelled a warning. He's had it in for us since he lost his house."

"But he doesn't even know Will Taylor."

"I wouldn't assume that. Besides, I didn't say he'd kill anyone. Jack Cullen's always been one to make trouble." Uncle Ross finished his coffee. "And who knows where trouble will lead, when it comes to an old codger like him."

"I saw him in the village yesterday."

"Yeah? Bet he didn't give you the time of day."

"He was pretty rude. Does he have any family in the area?" I asked. "I feel sorry for him, the way he looks like a scarecrow."

"Don't bother."

"But what if he does need help?"

"Let Cullen's kids deal with him. Although I bet they gave up, since they've tried to help him for years," Uncle Ross said.

"Jack Cullen's a miser. He doesn't want anyone's help. He let that house rot around his ears, and then when the city condemned it he fought them tooth and nail. The man belongs in a nuthouse."

"Well, I know you wouldn't kill anyone." I squeezed his shoulder. "I'm going to prove your innocence, no matter what any detective says about sticking to teddy bears."

"I dunno." My uncle sounded morose. "Mason acts like he's got no one else to pin this on. And you can't be running around Silver Hollow tracking down a killer. Might be dangerous. Who knows who wanted Taylor dead?"

"I won't let Mason railroad you into jail. He needs evidence, for one thing, and a lot more than circumstantial."

"Maybe they'll find fingerprints on the stuffing machine. If the perp wasn't careful, they will. Even with all these TV shows nowadays, people can be pretty stupid about leaving signs behind."

"Like that teddy bear," I said aloud. "The one left on the floor."

"You think it has something to do with the murder?" my uncle asked.

"I don't know. Two things I want to find out, though. Who was the last person to see Will alive. It had to be whoever was driving that car, the one who knocked down our mailbox. And second, what other enemies Will had besides you."

"Let's hope Mason clears this whole thing up before our business tanks."

On that subject, I had to agree.

Chapter 11

I headed to the coffeepot. Rinsed out the small amount left and fetched a fresh filter and whole beans from the pantry. Maddie ordered the best brand online. Once I ground enough for a full pot, I breathed in the heady fragrance. No fancy K-cups for us. Not yet, although I did prefer tea in the afternoon. I'd rather buy a machine that could brew espresso, lattes, tea, hot chocolate, the works—but only if it came with a barista.

Thinking back to when Jack Cullen met me on the street, I flipped the faucet handle and let cold water flow into the sink. "When I took Rosie for a walk yesterday at lunchtime, Jack Cullen threatened to sue me if she came near him."

"How do you think I knew he was snooping around?" Uncle Ross reached for the last bagel. "Rosie was barking like a fiend. I knew someone had to be outside on the grounds or by the factory. Not many people are around on the weekend."

"Was this back on Saturday or Sunday?"

"Sunday."

"Mads and her friends were shopping. What was I doing that day?" I filled the coffeemaker's reservoir and cursed under my breath. Water puddled on the counter and tile floor, so I mopped up and then pressed the start button. "I think I was home until five-ish, and then I met Mary Kate for dinner. She wanted a break before getting back to the grind Monday. How late was it when you saw Jack?"

"Getting dark."

"Ah." I had no idea whether the old codger knew Will Taylor or not. "What would Jack Cullen be doing around the factory, I wonder."

"Like I said, causing trouble." Uncle Ross crammed the last bite in his mouth and twisted on the tall stool, stretching his long legs out while leaning against the island. When he choked on a crumb, I had to slap him on the back several times. He coughed hard. "I thought he was up to some funny business. Didn't find anything."

"So did you tell Detective Mason about Teddy Hartman?"

"What's there to tell?"

"I suppose Deon told him how he saw Hartman and Will Taylor."

"No idea." He coughed again. "All I do know is Mason wasn't all that impressed with my alibi of being home Thursday night. Called it as flimsy as a fishing net."

"Did you call anyone? Did anyone call you on your home phone? Darn. They could have checked the phone records. Any neighbors who saw you at home?"

"No."

"Well, it's possible Hartman met with Will for something. Debbie Davison told me Will was pretty happy, that he'd finally gotten his way. Whatever that means." I explained my conversation earlier that morning. "Why else would he be so elated, if it didn't have to do with Teddy Hartman? Would Dad really agree about sending production overseas?"

"We can't jump to any conclusions."

"I suppose not." My stomach rumbled. I pulled open the

double doors of the refrigerator and set a variety of lunch-meats and cheeses out, along with mustard and mayonnaise, lettuce, several tomatoes, plus a jar of pickles. "Good thing we went to the grocery store recently."

Maddie popped in, beating me to the bread box. While she retrieved the bags of wheat and rye bread, Mason collected all the sewing ladies together and led the way to the study. We exchanged glances and began making sandwiches.

"I suppose you didn't get a hold of Pete Fox," my sister said.

"No, but I meant to call him again."

I let her finish the sandwiches, grabbed my phone, and headed away from the fan. I'd bet anything that Dave Fox, Pete's dad, was preparing a first-page story for his *Silver Hollow Herald* about the murder. In fact, I was surprised he hadn't shown up at our door yet. Pete's cell phone went to voice mail, so I left a second longer message. Odd that he hadn't called me back, because he usually let us know if he was coming in late. My worries deepened.

He and Deon Walsh were the same age. I knew Pete had earned a GED after getting in trouble and ribbed Deon for taking college classes. Pete seemed easygoing and relaxed at work in the factory, but I'd once overheard him arguing on the phone during break time. Something about owing money. Maybe Maddie knew more about him. Her high school years must have overlapped with his at some point. Deon's, too.

"Mads, what do you know about Pete Fox? Did he have any problems?"

She looked up from cutting a sandwich in half. "Not that I know. Why?"

"I'm wondering why he didn't call or show up with everyone else. His dad must have heard about Will's murder, too," I said. "That isn't like Pete, to ignore what's happened at the factory. I called twice and left messages. Why hasn't he called back?"

"Gee, I don't know. We should have asked Deon."

"Come on, Sasha. Sit down and eat," Uncle Ross said. He'd devoured half of a turkey, cheese, and romaine sandwich on rye in one bite. "Fretting won't make anyone call. I'm gonna give Alex a piece of my mind, though, when he does. Count on it."

Halfheartedly I nibbled on my ham and cheese. While Maddie related what little she'd told Detective Mason, my mind reeled back to the scene last night. Guilt flooded me; we'd all been so annoyed, dreading the meeting after work. My sister and I had been tense, waiting for Will to show, but I had to wonder where he'd gone after he left the office in the afternoon. And before the meeting I'd grumbled that he was "full of himself"—everyone had heard me say that.

Will Taylor wasn't the most popular man on our staff, but he was the company's sales representative. I usually kept my dislike hidden, although at times it popped out; perhaps I had been too vocal. Finding him on the floor, his eyes glazed and unmoving, his throat and cheeks filled with fiber—that was horrible. Someone had filled him, all right. Would one of our staff take matters into their own hands?

"No. It's not possible!"

"What?" Maddie held a sandwich halfway to her mouth.

"Uh, nothing. Important, I m-mean," I stammered. "Never mind."

My cheeks burned. Great. Now I was lying to my sister. It might be important, especially since Lois Nichols also had avoided coming to the factory this morning. While it might be true her husband had "taken a turn for the worse," what exactly did she mean? Wasn't he supposed to be in remission? Or so Lois told us the last time she updated us. Not that long ago.

I'd have to visit Lois and Harry Nichols. I hated to admit

it, but visiting sick people or hospitals was not my specialty. I never knew what to say. I had the same problem with senior citizens. Mom always dragged us to visit Grandma Helen, a crotchety old biddy compared to warm, friendly Grandpa T. R., who'd died when I was a teen. Children I could handle, easy. Even a tour group of thirty rambunctious kids.

"Hey, look at this." Maddie showed me her cell phone's display. "A photo of our shop with the police cars in front, on Facebook. It's pretty blurry, thank goodness."

"Who posted that?" I asked.

"It's on Debbie Davison's timeline. People are asking what happened."

"Ignore it. The less said, the better." Uncle Ross drummed his fingers on the island. "Damned technology. It's the only thing people pay attention to nowadays."

My cell phone rang—with the tone reserved for Dad— *Raiders of the Lost Ark*. Maddie and I both lunged for the thin case and knocked it to the floor. It bounced and clattered on the tile. Rosie jumped up to play the game; her paws sent it skittering toward the hallway. But I grabbed it before she snapped it in her mouth. The call had dropped, but I quickly speed dialed Dad's number and hit the speakerphone button.

"Dad? Dad, are you there?"

Mom's voice came through instead. "Sasha? I can barely hear you. And how come your voice is echoing?"

"I've got you on speaker, Mom. Maddie and Uncle Ross are both listening," I said in a louder voice to compensate. "Where's Dad? We've been trying to get you both, leaving text messages and voice mails. We've got serious trouble here."

"So I saw by your text. We're in the same boat, I'm afraid." She hesitated. Uncle Ross, Maddie, and I exchanged shocked looks. "Big trouble."

"What do you mean?"

"Your father's still in the hospital. The CCU – Critical Care Unit."

My uncle cursed. "I knew it had to be—"

"—wait. Just a minute, please."

Mom had muffled her phone somehow. Muted voices and other indistinguishable noises drifted through the speaker. I hated waiting. What in heaven had put Dad in the hospital? Was he on death's doorstep? I wanted to rush and pack a bag this minute.

"Hello?" Mom actually sounded cheerful. "Dad's improved so much, they're moving him to a private room. But he has double pneumonia."

"Double pneumonia?" Maddie's high-pitched squeal hurt my ears.

"Your father caught a bad cold a month and a half ago. Don't you remember? And you know how he is—"

"He never wants to deal with being sick," I cut in. "Or go to the doctor. But why didn't Will Taylor mention yesterday about Dad being sick?"

Yesterday. Before Will's gruesome death—that suddenly hit me. Mom sounded matter-of-fact over the phone, which I knew covered her deep worry. She'd never sheltered us from bad things, either deaths in the family or why Uncle Ross had been dragged into divorce court, even horrible crimes in the world. "Face everything with courage" had been her motto. But now, when push came to shove and it involved Dad, her high school sweetheart . . .

Maybe Mom couldn't drum up enough courage when it affected her directly.

"That's easy," she said. "Dad wasn't coughing when he met with Mr. Taylor. He looked fine, in fact. Walked around the whole trade show for two days, and when he finally felt sick we realized he must have gotten a fever. I told him I was taking him straight to the nearest hospital. He wanted to go home, but I said no."

"What about Will Taylor?"

"What about him? He'd already left, I think."

"So then what?" Maddie piped up. "After you took Dad to the ER."

"Probably had to drag him there," Uncle Ross muttered.

"Your father was so weak, the taxi driver helped me get him into the car." Mom sounded close to tears. "That was close to midnight on Sunday. We waited for several hours. By the time a doctor saw him, they admitted him right away. His fever was close to a hundred and three, and then he had an allergic reaction to one of the medications. That made things worse. I had no idea which antibiotics he'd ever taken before, and neither did our family doctor."

"Dad's never been sick much," I said.

"Yes. And they put him in CCU early Tuesday. What's today?"

"Friday."

Mom made a little moaning sound. "I'm exhausted. I haven't slept since we came here. And I didn't want to worry any of you with this."

I glanced at Maddie. "One of us should be with her," I whispered, and then raised my voice once more. "Mom, did you and Dad know about Will's plan to send production overseas? We're really confused by all that."

"Yes, Dad mentioned something about Will pressuring him to decide. I saw your text," Mom added, "but I couldn't deal with it right then."

"Couldn't deal?" Maddie sounded desperate. "But Will Taylor told us Dad agreed to everything, that jobs would be cut—including Uncle Ross's!"

"Wait, wait. Give me a minute. Oh, let me call you back."

Mom hung up before we could get an update. I paced around the kitchen island, half out of my mind with worry. Maddie immediately began loading dirty dishes in the dishwasher. Menial tasks always helped her to deal with stress. Uncle Ross sat with his large hands clasped before him, his shoulders slumped. His battered cap hid the bald spot in his thinning gray hair, and he stared at the willow basket of red-cheeked apples.

Odd to see him silent, almost pensive. That wasn't like him. The veins of his hands stood out, and his spotted skin reminded me of Grandpa T. R. Will Taylor may have thought Uncle Ross was old enough to retire, but he usually had boundless energy. Unlike now. I suspected he was worried about Dad—his younger brother and only sibling since Aunt Marie was gone. I would be just as worried about Maddie if anything happened to her.

"Dad will be all right," I said, trying to sound cheerful. "He's a fighter."

"I knew it had to be serious. It wasn't like Alex not to call, not after I left messages, yelled at him on his voice mail, told him he'd better not be thinking about cutting jobs. I even offered to buy the factory to keep everything the way it is."

"You did?" That made me smile. "You ought to tell Detective Mason that."

"He wouldn't believe me."

"I think it proves you wouldn't murder Will if you wanted to take over the business. But I'm sure you'd have fired him from his sales rep job."

"I doubt Alex would sell, for one thing. Plus I don't have that much dough. Unless we all pitched in, Deon and Pete and the ladies, to run the factory." He brightened at that idea. "Bet we could get a small business loan if it came down to that."

I nodded. "Maybe. So go ahead and tell Mason—"

"Tell me what?"

The detective lumbered into the kitchen, rubbing his eyes before placing his glasses back on his nose. He drew a stool out on the opposite side of the island. I noted Flora, Joan, and Harriet trooping to their cars beyond the window. The ladies all looked downcast, as if they'd sold their favorite puppy of a litter. Mason yawned and flexed his shoulders, then glanced at us both.

"So. What did you want him to tell me, Ms. Silverman?"

"That my uncle wanted to buy the Silver Bear Shop and Factory," I said with a touch of defiance. "Along with the others on staff, if my dad had actually caved in to Will Taylor. They would have fired him, not resort to murder, and then hired a new sales rep. So that proves he's not the prime suspect."

"Really." Mason glanced at Uncle Ross. "I hear you met with Deon Walsh's sister. That you planned to talk Alex Silverman into hiring her. Is that true?"

"She has sales experience," Uncle Ross said with a shrug. "Marketing, too."

"Makes me wonder if you expected Taylor's death."

"That's crazy."

"Devonna sells lingerie." Maddie leaned against the wall. "In people's homes, at hostess parties. I'm a good friend. She never expressed interest in a job here."

Detective Mason changed the subject. "I also learned that Lois Nichols had threatened Will Taylor during the staff meeting."

Uncle Ross scoffed. "Sure, she said about the same thing I did about killing Taylor. And she had a better reason to keep her job. Her husband has cancer. She can't afford to lose their insurance."

I spoke up before Maddie could. "But neither of them is capable of murder."

"All right. I've got everything I need for now. The shop

and factory will be closed until further notice. Remember, Mr. Silverman, don't leave town for any reason."

Detective Mason strolled outside. Rosie stopped growling when the screen door banged shut behind him. I patted her on the head. "Good dog."

"I suppose we'd better arrange for a notice in the newspaper about being closed." Maddie's dejection matched my own. "I'll take care of that in the morning. What about you, Uncle Ross? Should we do an inventory while we have the chance?"

"I dunno. Do we—"

He couldn't finish, since the *Raiders* tune blared from my cell. I jumped to answer, but my sister beat me. "Mom? . . . What happened? Is Dad okay?"

Both Uncle Ross and I rose to our feet, watching Maddie's face. She'd paled a little but kept saying, "Uh-huh," over and over again. I reached out to snatch the phone out of her hand, but Maddie twisted away. I mouthed the words, *Speakerphone,* but she ignored me. She could be as stubborn as my parents. Or me. And Uncle Ross, for that matter. Even Rosie.

"Okay . . . Okay, Mom, I will. Bye." Maddie clicked the off button and tossed the phone to me. I nearly missed. Without a word, she raced for the stairs. "I'm packing a bag! Get me the next flight to Newark, Sash. Please."

Uncle Ross stood. "I'm the one who ought to be—"

"You can't go. Detective Mason won't allow it," I interrupted. "At least Mads can stay at the hospital and let Mom catch up on some sleep. She'll keep us posted on Dad's condition and find out what he said to Will at the trade show, too. I've got plenty to do for the picnic on Monday."

He paced the kitchen in frustration. "I don't care. I ought to be flying to New Jersey. Alex is my brother. He might take a turn for the worse!"

"We can't jump to any conclusions. If it was life threatening,

Mason would have to let you go—but it's not. And remember, your Thunderbird is a traditional fixture in the village parade on Monday. Everyone expects to see you with all the teddy bears crammed in, and tin cans trailing behind the car."

Uncle Ross only grumbled at the reminder. I retrieved my laptop. I quickly checked for the cheapest flight with enough time to spare so Maddie could get to the airport. I entered in the credit card information and confirmed the details, then printed the boarding pass; I raced to the office to snatch it from the machine's output tray. The message light on the phone blinked like crazy. I didn't have time to listen to any of them, though, and raced back to the kitchen.

Maddie waited by the back door, looking adorable in a white skort, a top with red and white stripes, plus a red cross-body purse. Sunglasses perched on her head. She held the handle of a paisley Vera Bradley weekender bag to wheel behind her. My sister, fashionable and ready for travel on a moment's notice, even when stressed to the max.

"Six-oh-five departure, and don't forget security takes extra time" I said, waving the pass before handing it over. "Want me to drive you to the airport?"

"Nah, I'll drive myself." Maddie checked her watch and then refastened her sturdy sandals. "Four hours to spare. I can park and take a shuttle to the terminal."

"What did Judith say before you decided on a trip to New Jersey?" Uncle Ross asked. "Did the doctors update her on Alex's condition?"

"I asked, but then Mom started crying. She's so exhausted, she can't think straight. That's why I told her I would come right away. One of us should be there."

"Better you than me, I suppose," I said. "I'd probably make her more nervous. But do try and get an answer from Dad about what he and Will agreed on. Anything about the factory. Just call us, please. As often as possible."

"Okay, no problem." Maddie hugged me and pecked Uncle Ross on the cheek, although he scowled a little. "Hold down the fort."

She headed outside, car keys jangling. Rosie jumped down from the window seat and nearly slipped out before the door shut. I caught her by the harness and dragged her back inside. One hand shading my eyes, I squinted at the distant Christmas shop.

"Looks like Detective Mason is across the street again. On the porch."

"At least he's bugging other people." Uncle Ross ambled past me out the door. This time Rosie did escape; she squatted near a bush. My uncle shut the garden gate before she wandered off. "One thing I will say—Mason's sharp. I doubt Digger Sykes would have asked me such rapid-fire questions, catching me off guard and repeating things in a different way. He'll trip up others if they aren't paying attention."

Rosie and I waited by the gate, watching Mason jot in his notebook. Carolyn wasn't in sight, but both Debbie and Cissy Davison nodded a few times and interrupted each other in their interview. If they were even aware of it as an opportunity for the detective to gain information.

A car barreled around the corner and screeched to a halt before the shop. I saw Nickie Richardson jump out of the SUV, along with Kristen Bloom, barely five feet tall. They rushed up the steps; Mason motioned them all inside. The sun sank lower toward a bank of dark clouds, setting the Christmas shop's slate roof aglow. Where was Carolyn Taylor? I didn't glimpse her inside among the group of women.

Oh well. I whistled for Rosie. "Come on, girl. Suppertime."

Inside, her claws clicked over the tile. Onyx slunk around the island, clearly unhappy. She had every right to be. The last time my sister left on a trip, I'd forgotten to clean the litter box

and replenish the cat's dry kibble self-feeder. At least I'd remembered the gravy. I tore open a packet of cat food and set it
high on the tower. She leaped to the middle and climbed her
way slowly to sniff the bowl with caution. Onyx turned up her
nose and jumped to the floor. Rosie stretched along the window seat with a deep sigh.

At least one of us was happy.

Chapter 12

I fretted for the rest of the evening, which did turn stormy. Usually the patter of raindrops on the roof soothed me, but not tonight. I jumped at the occasional crash of thunder. That rattled my nerves. Why didn't Maddie text or call? Instead of pacing the downstairs, I flipped through TV channels, checked e-mail and Facebook, and finally gave up. I couldn't focus on anything. Frustration built inside me.

By ten o'clock, I took a decongestant for my sinus headache. Ate a few bites of a microwave dinner and tossed the rest. Searched for my secret stash of Girl Scout cookies in the freezer, took out a sleeve of Thin Mints, and began pacing. Within five minutes, I checked my cell again. I also held an empty sleeve in my hand. I couldn't remember eating the cookies. At least my headache had subsided to a dull throb.

After brewing a cup of chamomile mint herbal tea, I picked up Barbara Ross's latest cozy mystery book. I loved the Maine Clambake series, but my eyes swam. Reluctantly, I put the book down, walked around, checked my phone. Gaah.

I dialed my sister. "Hey, Maddie. Let me know you got

there safe, okay? I'm worried sick. Text, call, whatever. I just need to know. Thanks."

I hated leaving voice mail. Taking a deep breath, I headed for the office. I had to do something instead of walking around in circles and worrying. I ought to find the list of people signed up for Monday's picnic. Dealing with that might be a good distraction.

The office occupied the one-story addition Dad had planned when he and an architect met to design renovations. They'd matched the Victorian exterior's style and chosen gray vinyl siding for the entire building, new windows with black shutters, and new white doors. Mom moaned about the cost, but Dad was insistent. He wanted people to take note of the fresh look and the giant teddy bear he'd placed in an oversized rocking chair on the front porch.

The bear hadn't lasted more than a few years, battered by weather and faded by the sun. Twice a groups of kids had targeted it for pranks. Dad once found Mr. Beary in the park, sitting at a picnic table, and mended rips squirrels had made; another time the police discovered the bear on the courthouse roof. No one claimed responsibility. Three high school students confessed—several years after graduating from college— and chipped in to replace the giant teddy with Mr. Silver, now safe in our upstairs loft.

I passed the alcove where I kept my own so-called desk. A table, actually, with a butcher-block top and legs painted white, holding stacks of paper and a caddy with pens, scissors, clips, tape, twine, and ribbon; a shelf held small baskets, our tiniest bears, boxes of tea, candy, and other items to make gift or charity donations. Books crammed two other shelves, from classics to mysteries to biographies. My floral-patterned Queen Anne chair was the most comfortable in the shop, but I rarely had time to sit and enjoy it.

"Nyx, get off."

The cat loved it as well. She stretched first, her paws kneading the chintz fabric, arched her back slowly, and then slunk off the chair. Onyx padded her way to Maddie's desk and curled beneath it. The wide six-drawer wooden desk had little clutter on top, with a Rolodex near the phone. She was far more organized. An array of file boxes, decorated with Snoopy as the Red Baron, Joe Cool, or lying on his doghouse with Woodstock fluttering above, sat beside rattan baskets with reams of paper and other supplies; a low filing cabinet held bright yellow Gerbera daisies in a ladybug-painted planter. Cute, just like her Peanuts mug. The desk light reminded me of the jumping Pixar animation lamp with its angular arms and rounded head, only painted gold. Maddie had spray-painted it last winter on a sunny, cold day. She always found the neatest things.

I sorted through a variety of drawings, some with cats or dogs hugging teddy bears, or "bee" bears in yellow and black with wings. Another showed a picnic theme, with bears stashed inside wicker hampers. My sister had earned an art design degree but balked at working in that field.

The list of picnic-goers—the names in alphabetical order—was pinned to a strip of cork on the wall below a shelf holding children's books and bears.

"Ah. Her old Pooh bear." I took the well-loved stuffed animal down and swiped a smidgeon of dust from his red felt shirt. "Good old Pooh."

Her creativity seemed to be crammed into this small office. In comparison, Will Taylor's larger office next door had an entire brick wall perpendicular to the huge window and its glorious view of the side flower garden—too dark to see anything now, of course. Rain spattered the glass at a steady pace. An animal skin covered the polished wood floor beneath the austere metal and wood desk. I disliked the ugly modern steel and leather chair and the two barrel-shaped visitor chairs. A landline phone sat on the desk with a handsome Mission-style Tiffany lamp.

At the sound of an incoming text, I perched on Will's chair and scrolled down to read it. *Arrived safe, nice hotel. Taking a cab to the hospital now.*

Thank goodness. Maddie would figure out the situation with Mom and Dad and gauge how serious his condition was. I'd missed an earlier text message from Mary Kate Thompson. I dialed her number, but the call went straight to voice mail. Blarg. I checked the time and kicked myself. Ten o'clock! She was no doubt in bed already, since she rose at four in the morning to start baking at Fresh Grounds.

A flash of light through the wet windowpane caught my attention. I rose to glance outside. A small car, its headlights flickering, stopped in front of the Christmas shop. The rain had subsided to a fine mist. I didn't have a pair of binoculars handy, so I couldn't tell the type of car beyond its size, or who the late-night visitor might be. The building's only lights twinkled along the roof. I couldn't tell if Carolyn had returned to check the locks or if someone was trying to break in. Before I was tempted to dial 911, the car moved on.

Had it pulled into the Silver Leaf B and B? I couldn't tell. Maybe one of their guests wanted to know the shop's hours. It also might have been a friend of Carolyn's. I hurried to the front window, close by Maddie's desk, and checked out the Silver Leaf's small parking strip. Trees shadowed the cars. Only a few lights glowed upstairs.

Relieved, I returned to Will's office. Something about it bothered me. The size of the room? Yes, but also the garden view, and the brick on the wall that cost Dad a fortune to install. Will had insisted, though, claiming it added prestige to the "look" and his company title as Sales Representative. Ha. Few visitors ever came to his office. He always met vendors at shows. Come to think of it, Will rarely used this space.

One thing was certain. I'd move my sister's things into this room, paint the brick white, and take down half of the wall between this office and the smaller one. Maddie deserved a better view. A fresher décor for all the hard work she did for our business.

I punched the blinking message button on the phone. A woman's voice filled the room. "Hello? This is Mrs. Bishop. I'd like a refund for our teddy bear picnic tickets—"

"Oh no."

Four other women had left similar messages, all starting this morning around ten o'clock. Speechless, I listened to the worry underlying their terse voices and sighed. How could I blame them? Moms wanted to protect their kids. I'd probably do the same. After all, village residents might not realize the murder had occurred in the factory—not in the shop, not at the park—but until rumors were replaced by facts we'd suffer guilt by association.

I wondered if anyone would show up on Monday for the picnic. After jotting down the names on a notepad, I tore off the sheet and pocketed it. Then I stopped. Why hadn't Will locked his desk? That seemed odd. I took advantage of the opportunity to search for anything important. Chances were good he didn't keep much but the basics in his desk. I opened a side drawer. Business cards, check. Letterhead, check. Envelopes, check.

Pay stubs had been tossed into the bottom drawer. My eyes popped wide when I saw the figure before taxes. I didn't realize Will made that much for a salary. Maddie took care of payroll. Once, before Dad hired Taylor, I'd cut the checks and handed out the envelopes to the staff. I vowed our next sales rep would start at the bottom of the scale, for certain, and never earn more than I did.

After rummaging through the other side drawer, holding business letters for the most part, I stopped. All of them were dated over the last few weeks. All of them had been sent by longtime suppliers of our fabric, thread, eye studs, tags, and the fiberfill stuffing. And the companies all thanked our business for being a loyal customer, with hopes that he would reconsider the decision. Uh-huh. Apparently Will had canceled our contracts without telling Dad or any of us. That was further proof that sending production overseas was a done deal—in Will's eyes.

Now we'd have to call and explain it was all a mistake.

Ugh. I was terrible at such tasks, keeping conversations on track, and had been flustered talking to Detective Mason. Uncle Ross would have to deal with our vendors and explain—without details—about Will's death. And renew the contracts.

The narrow middle drawer held an assortment of paper clips, a box of staples, pens, a small bottle of liquid white-out, even earphones with a tangled cord. Plus a prescription bottle with Blake's Pharmacy label and a few pills left—I recognized the drug as a blood pressure medicine, since Dad used the same one. A plastic comb missing a few teeth lay atop one of the teddy bear key rings we sold in the shop, with a tiny brass key. Hmm.

I glanced around and saw a small wooden box on a high shelf. Lucky for me I was tall enough to retrieve it. And the key fitted and turned. I removed a business card. The rectangular, glossy-coated cardstock had a plush bear printed on it, gold edging, and a row of red hearts. Below that was Teddy Hartman's name and phone number printed in large black letters.

I flipped the card over. A note had been scribbled on the blank side. *Lunch Thu 9/3.* I smiled. This was proof that Will Taylor had arranged to meet the toy company owner before his trip to New Jersey.

Chapter 13

The morning sun warmed my face. After stretching out on the mattress, I checked the clock. Still a few minutes before—oh, wait. The shop was closed. I scratched Rosie behind the ears. She moved her head closer, yawned, and stretched her legs stiff and straight. Oddly enough, Onyx was curled at the bed's foot. I reached for my cell, read a few texts from last night, and then punched in my uncle's number.

After four rings, he answered with his usual greeting. "What?"

"Mads kept vigil by Dad's bedside while Mom slept at the hotel. He's responding to the new antibiotics. They'll transfer him to a regular room sometime today."

"You called me at this ungodly hour to tell me that?"

"It's ten after nine, Uncle Ross."

"I figured you'd sleep in this morning. We're closed, remember."

"We've got more problems." I explained searching Will's desk and then rattled off the list of companies we needed to call next week. "Maybe we can find out what Will told them exactly."

"So he jumped the gun, eh? Slick no-good bast—"

"I also found Teddy Hartman's business card in his desk, and they set a time to meet. I'm going to show Detective Mason. But someone's gotta call our vendors."

"Yeah, I'll do it on Tuesday."

Uncle Ross hung up. I jumped in the shower and donned khaki shorts with a muted coral T-shirt. I considered changing to a black one. After all, one of our employees had died. Would it make sense to show that respect now, or should I save it for the funeral? Then again, I'd wilt. Eighty-plus degrees in black? Ugh. Too hot.

I fetched a tan straw fedora, dark sunglasses, and chunky wooden bracelets. Maddie's, in fact. My one nod to style. After a restless night with recurring dreams of tornados, I felt off-kilter. Coffee. I needed a triple-shot espresso but vowed to function without it—if possible. Too much caffeine and I'd be a walking zombie. Had Mary Kate heard about the cancellations for the picnic on Labor Day? I dialed her number.

She answered with her usual cheerful greeting. "Fresh Grounds, may I help you?"

"Tell me you baked those puff pastry apple blintzes this morning."

"Sasha! I'll save one for you, okay?" Mary Kate lowered her voice to a half whisper. "Sorry I missed you last night. But I overheard Cissy and Debbie Davison yesterday, talking about the wild night they had at Quinn's Pub. They were so freaked out over Will's murder. And of course, everyone here believes your uncle's guilty."

"Oh, man. That's not fair."

"I know. Even Uncle Gil overheard the bit Ross said about gutting Will Taylor like a fish. But Cissy and Debbie were all worked up because a detective interviewed them for hours. And today, they're not able to help Carolyn at the shop."

"Why would she open the store at all?" I shook my head, trying to figure that out. "Never mind. Some people want to cancel their picnic reservations for Monday."

"Oh no! Really?"

"I guess I should have expected that. I'll gladly refund people's money, but I'm not changing my cookie order. Plan on the same number, okay? I'm sorry about the fancier design. The first one was sweet, and I think the kids would have loved them. But Maddie mentioned asking if you could get Wendy Clark to help decorate the bears with sunglasses on their faces. Or something more summery."

"Well, a fancier sugar cookie will impress the adults."

"That means people will expect over-the-top ones at the October tea party."

Mary Kate laughed and then said something to her husband in the background. "I think people are crazy to miss the picnic. It's not like Will Taylor had anything to do with planning it. And the park is nowhere near the factory."

"I'll refund their money, no matter what the reason."

"Let me see what I can do about spreading the word. A few moms I know didn't get a chance to make a reservation, so maybe they'll take the canceled ones."

"That would be great, thanks."

Rosie whined, waiting by the door, so we headed downstairs. After a visit outside, I ate a hard-boiled egg while Rosie wolfed down her kibble. Then I sat down with the list I'd found on Maddie's bulletin board. Each reservation had a phone number, so I called the ones who hadn't canceled already. For roughly two-thirds of the calls, I left voice-mail messages—confirming that the teddy bear picnic would still take place and asking them to please return the call if their plans had changed. The few who answered sounded relieved that I was willing to refund their money, but only one accepted the offer.

I politely refused to answer any questions or hints about Will's murder. No one pressured me, thank goodness.

After sticking the list beneath the fruit bowl, I headed outside with Rosie. She trotted beside me on the narrow sidewalk along Theodore Lane. Thankfully the parade of cars had ended yesterday afternoon. Except for the yellow crime scene tape flapping in the warm breeze, things looked normal for a Saturday—at least in the aftermath of a murder on our property. But I shivered. Maybe waiting to reopen the factory wasn't a bad idea after all.

The Silver Leaf Bed and Breakfast's parking lot was crammed now, with a few cars lined up in our parking lot as overflow. The village clock struck ten. Even at this distance, I could hear the chimes. The council added the carillon tones two years ago, allowing visitors to listen for the hour and gauge how much longer they could shop. Glen and Jenny Woodley had installed a lovely gazebo in their side garden; right now a young couple sat in wicker chairs reading books. Too bad I couldn't relax like that. I glimpsed a five-year-old and a toddler chasing geese over the lawn beside the garden, their parents keeping close watch.

A Dexter County SUV stood in front of the Holly Jolly Christmas shop. Rosie and I crossed the street. The Michael Bublé version of "Have Yourself a Merry Little Christmas" drifted through the screen door—Carolyn's favorite singer. I hesitated, wondering if I should extend our support and sympathy for her husband's tragic death. Mason had questioned the Davison sisters yesterday along with Nickie Richardson and Kristen Bloom. What had he learned?

Curious, I lingered near the porch steps. Rosie sniffed the pots of red geraniums. No lights twinkled along the rooftop, and the trees inside didn't sparkle with color, either. A light breeze rustled the ferns hanging on the porch. I noticed Detective Mason in the window, but he faced the shop's interior. Carolyn flitted by the screen door, in her usual black dress. She must have spotted me since she rushed outside with a cry of relief.

"Oh, Sasha!" Her heeled sandals clattered on the steps. Carolyn practically threw herself into my arms while sobbing. "How horrible, and to think you found Will!" Tears streaked her face, her blond curls were a mess, and she dabbed her blood-shot, swollen eyes. Even her cheeks looked puffy. "I'm such a wreck! I can't believe this is happening."

"I'm so sorry—"

"Ms. Silverman, Mrs. Taylor?" Mason beckoned from the porch. "Please, come inside. It's better if you don't linger out in public."

His firm tone meant business. A few Silver Leaf guests stood in front of the bed-and-breakfast, whispering and pointing. Carolyn sagged against me, a handkerchief crumpled in one hand, so I helped her up the stone steps. Unfortunately, Rosie started barking and lunging against her leash.

"Let her come in, please! Oh, you darling—he looks like a teddy bear."

"It's the way they shape the ears for grooming," I said. "And he's a she."

Carolyn stooped to bury her face in Rosie's curly hair. My dog shook herself free and made a beeline for Mason's leg. I managed to catch her. Thank goodness. She growled at him from afar, since I held her close by me. The detective merely checked his notebook, waiting until Carolyn had calmed down, but he put a low table between him and Rosie.

"Don't you like dogs?" I asked.

"I have three," Mason said shortly. "Two Labs and a pointer, all male. Your pooch probably smells them on my clothes."

"Oh."

Carolyn smiled and fetched a treat from a jar. "What's her name, Sasha?"

"Rosie."

"Of course she is! Sweet, sweet Rosie." She crooned over my pet, who crunched the bone-shaped biscuit in two seconds flat. "Good doggie."

"Mrs. Taylor, we can discuss this at the police station if you prefer—"

"Oh no, Detective. Here is fine." She glanced at me with a pleading look. "Sasha, will you please stay? I don't believe what everyone's said. Your uncle wouldn't hurt a fly. He acts like a bear, but he's really a big sweetheart."

I blinked. "Uh—thanks."

Mason glared at me. "Don't you have somewhere to be, Ms. Silverman?"

"Let her stay! What exactly did you need from me again, Detective?" Carolyn wrung her hands. "I told you Will came home suddenly from his trip. He didn't even call me from the airport. Not that he hasn't done that before, of course, but I refused to change my plans. I suppose I should have, but my friends and I had our hearts set on meeting for dinner. We hadn't spent time together for months."

"I see." He wasn't taking notes, though.

"Will knew it, too. But the world revolved around him." She caught her breath and pushed a stray curl behind an ear. "That sounds horrible, doesn't it! But we had our problems, like any married couple. I wanted him to join me for counseling, but he kept saying he didn't have time."

"Did he ever mention meeting Teddy Hartman?" I asked. Mason flashed me another warning look, but I hurried on. "I found this business card in Will's office. They met on Thursday for lunch."

"I'll take that as evidence." He snatched it out of my hand, read the back note, and then pocketed it. "Now—"

"Teddy Hartman? I've heard his name before," Carolyn said, "but Will never talked about meeting him. Doesn't Hartman own a toy company?"

"Yes. Bears of the Heart," I said. "One of our biggest competitors."

Mason cleared his throat. "It may have nothing to do with this."

"Actually, it might." I didn't care if the detective resented my presence while I related how Hartman had been seen in Silver Hollow and stayed within driving distance. "You ought to check out Weber's Inn. Hartman might still be there."

Carolyn gasped. "You mean Teddy Hartman came here to Silver Hollow?"

I shrugged. "Yes. Maybe they negotiated working together—"

"Pure conjecture," Mason interrupted, but Carolyn slumped into a chair.

"What if that man killed my husband? How horrible! And they're doing an autopsy on Will. Cutting him up like—"

She broke down, pulled a white teddy bear from under her hip, and then hugged it to her chest. Mason looked furious, as if I was ruining his chance of questioning her without all the waterworks. Maybe so, but it wasn't my fault. Carolyn wept harder.

"I'll check on Hartman later," he said. "Now if you don't mind—"

"No wonder Will was so . . . so secretive about everything." Carolyn hiccupped louder. "He'd been n-nervous for the past m-month. I couldn't get him to . . . tell me anything. And then. On Thursday. He came home. Wanted to celebrate."

She gulped a breath and then rushed on. "Will swore he made the biggest coup in his life. That we could pay off all our debts, sell the house, and buy a bigger one. Plus a new car! I didn't believe him."

I turned to the detective in triumph. Mason didn't look convinced. "You might want to check the front of Teddy Hartman's rental car. See if there's any damage."

"Maybe."

"Oh, and I saw a car last night stop in front of this shop."

That piqued his interest. "Did you see anyone getting out of the car? Prowling around, checking the doors and windows?"

"No."

"All right then. Thank you, Ms. Silverman. You can go."

He ignored my frown and flipped through his notebook. Carolyn had finally quieted and was petting Rosie. I couldn't very well yank my dog out of reach; she wagged her tail, distracted by the kissy sounds Carolyn made, and didn't notice Mason sneaking around them both. Smooth move on his part, because I didn't need to deal with a dog bite case.

But Carolyn shot to her feet as if someone had stuck a pin in her rear. "Oh! I remembered something. I did see a prowler."

"What's that, Mrs. Taylor?"

"That man, the one who's always smoking a cigar. He owned the house they tore down next to the teddy bear factory. He stopped by this past week, asking when Will would be back from his trip to New Jersey."

"Jack Cullen," Mason said, his tone weary. "Is that who you mean?"

"Yes, that's the one. I saw him Thursday afternoon with a wrench in his hand," she said with a nervous wave. "Kind of scared me, since I was ready to close the shop. Mr. Cullen headed toward the factory, too, like he had to fix something. But he went around it. I didn't care. I was glad he was gone."

"All right, then. Getting back to your night at Quinn's Pub," Mason said. "Who do you remember seeing there?"

"I told you already!" Carolyn pouted and pushed her blond curls off her face. "All my friends. Plus Ross Silverman, Deon Walsh and his sister. After three drinks it all turned fuzzy."

Rosie growled at Mason, who ignored her, and then accepted another treat from Carolyn. I kept tight hold of my dog's leash. "Did Will have any enemies?" I asked.

Carolyn's eyes widened in surprise. "No. Everyone liked Will."

"Really?"

"Well, except for your uncle. I suppose." She stooped to pet Rosie. "Oh, don't bark at the policeman, you sweet baby. He might put you in jail."

"Time to go." I'd caught Mason's venomous stare and whisked Rosie out of reach—from them both. "If there's anything Maddie and I can do, Carolyn, let me know."

She looked forlorn. "Thanks, Sasha. Things have been so crazy since yesterday morning. I didn't even know Will hadn't come home Thursday night. When Digger Sykes told me what happened, I couldn't think. My head hurt so bad. I had the worst hangover ever. . . ."

I stepped onto the porch. "All right. Good-bye," Mason said, and pushed the wooden door half-closed.

He blocked my view, standing with his back to me. I knelt and fiddled with Rosie's harness, listening while he went over the "pity party" timeline again. When had Carolyn and her friends arrived at the pub? How long were they together, who'd gone to the bathroom and when, with whom, whether anyone saw them, and what time they'd left, et cetera. He was certainly as thorough as Columbo.

Not that Carolyn could tell him much, being so drunk. I hadn't expected him to question her again. Another thought struck me, one that gave me a measure of hope.

Maybe Mason had put someone else ahead of Uncle Ross on the suspect list.

Chapter 14

I had to wonder if Mason suspected Carolyn—except she had an airtight alibi. With so many friends surrounding her, and she'd been drunk to boot. I hoped I'd turned his focus toward Teddy Hartman instead of Uncle Ross. I sighed. Or anyone but my uncle.

I headed toward the village. From what little I knew, Kristen, Carolyn, and Nickie were a tight trio of BFFs in high school. Debbie, younger than me but a year older than my sister, joined the group whenever they planned to party.

Kristen Bloom, serious in nature, energetic from jogging two miles a day in a variety of skimpy bike shorts or exercise outfits, co-owned the Silver Scoop Ice Cream Shoppe with Isabel French. Isabel was the exact opposite, tall and curvy, always smiling, and a natural dealing with customers; she created the clever names for their delicious confections, both hard ice cream and soft-serve custard—like Strawberries & Cream, Berry Cherry Pie, Campfire S'Mores, Over the Blue Moon, and Peachy Keen. That was Maddie's favorite, chock-full of fruit from Richardson's Orchards. Mine was Chipperoo, with chocolate chips and cookie pieces.

Kristen and Isabel had turned a former run-down candy store into the Silver Scoop with a sweet pink and green awning and décor, white ironwork tables and chairs, plus a drive-through lane. A sound business decision given the car and foot traffic combined in the village.

Carolyn Taylor had been jealous of Kristen and Isabel's success a few summers ago when they first opened. Summer was peak season for the Silver Scoop. The Holly Jolly's business peaked in winter, although it always looked busy. As for Nickie, she'd married into the sprawling Richardson clan. Tom and Cleo Richardson had expanded the family farm into a thriving multiple-season, multiple-product business enterprise. Their five kids and a passel of grandkids all helped keep things running smoothly.

Richardson's farm consisted of a huge apple orchard, with acres and acres of pruned trees, all varieties, plus other fruit trees, vegetables of all kinds, and a huge pumpkin patch. Their fall events—hayrides, a haunted house, a corn maze—added to the cider press and bakery. Everyone for miles around made annual pilgrimages to Richardson's in the spring, summer, and autumn. Nickie helped run the bakery; she looked far older than Carolyn and Kristen, however, due to her prematurely gray long hair. Plus she chain-smoked and had a serious love affair with tanning beds. No doubt due to being cooped up inside an air-conditioned building every summer.

"What an adorable dog," a woman said, and stooped to pet Rosie.

"Thank you—"

"Looks just like a teddy bear!"

Rosie wagged her tail when the woman produced a cookie—luckily, not chocolate. My dog scarfed it down before I could protest. When the woman slipped inside the health-food store next to the church, we crossed Kermit Street. Rosie trotted happily along to Fresh Grounds.

I'd been puzzling over what Carolyn had said about Jack Cullen. Why would he want to know when Will Taylor was coming back to town? Had the two of them been cooking up some kind of trouble for our shop? Had Mason questioned our former crotchety neighbor yet? Uncle Ross and now Carolyn had seen Jack Cullen skulking around the factory with a wrench.

Two more women walked past, avoiding my dog by a wide margin. One had platinum blond hair piled high on her head, skittering heels, and a slinky black silk dress. The brunette carried a pink-and-white-striped box from Vivian Grant's bakery.

"Did you hear about the murder yesterday? I never expected anything like that would happen here. In Silver Hollow, of all places," she said.

The other woman nodded. "What's the world coming to, really."

"I blame the violence on television," I said aloud. They glanced my way, mouths agape. "You know, the zombie stuff. *The Walking Dead*? How about *Breaking Bad*?"

Both women crossed Main Street without saying a word. I snorted. They'd looked at me from head to toe as if I wore an orange prison jumpsuit. Clearly they weren't locals and didn't appreciate anyone joining their conversation. Unlike most village residents, who would have stopped for a good jaw either outside or in line at Fresh Grounds. The two headed to The Birdcage, a shop offering seed, lawn art, and related items.

My phone jangled with the ringtone I used for Uncle Ross—"Scuttle Buttin' "—a jazzy guitar riff from his favorite musician, the late Stevie Ray Vaughn. "Hey—"

"Sasha, where are you? You've been gone for over an hour."

"I'm on Kermit near Fresh Grounds." I peeked inside the

coffee shop, where Mary Kate looked frazzled with a crowd of customers. Maybe I shouldn't bother her when she was so busy, so I turned and walked past Ham Heaven's parking lot. "What's up? News on Dad?"

"No. I finally found out why Pete Fox went missing." Uncle Ross's voice sounded tight, so I knew something was bothering him. "Remember I called Dave Fox about putting a notice in the paper about our shop being closed. He told me Pete drove into Detroit Thursday night and was arrested. He's being held in the Wayne County Jail. Stupid kid."

"Good grief. What did he do?"

"A drug bust. When you go looking for trouble, it always finds you."

"Drugs?" I'd often wondered if Pete was the type to dabble in marijuana. "Buying what? Pot, or worse?"

"Caught him with a huge stash. Never came to work affected, I can tell you that, or I'd have canned him then and there."

"What a shame."

"Dave's doing a special one-page edition. It won't have a lot about the murder, so he told me. Not with trouble in his own family."

"I doubt that will keep gossip at bay, though. I saw more on Facebook than the post Maddie noticed yesterday." I scratched my leg. "I'm going to talk to Lois. I'll be back soon. Unless there's something you need me to do."

"No, go ahead. Gil Thompson said it's bunk about Harry taking a turn for the worse." Uncle Ross snorted. "Lois probably made that up, especially if she heard about Will's murder. Probably wants to steer clear of it all."

"Call or text if you hear anything about Dad, okay?"

He hung up, as usual, without saying good-bye. When I passed Amato's Pizzeria, the tantalizing scent of tomatoes, garlic, and cheese wafted through the open screens. My stomach grumbled. The Silver Scoop didn't look swamped yet, but would be soon due to the hot weather. Rosie and I crossed the street toward the cottages tucked farther back under a stand of trees; they each had white clapboard siding, wood shutters to match their painted doors, and a porch stoop.

Lois and Harry Nichols lived in the middle one. Two upstairs dormer windows poked from the roof. Their kids were grown, however, and had moved away from Silver Hollow. A girl and a boy, from what little I knew.

I loved adorable Cape Cod houses. I'd wanted to buy one after getting married, ditching the apartment where Flynn and I bumped into each other every minute. A cozy house with a white picket fence surrounding it, a vegetable garden in back, and flower boxes below all the windows overflowing with colorful petunias. So much for dreams.

I climbed the stoop and knocked on the blue door. The lawn looked overgrown, as did the shrubbery. No doubt with Harry's illness, Lois had to handle all the work inside and out. I tapped a foot, impatient, until she finally answered. She looked surprised to see me and stepped out on the stoop instead of inviting me inside. Perhaps her husband wasn't doing well. Lois wiped her hands on a checkered kitchen towel.

"Ms. Silverman—"

"Sasha, please. How is your husband today?"

"Oh." She looked startled, as if she'd forgotten about Harry. "Much better."

"Good."

Lois resembled a typical housewife in a frumpy plaid cotton dress plus fuzzy pink mules on her feet. I'd never seen her in anything but black slacks or a loose skirt below her silver T-shirt. Then again, I'd never visited her or any of the other sewing ladies at home. We respected our employees' privacy. I wondered how to broach the subject of the murder and Detective Mason, but Lois beat me to the punch.

"The police came here yesterday evening. A detective. He asked me about what I said at the meeting Thursday, that I'd kill Will if he took our insurance away." She sounded resentful. "Who told him that?"

"I don't know."

"He questioned everyone, didn't he? That's what I heard from Flora."

"Yes, but I—"

"Someone must have mentioned it! I don't know why he would come here asking about that, when your uncle threatened him worse."

I held my temper in check. "Yes, I understand that."

She sailed on as if I hadn't spoken. "Everyone knows Ross Silverman wanted to get rid of Will Taylor. For months."

"It doesn't matter what was said at the meeting," I said, hoping to sidetrack her. "We're certain that neither you nor my uncle had anything to do with the murder." Rosie paced back and forth, sensing Lois's tension. Mine, too.

"Harry and I talked that night. After the meeting." She sounded close to tears. "I've worked five years at the factory, so how could Taylor dump us like garbage? Thank goodness he's dead. We all worried over the past few months that he'd get rid of us."

"But why?" I asked. "We never heard anything before Thursday."

"I overheard him talking on the phone," Lois said. "Long before he left for New Jersey. He said he'd managed to keep things secret, and that everything was ready. That a factory had been chosen in Shanghai, and he was going to rent it."

"Did Will mention anyone's name during the conversation?"

"No. Remember when my sewing machine went on the fritz?" She rubbed her lower back. "The repairman took forever, so I walked around the shop a little. Kind of lingered by the office, and that's when I heard him on the phone. He wasn't happy to find me outside his door."

"Hey!" a voice bellowed from inside. "Lois!"

"Oh, that's Harry. I'd better go," she said, half in apology. "I have to make lunch now. He sleeps late, so his mealtimes are all out of whack."

"I won't keep you, then. Thanks for chatting."

"Ms. Silverman—Sasha. Please believe me," Lois said, but was unable to meet my gaze. "I did get upset at the meeting, but only because we might lose our health insurance. I'd never hurt anyone, though. Even if I did lose my job."

"I do believe you." Not that it mattered, since she had to convince Detective Mason. "Are you able to help at the shop on Labor Day?"

"I thought the police closed the business."

"We're going ahead with the teddy bear picnic. I'm hoping we can open the shop for our annual sale on Monday. I can get one of the other ladies, though."

"No, I'll come in by ten." She hurried inside after Harry bellowed again.

I descended the steps to find Rosie squatting on the lawn. Oh no. Lois had already disappeared. How embarrassing. Must have been all the extra treats. And while I always carried a bag or two whenever I walked my dog, I'd forgotten to grab one earlier. I did need coffee after all. Next stop, Fresh Grounds. Plus Mary Kate might give me some word on whether any of her friends had taken the canceled spots at the picnic.

I checked all my pockets and found a half-used tissue, which was better than knocking again and asking for a plastic bag. Rosie pulled at the leash, anxious to chase a squirrel, making it tough to scoop the droppings. Loud voices drifted through the cottage's open front window. Lois cursed a blue streak. Whoa. She'd never used such colorful words at work.

"Losing the insurance don't matter! What we need is

money," Harry said. "The Quick Mix would pay twice as much. Quit that job at the bear factory."

"I'll do what I want," Lois snapped. "You're in remission. Why can't you go back there if you're so worried about money?"

"How do you think I got this stupid cancer? Breathing in all that wheat and cornmeal dust!"

"The least you can do is help around here. It won't kill you to mow the lawn or sweep the floor. All you do is eat and watch TV all day—"

"Oh, you can't wait to put me in the ground."

"Stop, or you'll find yourself there sooner than you think." Lois's tone had turned nasty. So different from our conversation five minutes ago, threatening, almost evil. "You keep pushing me, Harry, and I swear you'll be sorry."

"You don't want to end up at Huron Valley again, do you?"

"Shut your piehole!"

I hurried across the grassy lawn, forgetting all about the tissue and its contents, but no way was I going back to retrieve it. Mortified by eavesdropping, my face burned. How could that be sweet, placid Lois? A woman who sewed teddy bears for children, quiet and efficient. Uncle Ross never mentioned any trouble with her work. So Lois had lied about her husband being worse. And he clearly didn't care if she lost her job.

Pete Fox was in jail on a drug charge, and now I'd heard the real Lois Nichols. Plus Will had gone ahead with plans to rent a factory in China, even before Dad agreed to send production overseas. Everyone had their secrets, apparently. Things seemed to be falling apart at the seams, like that abandoned teddy bear we'd found near Will's body by the stuffing machine.

Was I being naïve? Did our employees know about my tempestuous marriage, or had the details been fodder in the gossip mill over the past seven years? I wondered if Maddie might be harboring a few secrets of her own. My popular kid

sister had dated boys right and left in high school, during college, right up until the last guy she recently dumped. But she'd
posted all her status changes on Facebook.

Single. In a relationship. Single. Et cetera . . .

Maddie was far more open than me over the years, but she
had been acting fairly moody of late. She never shared information about her relationships. Then again, I hadn't explained
everything to her about what happened with Flynn. Maybe
that was a mistake. I hated to think our sister bond wasn't all
that close as I once thought. We could change that, though. I
added a long heart-to-heart chat with Mads to my list. Along
with redecorating Will's office for her use.

Two kids screamed shrilly behind the house next door. A
third sent up a long wail. The mother yelled at them to shut up
or she'd give them something to cry about. So much for the
simple life in sweet, picturesque Silver Hollow.

It had more than a hint of tarnish.

Chapter 15

I headed across the street. The bakery with its pink-and-white-striped awning and a window box filled with pink geraniums helped offset the unpleasant taste in my mouth. Until a motorcycle roared past from the Silver Scoop's parking lot, spewing black exhaust and a swirl of gravel toward my feet. A skittering stone hit my ankle. Ouch! I rubbed the scraped skin. Better me than my dog, though. Two cars honked long and loud; a teen riding a bike stuck out his middle finger at them both. The idyllic street scene was ruined once more.

Rosie shook herself from head to tail. I wanted to do the same.

Instead I headed to the Silver Scoop's side patio, hoping to find Kristen Bloom. I wondered if her story about the "pity party" jived with Debbie Davison's version. I was in luck. Kristen sat in back under an ironwork table's umbrella, chatting on her cell phone, a salad before her. I figured she could watch through the side door while her employees raced around one another, filling orders at the counter and drive-through window in back. Always watchful.

I fetched a triangular paper cup from the stack by the outside drinking fountain. My sweet Rosie slurped from the filled cup like she'd found a desert oasis.

"Poor baby. I should have brought your water bottle," I murmured aloud.

"Hey, Sasha!"

Surprise, surprise. Kristen waved me over. Easy, since I hadn't come up with an excuse to chat with someone who usually shunned conversation. I sank on the ironwork chair opposite. I should have ordered a slush or a creamy milk shake, but resting was less calories. Kristen's tiny frame unnerved me, anyway. Especially given her full Lotus pose. Looking at the marks on her slim calves from the metal chair made me wince; my butt hurt, and I had plenty of padding. Who had that kind of incredible flexibility without killing themselves to attain it?

Rosie wouldn't sit on the hot pavement, so I lifted her into my lap. "Business will be booming today," I said.

"Great weather for us." Kristen grinned and then leaned forward to whisper, "So it's true? You found Will Taylor strangled, on the factory floor?"

I fixed my gaze on the ice-cream flavor chart. "Dead, yeah. I hear you spent Thursday night with Carolyn at Quinn's Pub. Cheering her up, which she probably still needs. Poor thing."

"Yep." She took a huge bite of salad. Somehow she could still talk out of one side of her mouth without grossing me out. "Got drunk as skunks. Fun. Bit much, though. Paid for it, too." Kristen swallowed, adding, "Trying to get my two miles in the next morning was a killer."

"I heard the case detective questioned you."

"Like cheeseburgers on a hot grill! Good thing we had nothing to hide." She used a pinky finger to push a strand of blond hair out of her eyes. "That guy is tougher than he looks. I dunno how many times he kept asking the same question but in different ways. Poor Carolyn. She was half out of her mind anyway. You'd think he'd cut her a break, her husband being offed! But no. He asked about every minute, from the time we got to the pub to the time we left."

"Wow."

"Tell me about it. I mean, sure, Carolyn went off to the restroom to barf. She was gone so long, I thought maybe she'd fallen into the john. Sicker than a dog!"

"So was Debbie, right?"

"Yeah. We all had too much to drink."

That reminded me to call a friend who often met me after work. Being a nurse, Laura Carpenter could answer questions about a murder victim's time of death. I had no idea how long it took for a dead body to turn stiff, or whatever. Will's gray pallor haunted me as it was.

"—but I won't throw up. I just can't," Kristen went on. "Even though I drank about a gallon of sangria." She unfolded her legs and sat straight. I pushed my shoulders back from a slouch, seeing her ramrod posture. "We ate like pigs, too. Calamari appetizer, then burgers, fries, onion rings, more rounds of drinks, dessert. That pub makes a mean cheesecake."

"I know." I couldn't imagine her eating a decadent dessert. But I also didn't mention how Brian Quinn, the owner, had a standing order for cheesecakes from Mary Kate Thompson, not the Pretty in Pink bakery. "I see you've got a new ice-cream flavor."

"What, the Salty Honey Bee? Yeah, it's sort of like salted caramel with a vanilla base. Wanna try it?" Kristen waved to the clerk behind the counter, who nodded. "We use Debbie Davison's clover honey, too. Good stuff, reasonably priced."

"I ought to ask her about selling her honey at our shop."

"She'd love it. Bears and honey go together like cream and sugar." When Kristen beckoned again, one of the teens brought out a small cone with a single scoop of vanilla ice cream. "Hope you like it."

"Mm." The ice cream was threaded with gold and studded with salt crystals, but I thought the flavor was a bit salty for my taste. Too bad it didn't have crushed cookies in it. I steered our chat around to Thursday night. "My uncle said you all had a blast at the pub with Carolyn."

"We did." Kristen shoved her cell toward me. "Here, see for yourself."

I swiped through three photos. "Nice." Carolyn was laughing in every single one, a drink in hand and an arm around a different friend. "She sure needed it."

"I haven't had a chance to upload them to either Instagram or Facebook yet."

"Only three photos. Because you arrived late?"

"Are you following up for that cop?" Kristen's eyes had narrowed, although she kept her smile fixed—a shade short of friendly. "I had a Zumba class, so yeah. I came late. I'd have taken more photos, but my phone died."

"Well, thanks for the sample." Since her suspicions seemed high, I rose from the chair with a firm grip on both Rosie's leash and the ice-cream cone. "Next time, I'll join you guys for a drink or two at the pub."

"Yeah. Sure."

By her flat tone, I got the impression there'd be no invitation. I dodged the crowd lined up at the counter. Kristen had pulled out her cell phone and turned sideways to the wall, her back arched. She often did stretching exercises whenever she could squeeze in a free minute or two, at the shop, the grocery store, even in church. I'd always yearned to be tiny and thin like her. But that kind of skinny took work—time and effort I didn't want to take. I was happy walking my dog. And resorting to a treadmill at the gym.

Who was I kidding? I always turned down Maddie's invitation to join her for a workout and curled up with a book, a cup of tea, and a cookie instead. Okay, maybe two or three.

I dumped the Salty Honey Bee in the trash out front. Definitely cut the salt.

Rosie scarfed up an ice-cream cone some kid had dropped on the sidewalk. After that, we walked to Fresh Grounds. My heart sank when I saw the line snaking out the door. It would take twice as long to get coffee. Instead Rosie and I headed next door to The Cat's Cradle Books, where Rozelle Cooper bagged up a customer's purchases. Elle had married my cousin and was my other best friend besides Mary Kate. She kept her naturally curly dark hair pulled back from her heart-shaped face, sans makeup except for pale pink lip gloss. One quarter Ottawa and Chippewa Native American, her aquiline nose and the golden hue of her skin gave her an earthy charm.

Her voice boomed with a cheery ring. "Sasha!" Elle grabbed my arm and dragged me toward the counter. "And right here's the woman you need to talk to about the picnic. Sasha Silverman's in charge. You have room because of a few cancellations, right?"

"Yes, we do. It's fifteen dollars."

"Per person?"

"For a family up to six. Ten bucks for two to three people." I crouched near the little boy who'd reached out a hand to pet Rosie. "Always ask first if a dog's friendly, okay? She won't bite. Go ahead and scratch behind her ears. She loves that."

Instead he threw his arms around my dog, giggling when Rosie licked his face and neck. "It tickles!"

"Good doggie." The woman rummaged in her purse for a few bills. "Here's the fee then, and I'll bring my sister and her kids. I'm so glad I ran into you! Some of my friends told me a few weeks ago about the picnic, and I'm glad we can join in the fun."

"I don't have any reservation slips with me—"

"Here, I've got you covered." Elle wrote out a paid-in-full

receipt on a slip of paper and handed it to her. "Bring that on Monday with a packed lunch and as many teddy bears the kids want to bring. We'll have signs directing everyone to the right shelter. Sasha's providing the lemonade and cookies."

"Great! See you then."

The woman hurried outside with her little boy in tow. Elle grinned. "There. One cancellation filled. I bet Mary Kate has a few more. She told me earlier today how you found Will Taylor in the factory. Pretty gruesome."

"You got that right, girlfriend."

I plopped down on a chair while Rosie nosed the shelves. Elle fetched a ragged bunny from behind the counter, so my dog stretched out on a rug for some serious chewing. I loved this bookstore. Its oak planks salvaged from an old church matched the floor in Fresh Grounds; wall-to-wall shelves, a play area for kids, and the varnished wooden board across a double row of cubicles that served as the counter made it cozy. The cubicles had cushions. Charlie the tuxedo cat was always curled up inside. I guessed Whiskers must be hiding.

My cousin Matt worked days at the Quick Mix while Elle ran the shop. She was a natural with customers. She'd added a pair of cozy armchairs in the bay window on either side of a table display of books to draw customers from the street. Besides children's books, they sold all kinds of mystery, thrillers, romance, fantasy, science fiction, and even nonfiction. A selection of family games lined a long shelf behind the counter. An arched doorway led to the adjoining coffee shop and bakery. Noise was an issue, but the exchange of customers offset that disadvantage.

"I saw this online." Elle showed me her iPad with a local news report about the murder. Dave Fox was listed as a source in the article. "No real details. Police want to keep all that to a minimum, I suppose."

"Can I ask you a question? What is Huron Valley?" I asked. "Like if someone said, 'You'll go back to Huron Valley if you're not careful.' I'm just curious."

Elle raised her eyebrows. "Could be a bunch of things. 'Huron Valley' refers to the area around Ypsilanti. There's the Humane Society, a hospital, and the school district. Oh, and there's a women's prison. The Huron Valley Correctional Facility."

"Bingo."

"What do you mean?"

"I can't say right now. Sorry."

The information was disheartening. I realized now that Maddie hadn't dug deep enough when it came to Lois Nichols's background check. While she sounded sincere ten minutes ago, literally begging me that she had nothing to do with Will Taylor's murder, the hair on the back of my neck prickled with uneasiness. What the hell. Had we harbored a murderer in our midst?

Detective Mason's words haunted me. *But he lived right next door. . . .* Even though plenty of people fudged the truth all the time, I had little experience on knowing whether someone was lying through their teeth.

And that scared me half to death.

"Hey! How's it going?" Mary Kate popped through the arched doorway, holding a square plate. "Here's your apple blintz. The very last one, lucky duck."

"I am eternally grateful. Coffee?" I asked. The first bite oozed cinnamon and sweetened apples, plus crunchy pastry. Rosie stretched up, paws on my knees, sniffing hard, but I gently pushed her down. "Not for doggies. Sorry."

"I'll get her a peanut butter biscuit." Mary Kate soon brought back a cardboard cup within minutes. "Mint mocha, skinny. I put whipped cream on it anyway, and chocolate syrup drizzled on top."

"Mm. You're a lifesaver."

"And here's Rosie's treat." She held out a round cookie baked for any dogs who had to wait outside while their humans enjoyed the coffee, treats, and camaraderie inside Fresh Grounds. "What a good girl. What's the matter, Sasha? You look really down. Of course, after yesterday, we expect that, but—"

"She has a friend in Huron Valley Correctional Facility," Elle interrupted.

"I do not!" I laughed with them. "All right, I should know teasing when I hear it. But when someone mentioned the name 'Huron Valley' I didn't know what they meant. It didn't sound good."

"It's the only women's prison in Michigan."

"Stop it, Elle." Mary Kate snapped her fingers. "Drink up. Get happy again."

I sipped the coffee with my eyes closed. The thought of Lois Nichols in prison shook my faith in Maddie's instincts. She wouldn't have hired someone with a prison record, would she? I set the cup down and texted my sister, hoping the little ding of an answering text would relieve some of my tension. Then I savored the last few bites of my apple blintz for a longer time. Mmm. So good. I flexed my shoulders. Relaxed. Carbs worked magic on my stress.

"I need an intervention, too." Elle poured out a handful of colorful candy-coated chocolates from a glass jar on the counter. The top clinked when she shut it. "Don't tell Matt. I'll buy him another package at Costco. But ever since I heard about Will Taylor, I'm popping these like pills. I'm so nervous. What if a serial killer is loose?"

"Oh, Elle," Mary Kate said with a laugh. "I really doubt if it's that bad."

"I'm waiting for the other shoe to drop," I said. "What if someone's trying to make trouble for us? Someone with a grudge, like Jack Cullen."

She looked puzzled. "I don't know. He can barely lift a

coffee cup. I'm sure he didn't have anything to do with Will's murder."

"Maybe you're right. But why would he be snooping around the factory?"

"Because he's a nosey parker," Elle said.

"Oh, I have two families to make up for those cancellations," Mary Kate said.

Relief washed over me. "That's three out of five. All right, ladies. What can you tell me about Will Taylor having a girlfriend? Is it true? Do you know who it might be?" I noticed that Mary Kate and Elle exchanged meaningful glances. "I want all the dirt."

"Ooh, dirt! Dirt!" Elle closed the adjoining doors to the coffee shop. "I hereby call an official meeting of the Guilty Pleasures Gossip Club."

She also flipped the sign on The Cat's Cradle door to Be Back Soon and perched on a stool by the counter. Rosie curled up at my feet on the rug for a nap, so I stretched out my bare legs with a contented sigh. Uh-oh. Should have been more awake with that razor in the shower. Thank goodness I was among friends who wouldn't notice the strip of fuzzy leg hair I'd missed.

"Come on, then. After all that's happened, I could use something juicy."

Mary Kate raised an eyebrow. "Well. From what I heard back in May, Carolyn was so busy with her shop, she never realized Will was coming home later and later and skipping meals. Debbie Davison—she supplies us with honey for the tea we offer, plus for baking—once told me she saw Will's Camry following Vivian's car—"

"Vivian Grant?" I squeaked.

"Yep. In a few weeks, most people knew they had a thing going."

"Everyone except Carolyn," Elle added.

"And me, apparently. So how did she find out?" My curiosity rose, but my phone rang then with its cheery piano *Peanuts* ringtone. Maddie loved her Vince Guaraldi CD as much as her Snoopy collection in the office. "It's Mads. Hang on a minute, okay?"

My sister sounded rushed after I answered. "Hey, Sash. Dad's in his own room now, but I can't talk long. Mom said the doctor should be here any min—"

"Wait, listen. Did you know Lois Nichols might have a criminal record?"

"No way is that possible! I'm careful about checking all their references and previous employment. Oh, here's the doctor. We'll talk later."

Frustrated, I slipped the phone into my pocket. So Maddie hadn't known. Lois's arrest and conviction may have been long ago, and she might have omitted the facts on her employment application. I figured Detective Mason would nose out the truth, though, on his own. I turned back to my friends, updated them on my dad's condition, and then finished my coffee.

"Okay, let's get back to the gossip."

"Well." Mary Kate's eyes shone. "Didn't you hear about the huge food fight at Pretty in Pink?"

"What? When was this?"

"Late June, I think. Where were you?" Elle asked. "Wait, you and Mads were helping your parents move into a new condo in Florida."

I nodded. "Sure missed something big. How come I didn't hear anything after we came back, though?"

"That's because you jumped into the Fourth of July teddy bear parade," Mary Kate said. "So Carolyn finally figured out that Vivian Grant and Will—"

"What would she see in him?" I still had trouble believing it.

"Takes all kinds," Mary Kate said with a laugh. "Garrett saw Caroline storming into the bakery. I don't know why he was walking past that day, but boy howdy, did things spiral out of control! What a mess."

"I remember," Elle said. "He and Uncle Gil were volunteers at that Habitat for Humanity house. Near the curve on Kermit Street."

I nodded. "Oh yeah. Uncle Ross volunteered, too, but he hurt himself and left early. But a public food fight at Pretty in Pink? Wow."

"Yup," Elle said. "I don't know how Carolyn finally found out about their affair, but it all started on a Saturday, around the midafternoon slump time. She slammed the door so hard it shook the whole building, according to Wendy Clark."

"Yeah, stopped Garrett right in his tracks," Mary Kate said. "He figured something must be up, so he called the cops."

"Wendy Clark called first. I love those gorgeous lace cookies she decorates for Vivian." Elle poked Mary Kate. "Is she helping you with the teddy bear cookies for the picnic? Cool! You ought to steal her away from Pretty in Pink. She's getting tired of Vivian's bad moods, from what I've heard."

"We've talked, but keep that under your hats."

"Anyway, Wendy said Carolyn marched into the shop and screamed, literally screamed, that Vivian had no right to be 'boinking her man,'" Elle continued.

"Whoa," I said. "No kidding?"

"Then Carolyn unhooked the half door and came into the back, where they did all the baking and decorator work—"

"And started throwing icing bags, cupcakes, you name it," Mary Kate cut in.

"Wendy was so shocked. She blocked Carolyn's access to the wedding cake she'd just finished decorating." Elle rubbed her hands together. "Imagine if Carolyn had thrown that! She was ranting about seeing Will and Vivian stark naked in her kitchen, doing the nasty right on the table. Ugh, ugh, ugh. And no doubt in her bed, of course."

Memories flooded back, bad memories. I swallowed hard. I'd never told my best friends about finding my ex in our bed with his paramour. The thought of sleeping there or in any room of our apartment turned my stomach; I could definitely sympathize with Carolyn Taylor. Despite Flynn's pleas, I'd packed my bags and left for good. Nothing he said or did changed my mind. His usual flowers, candy, and jewelry no longer worked to ease that pain.

Trust couldn't be bought.

I banished all that to a locked room inside my head. Tried not to think of how Flynn had failed me once again after I'd swallowed my pride and called him for help. He hadn't lifted a finger to track down my parents. Always too busy, then and now.

"So that's it? She threw icing bags and cupcakes?"

"Oh no." Elle grinned. "Carolyn did a smackdown, right on the bakery floor, trying to rip Vivian's hair out. Yelling and screaming bloody murder—"

"By that time, the police arrived," Mary Kate added.

"Yeah. Digger Sykes said Vivian and Carolyn had frosting in their hair, on their clothes, and cake crumbs were every-where. What a mess! Wendy said it took days to clean the bak-ery so they could pass health inspection again."

"Carolyn posted a ton of selfies, too, on Facebook."

"Get outta town!" I blew out a long breath. "On her time-line?"

Mary Kate giggled. "Yes! A few are still there. Carolyn snapped photos of all the damage and posted them. Her friends all clicked 'like' and commented how she was so courageous. My brother told her it wouldn't look good in case Vivian sued her for slander, so she took them down. The ones showing the bakery's name, anyway."

"Here, take a peek."

Elle handed over her cell. I scanned through half a dozen photos showing the bakery's interior, which looked like a tornado had hit. One showed Carolyn standing in front of the scalloped pink-and-white-striped awning, with frosting in her hair and coating her eyelids; she held one arm flexed in a pose like a weight lifter pumping iron, with a huge smile on her face. Her timeline was loaded with selfies, showing Carolyn inside the Holly Jolly Christmas shop, eating one of her gingerbread cookies, posing with customers, you name it.

"We all thought her business would suffer," Mary Kate said, "but it slows down in summer anyway. Even though it looks like she's working nonstop."

"Carolyn told me she started selling online." Elle tossed my empty cup in the trash. "I've seen her at the post office sending off boxes and packages."

"So, why didn't they get divorced?" I asked. "I know Will was tired of Carolyn's stalking him. You'd think he'd file if he refused counseling."

"He preferred playing around. I heard Jenny Woodley met him for dinner, probably on the sly, in Ann Arbor."

"Ooh. Rumor only, or is there proof?"

"No idea."

"I heard the Silver Leaf Bed and Breakfast is strapped for cash," Mary Kate said. "They're always running some kind of promo to get bookings. But let's get back to Carolyn and Vivian."

"Well, she demanded that Will end the affair with Vivian. I'd have divorced him," Elle said. "They don't have kids, so that would have been easy."

"But." Mary Kate glanced out the window, her reddish-blond ponytail swishing behind her head, as if making sure no one would overhear. Her blue eyes sparkled with excitement and her voice dropped to a whisper. "This is very hush-hush. Do. Not. Repeat. Pinky swear."

We agreed, linking fingers, and waited for her to continue. "Carolyn may have signed a prenuptial agreement," she whispered, "that guarantees her almost nothing, except for the Holly Jolly shop, if they divorced. But you didn't hear it from me."

"Your brother told you that?"

"Shh! Mark would kill me if he knew anyone else found out. So you don't know anything, right?" Mary Kate blinked half a dozen times rapidly, on purpose, making me laugh. "I'll see if I can find out the actual terms, because I'm curious. You knew she opened the shop after her first divorce."

"Yeah, that's old news," Elle said drily. "So what was it like, finding Will dead?"

"Oh, come on." I shuddered. "You don't want to know. Trust me."

"But we've never seen a dead body—"

"Speak for yourself," Mary Kate interrupted. "My grandma died in her sleep. In my bed, over the Christmas holidays. Mom bought me a new mattress, but I couldn't sleep until she let me switch rooms with Boomer We didn't tell him, though."

"Ha! Your brother would think it was cool," Elle said. "A dead body wouldn't faze him at all, especially now that he's a Marine."

"Boomer's an IT specialist."

"Trained for stealth assignments. Snuck up behind me the last time he came home on leave," she said, "and I jumped so high, I almost hit the ceiling."

We all laughed. I loved chatting with my friends whenever possible. We hadn't shared in a major gossip fest in a while, but my sense of relaxation quickly dissipated. Carolyn's prenup as a motive for murder sobered me. Fast.

"I wonder if Detective Mason knows about what happened at Pretty in Pink," I said slowly. "It's bound to come out if it was that major of a catfight."

"Oh, you better believe it was. Major-major. Colossal," Elle said.

Mary Kate nodded. "Titanic."

"Well, Carolyn was with friends all night at the pub." I stood, smoothing my khaki shorts. Rosie rose, stretched, and shook herself, clearly ready to go until Elle scratched behind her ears. "And that cake wrestling match didn't sink either of them in terms of their businesses. I hope this murder doesn't ruin ours."

"It won't," Mary Kate reassured me, although I had my doubts. "I've been asking all the customers I know—not the strangers, of course—if they've heard anything. Or if they saw any cars in your parking lot Thursday night."

I smiled at my friends, hoping they wouldn't notice how worry plagued me. "Thanks for the laughs today. With what's happened at the factory, and with Dad in the hospital, it's been pretty crazy. I'll see you both Monday at the picnic."

"Where you'll be in for a triple dose of stress," Elle said, half-joking. "But don't worry. Our Mary Katherine is a whiz at baking and a great mom. I'll let her deal with all the scream-ing kids, broken cookies, and skinned knees."

"You'll saddle Matt with the kids," Mary Kate retorted, "and sit at home—"

"Will not!"

"Quit bickering, you two," I said. "I feel like the mom in this club."

"The Queen. Queen Alexandra." Mary Kate retrieved my empty plate. "Gotta run, girls! Closing time, and you know what that means. More work."

I poked Elle in the shoulder. "I'd open up again if I were you, or you'll lose business. Looks like a mom with her kids waiting outside."

She jumped up, turned the sign around, and ushered the group inside. "I'm so sorry! I didn't see you out there. Minor crisis here, but it's over."

"That's all right. We'd like a picture book—"

"Oh, doggie, doggie," the youngest child crooned. Rosie licked the boy's hand.

I quickly left before the kids could latch on to my dog. They looked disappointed, but Rosie had been sitting long enough. I didn't want her to get anxious and nip anyone. I led her past the Fresh Grounds window. Mary Kate waved from inside; she helped Garrett package leftover muffins and bread as donations for the church pantry.

I guided my restless pooch to the street with plenty of food for thought.

Chapter 16

Rosie nosed every bit of litter along the way home while I dawdled. Thinking hard. About Uncle Ross, who wouldn't have killed Will Taylor even if the jerk begged him to put a gun to his head. I knew that in my gut. My uncle loved hunting—gun and bow—in the fall, but he'd never kill a human being. Or stuff him with fiber.

I wondered if Detective Mason would tell me the autopsy results and the exact time Will had been murdered. Patience, that's what I needed. I kicked a pebble from the sidewalk. A sparrow fluttered from a low bush toward the sky, startling me.

"Oops. Sorry, little bird." I needed to get a grip. "Come on, Rosie."

We walked on. Next I considered Lois Nichols, who had a secret past. What crime had sent her to the Huron Valley Correctional Facility? Robbery? Assault and battery? Murder? Had that been what her husband meant? I couldn't imagine Lois coming to the factory Thursday night, lying in wait, ready to take steps to prevent losing her health insurance. How would she have known Will planned to come that night? And she couldn't get inside without a key.

That wasn't impossible, though.

And then there was Jack Cullen. Why had he been snooping around the factory, wrench in hand? He'd bugged Carolyn about wanting to see Will. Too bad Mason never mentioned if the killer had gotten into the factory by prying open the back door. My sister and I hadn't thought of checking around the building. We'd been too numb, unable to process Will's death. But if the killer didn't break in, then Will must have let him or her inside. Unless he left it open for any stranger to walk in unannounced.

Come to think of it, the door wasn't locked when my sister and I arrived. I doubted if Mason thought this was a random killing, though.

What about Carolyn Taylor? A businesswoman like Maddie and me, focused on success, but clearly distraught over her husband's affair. And with a disadvantageous prenuptial agreement that would push anyone over the edge. Unfortunately, her alibi was airtight. Mason had verified it. Kristen Bloom mentioned being grilled about the "pity party" and I'd witnessed him raking Carolyn over the coals as well. Could she have left the pub without being seen? With enough time to kill her husband and get back? Plus she was drunk out of her mind.

Was Teddy Hartman a long shot? Sure, he would have jumped at the chance to help Will take over our company. Maybe they even planned to merge the two bear factories. So why would he kill Will Taylor? Plus I'd never established whether Hartman had been seen in the village the day of the murder.

I didn't know what to think anymore.

"Sasha!" Startled, I almost stumbled into the sharp brick

corner of the drugstore. Ben Blake had emerged from the side door. "You okay?"

"Yeah. Just clumsy, as usual."

Ben grinned and fastened the iron grille's padlock. Rosie jumped against his jean-clad legs with excitement until he rubbed behind her curly ears, flashing the million-dollar smile that charmed customers, family, and friends alike. He stood half a head taller than me, his brown hair shorter than I remembered, hazel eyes gleaming, and still as handsome as in high school. We'd been good friends since then; Ben had played quarterback until he'd blown his knee during our senior year. After his girlfriend dumped him before prom, Mary Kate, Elle, and I had all gone to the dance with him—supporting him when he hobbled in on crutches.

The scholarship at UM might have vanished, but Ben quietly worked his way through college and pharmacy school. After a spell with a chain drugstore in a Detroit suburb, he returned to Silver Hollow. Residents needed a close drugstore instead of driving miles away to Ann Arbor or Jackson. And we'd renewed our friendship when I'd returned, minus my wedding ring.

"A shame about Will Taylor," Ben said, "but I also heard about your dad ending up in the hospital. Is he going to be okay?"

I leaned against the wall, suddenly weary. "You're the first person who's asked me that, did you know? Thanks for your concern."

"Well, I'm medically inclined. And nosy." He grinned.

"Double pneumonia. He's improving, but I haven't heard otherwise—wait." After checking my phone, I sighed in relief. "No missed texts. My sister flew to New Jersey last night. I guess everything's going well and the antibiotics are working."

"Glad to hear. Let me know if you have any questions about the specific drugs," he added. "Have you had dinner yet?"

"No." I glanced down at my outfit and at Rosie. "Did you

mean catching a burger or something? I'd have to take the dog home first."

"How about I bring a pizza over? Unless you want Chinese."

"Either sounds great. You choose."

At his pleased grin, I suddenly panicked. This couldn't possibly be a spur-of-the-moment date. No way. I hadn't had time to consider anyone for a serious relationship since my divorce. Not that Ben wouldn't make a great boyfriend. Or husband. But not for me. He was like a brother to me and my friends.

"Sure you don't mind coming close to the scene of a murder?" I teased.

"Ha. You're standing right where the cops almost caught someone who broke into my store. Gave them the slip, although I don't know how. I'll tell you the story later. Give me forty-five minutes to an hour and I'll be over."

"Okay, thanks."

Ben headed to his car across the street in the church parking lot. I scurried home at a faster pace than normal, which delighted Rosie. The Holly Jolly Christmas shop was closed tight, although the lights along the roof twinkled. Carolyn left them on at night, summer and winter. We'd considered adding a few strings of teddy bear lights but rejected the idea as too cheesy. We always hired someone to outline the house with white lights in December. Maybe I'd leave them up for the year. That might be pretty.

Uncle Ross had dragged the dented, broken mailbox and post to the side. It looked so sad. A new mailbox in the shape of a teddy bear would be neat, with the jaw pulling down. Cute or horrifying? Maddie would know how to design it classy and avoid a trashy or cheap look. I'd leave that to her when she returned.

I rushed in the back door and half-tripped over Onyx, who purred like a tank engine. She always turned on the charm when Maddie was gone. I fed her, hoping I'd remember to clean her litter box in the basement later. I swept the floor and tidied the island, stashing the picnic fliers in a basket. Housework wasn't my strong suit. It wasn't a suit in my deck of cards at all, to be honest. Then I raced upstairs to shower and wash my hair. Walking in the summer heat had been exhausting. I felt so refreshed afterward.

I wrapped my head in a towel, donned my terry-cloth robe, and wondered if I should call my friend Laura. We'd met in college our freshman year. Laura chose nursing while I'd pursued business. She was great fun as a bridesmaid, joining Elle and Mary Kate in the wedding party. Laura had warned me about Flynn's old friend Angela, who'd been pretty frisky with all the ushers. If only I'd listened. Apparently Flynn had dabbled in hot and steamy sex with Angela before the wedding and whenever possible afterward.

I dialed Laura's cell number.

"Hey, girl," I began, but then recognized her voice mail's automatic message. Drat. "It's Sasha. Call if you get a chance, and thanks."

Within a few moments, a text notification dinged. *On vacation, Sturgeon Bay, will call you next week.* Double drat. Laura would have called if I'd said "emergency," but she deserved her vacation. Especially in Door County, Wisconsin. We'd gone there together one summer, enjoyed the wineries, and toured a lighthouse or two; mostly we read books on several beaches when it didn't rain. My second favorite spot.

Number one, hands down, was Mackinac Island—the turtle-shaped gem nestled between Michigan's Upper and Lower Peninsulas. I hadn't been on a weeklong vacation in a while. Maybe I was overdue. The "sisters" weekend up north couldn't come soon enough. My stress level sure called for it.

I'd hoped Laura could answer my questions about autopsy procedures, time of death, and all that. I checked the clock.

Only ten minutes before Ben arrived. Too hot for ratty jeans, so a loose crinkle skirt would keep me cool. Maddie had ironed my tan, rust, blue, and white striped shirt yesterday along with her capris. At times I didn't appreciate my sister being a neat freak, but it came in handy sometimes.

I left my hair damp and loose and padded barefoot downstairs. Luckily, I found a liter bottle of Coke in the fridge, some beer Maddie kept around, and several cans of ginseng-flavored iced tea, my favorite. Rosie barked—perfect timing. I opened the door to Ben; he sported a faded Ferris State T-shirt, jeans with holes at the knees, and deck shoes. He carried in a large bag along with the square box from Amato's Pizzeria, which smelled heavenly.

"Hope you like barbecue chicken pizza."

"Mmm. With red onions?"

"Yep." Ben entered the kitchen. Rosie followed, sniffing hard, tail wagging. He slid the box on the island and then extracted a large lidded bowl. "Greek salad, too. I'm starving."

"I have Coke, beer, or tea. Help yourself." I gathered plates, flatware, and napkins and then checked the freezer drawer. Ice cream, perfect for dessert. "Let's sit in the kitchen. Too buggy outside."

"That's right. I remember you prefer a hotel, not a campground."

"I like campfires. If the smoke doesn't get to me," I said. "Thanks for bringing dinner. I'm not sure when Mads is due back, so you saved me from a bowl of cereal."

He laughed. "Dig in."

We did just that. I indulged in two pieces of crusty pizza first, dotted with chunks of chicken and layered with cheese, slathered with spicy barbecue sauce, before enjoying salad with feta, Greek olives, and more red onions dripping with vinaigrette. We didn't talk much, only catching up on family matters. Ben's brother, Mike, practiced estate planning and probate

law at Blake and Branson, plus he represented the village bank;
Mark Branson, Mary Kate's brother, handled divorce and family law. They advertised as Mike & Mark, Legal Eagles.

Ben wiped barbecue sauce from his jaw. "I never asked you
before about how Teddy Roosevelt is linked to teddy bears. I
suppose I can look it up on the Net—"

"Nah, that's easy." I launched into the long explanation,
figuring it was a good review since we often got asked that during
tours with adult visitors. "The president went on a bear-hunting
trip late in November of 1902, but never saw a bear. They didn't
want Roosevelt to look like a failure, though, so his attendants
cornered a black bear, clubbed it, and tied it to a tree."

"That wasn't easy, I bet."

"Hounds chased it down, apparently. President Roosevelt
considered that unsporting and told them to kill the bear due
to its injuries. A cartoonist turned the episode into a political
issue. Other cartoons followed, although the bear eventually
changed to a cub. So the following year, when a toy maker
came out with the teddy bear, everyone stuck the nickname
Teddy on the President. Despite how much he really hated it."

"I never knew all that."

"But you knew Kermit Street is named after his son, not
the frog."

"Yeah, I did. Who was the toy maker?"

"Morris Michtom. He saw the cartoon and created the
first teddy bear—at least in the States. He also asked the President for permission to use the name Teddy for his bear and
sent one to the White House. Everyone wanted a teddy bear
after that."

"Of course." Ben winked. "My mom has my teddy bear at
home, somewhere."

"Did you know in Germany, right around the same time,
Richard Steiff created a toy bear and exhibited it at the Leipzig
fair? They didn't have the Internet like nowadays, so no one

really knows who came up with the first teddy bear," I said. "We've tried to make our bears look as real as possible. That's why we only have tiny bears in blue, pink, green, yellow, and other colors."

Ben surprised me with a sudden question. "Sorry to change the subject, but did you ever see Alan Grant and Pete Fox together? Like hanging out around the village. Alan's mom owns the Pretty in Pink bakery. He makes deliveries for her, too."

"Yeah, I know." I hesitated, wondering if I should reveal what Uncle Ross had mentioned earlier about Pete. "So you think they're friends?"

He leaned back. "Must be. I've seen them at the Silver Screen and McDonald's. Alan still lives at home. Not that ambitious for a twentysomething, in my opinion."

"You know Pete's dad runs the local newspaper." I stole a cucumber slice from the salad bowl and crunched on it. "I remember seeing a small article in it about your pharmacy break-in."

"Much bigger write-up in the *Ann Arbor News* back in June, when it happened," Ben said. "The cops didn't find any fingerprint evidence, or anything else, but I think both Pete and Alan had something to do with it. Alan at least."

Again, I debated going into an explanation. I trusted Ben, but Uncle Ross might be mistaken. I'd hate to pass on bad information. "Why would you think that?"

"It's difficult to explain—"

"Wait, let me dish out dessert first. Or did you want more pizza?" When he shook his head, I carried the soiled plates and flatware to the sink and grabbed two clean bowls. "Vanilla, chocolate mint, or cookie dough?"

"Chocolate mint," Ben said. "I can scoop if you like."

"Sure. One vanilla, one chocolate for me."

I wrapped the two leftover pieces of pizza in foil and stuck them in the fridge. I rinsed and put the dishes in the dishwasher, refilled our drinks, and then scrounged up some short-bread cookies from the pantry to accompany our ice cream. They crumbled a little, since I'd bought them weeks ago, but tasted fine as a topping. I sprayed a circle of whipped cream over our bowls, then added a few drizzles of chocolate syrup and colorful sprinkles. Yum.

"Wow. A better sundae than at the Silver Scoop."

"But I don't have maraschino cherries," I said with a laugh. "Sorry about that."

"So, to get back to what happened." Ben perched on the stool again, spoon in hand, and took a huge bite. "When I worked at the big chain drugstore, we kept the controlled sub-stances under lock and key. There was always lots of traffic in the store. Plus bulletproof glass between the pharmacy and customers added to security. But we rarely had the chance to breathe or take a lunch break. Most pharmacies, even mine, are also registered in MAPS."

"What's that?"

"The Michigan Automated Prescription System database. Monitors all the Schedule Two to Five drugs dispensed by doc-tors throughout the state, and makes it easier to track abuse."

"That's good to know," I said, taking small bites of ice cream. "Last time I filled a prescription for my mom in Florida, some guy got all mad when the pharmacist wouldn't give him a refill. It said no refills right on the label. He was downright nasty."

"I've got stories that would make your hair curl. In my small pharmacy, it's much tougher for anyone to scope out where the drugs are kept."

"Why is that?"

"We keep controlled drugs mixed in among the other stock. Makes it harder for a thief to find anything without tak-ing a huge amount of time. That's why the cops almost caught them."

"You make it sound like a bank robbery—"

"Crime is big when it comes to drugs." Ben scraped his bowl, having inhaled his dessert. "I know the customers coming into my store. They stick to picking up their prescriptions, and maybe a new bottle of aspirin. I'll take being an independent over working in a big chain any day."

"I bet it's quieter."

"And I'm a lot saner. I had enough craziness after losing my dream of a pro football career. Getting through pharm school and then licensing exams was rough. I'm no quitter, though. We all get slammed. You had it rough a while back, too. Your divorce, I mean."

" 'Rough' is a mild word. Try 'nightmare.' "

"Yeah, I saw some of the photos and comments Hanson posted on Facebook," Ben said. "Pretty grim. I can't believe he blamed you."

I swirled what was left of my chocolate mint into the vanilla. "I'd rather not talk about it, if you don't mind."

A long awkward pause dragged out between us. I hadn't meant to cut Ben off that way, but the last thing I wanted was to talk about Flynn. My life would have been so different if I hadn't been so blind, so head over heels in love, so trusting.

Ben cleared his throat while I finished my last bite of ice cream. "I know firsthand what it's like to be betrayed. Had a few relationships that went sour over the years. But did you know I'm seeing Wendy Clark now?"

"No, that's great," I said, covering my surprise. "She's helping Mary Kate Thompson with decorating cookies for the teddy bear picnic."

"Yeah, she told me." He looked sheepish. "Lisa, my sister-in-law, set us up on a blind date. That was the night of the break-in, actually. Alan Grant came in a few times that week. Didn't buy anything. I sensed he was checking the aisles, and the pharmacy counter setup. That's why I suspected him right off the bat."

"You have a security alarm at your store, right? Mom said the buzzer almost gave her a heart attack last summer."

Ben nodded. "Yeah, but it's outdated. The cops told me to put in that ironwork grille. Usually small pharmacies like mine aren't on the radar for criminals."

"Usually, except in June. You promised to explain."

"The alarm wasn't tripped—it's outdated, I know that now, and I've replaced it. Like I said, it's too hard to find controlled substances among the other stock, so they failed. When the police showed up, they found the place trashed. But nothing was taken beyond a few bottles of codeine."

"I bet that wasn't fun cleaning up." I set my bowl aside.

"Yeah. But Digger Sykes messed up any possible prints. That's why they couldn't tell who broke in. Fool couldn't find a lost cat in a tree," Ben said. "Good thing the county sent a detective to handle the murder investigation."

"But just because Alan and Pete are friends doesn't mean one of them—"

"Broke into my drugstore?" He laced his fingers together. "I don't have any proof, of course, but it seems odd they both hang around the high school. They couldn't have friends that young. And they always carry backpacks. I think they're dealers. The street value of opioid drugs is incredible. Vicodin, Percocet, OxyContin—like forty to eighty bucks."

My jaw dropped. "A bottle?"

"Each pill." He laughed at my sharp gasp. "Yeah, incredible. Pot is a gateway drug, in my opinion, and it ought to be a controlled substance. There's a growing problem with heroin abuse here in southeastern Michigan, in case you didn't know."

"I guess I better tell you that Pete Fox is in jail." I noted his raised eyebrows. "Yeah, Thursday night. Caught in Detroit with a stash of marijuana and more."

"Guess I was right, then." Ben waved a hand. "Sorry for all the shop talk."

"I don't mind. It's way different from teddy bears."

"But you haven't mentioned one thing about how you produce them."

"What's there to tell? After cutting all the pieces, we sew them, stuff them, tag them, display them, sell them," I said. "And then start all over again."

"There must be more than that to the business."

"How about this, then? We found a teddy bear on the factory floor near Will's body. With a seam split open. We didn't know what to think, unless he was trying to fix it. But that seems doubtful."

"Oh? Why is that?"

"Will Taylor never cared about the toys. Only profits."

"So what does that mean?"

I shook my head. "I don't know. Yet." We both fell silent.

Ben stroked Rosie's head. "Sasha, I never forgot what you and your friends did for me back at prom time. I wish I'd said something at that Christmas party when you met Flynn Hanson."

"You were there?" My voice broke. I'd almost forgotten that fateful holiday. Once Flynn arrived on my radar, everything and everyone else had faded. "I'm not even sure who invited him. Wish they hadn't. Boy, would my life be different."

"Yeah. But I heard about him cheating on you. Wendy and I—we want you to know we've got your back. Especially given what's happened with Will Taylor." Ben stood and cleared his throat. "It's late and getting dark out. I'd better head home and walk my dog. He'll be raring to go by the time I get home."

I'd scrambled to my feet, still embarrassed. I hadn't even noticed the twilight had faded to darkness. The kitchen light had flipped on automatically. "What breed?"

"Norwegian Elkhound. Two years old, but he gets antsy if I leave him too long. Wendy has a little Chihuahua. You should see the two of them together. It's hilarious. Maybe we could

meet you and Rosie at the dog park and let them run together."

"That would be fun." I meant it, too. "Rosie loves it at
Paw Run. And thanks for your support and understanding."

Rosie and I followed him outside to the porch. "Okay, girl.
Bedtime."

My sweet dog did her business quickly and returned inside
ahead of me. Ben's tale of the pharmacy break-in was trou-
bling. Was Pete Fox involved with Alan in selling drugs? He
had been arrested, after all, and on Thursday night. I needed to
find out what time that had gone down, if Detective Mason
knew. And what about the teddy bear we'd found on the factory floor? I wondered if the police had tested it yet for traces
of drugs inside the cavity.

That might be the real reason behind Will's murder.

Chapter 17

"Uncle Ross! Wait." I clattered down the steps of the First Presbyterian in my favorite red kitten heels. When he pulled the Thunderbird over to the curb and then shifted into park, I slid into the front seat. "What? I'm being careful."

"You wore that to church?"

I glanced down at my red polka-dot skirt. It wasn't that skimpy, so I checked my white blouse. All buttoned up to my layered gold necklaces. Even my straw hat with its red ribbon bow seemed tame. My uncle wore his usual grubby cap, a wrinkled blue cotton shirt with rolled-up sleeves, and khaki shorts. I couldn't unsee his hairy legs, large knee knobs, and white tube socks covering his feet, stuck into ancient sandals.

"What's the problem?" I waved a hand to cool off my face and neck.

"The last time I saw you heading to church, you wore cut-off jeans and a tie-dyed shirt. With a baseball cap. Made me think you were going to a Tigers game. Your sister looked like she was going to a wedding next to you."

"I don't always dress casual. Mads would look good in a clown suit and red nose." I'd tucked a slip of paper under his visor. "Here's the list of our suppliers for you to call, with the numbers and contact persons. You can explain that Will was mistaken about our plans."

"More than mistaken, that stupid—"

"Don't speak ill of the dead. If we're open on Tuesday, and Mads is back, then she'll make the calls. Have you heard anything about Will's funeral?"

"Nope."

"I was just wondering. I looked for that special edition of the *Silver Hollow Herald,* but Dave Fox hasn't brought it out yet."

"There's been enough coverage about the murder on television, for pity's sake," Uncle Ross growled. "Is that all you wanted? I'm meeting Gil for lunch. If that detective shows up and harasses me again, I'll put a bug in Chief Russell's ear about him."

"What about Pete Fox? What are they charging him with?"

"Possession with intent to sell. Not just pot, but pills and some kind of white powder. Either meth or heroin. They're testing it."

"Okay, thanks." I hopped out of the car and leaned down through the open door. "Any idea where Dave Fox might be?"

"Around."

So unhelpful. Uncle Ross locked the car and ambled across the street. I swiveled and peered down the block, wondering if Mary Kate or Garrett might know. Dave Fox's newspaper office was on the other side of the Village Green. My heels wouldn't be comfy for such a hike, so I headed home to change first.

I'd run into several friends of Maddie before the service, who clamored for news after hearing about her sudden trip to New Jersey. If only I had something to tell. Two of them confirmed being at Quinn's Pub on Thursday night; they'd seen Carolyn Taylor but hadn't paid much attention to who else was there. I'd sure like to know what time Will was murdered and how exactly he'd been killed. Was he stuffed to death? Hit on the head? Drugged? Strangled?

Then again, Mason told me to stick to selling teddy bears.

Barbara Davison, Mom's friend, had also pestered me about Dad after the service. I was surprised to see her in the village. She and her husband usually avoided Silver Hollow over the Labor Day holiday by going up north. I had nothing to report. Mom had called Barbara several times since Tuesday to commiserate about Dad's condition. Huh. But her own kids seemed to be low on the information totem pole.

I walked faster, around the corner and past the Holly Jolly Christmas shop—usually closed on Sundays. Today the door stood wide open. Cissy Davison stood behind the counter, yakking on her cell, a laptop open in front of her. How odd. Her own boutique, The Time Turner, filled with unique items plus odds and ends like metal sculptures, pottery, and paintings, was always closed on Sunday.

Compared to her pixieish sister, Cissy could have walked out of a 1930s starlet movie magazine. Her straightened blond hair swung low over half her face, Veronica Lake style, and bright red lipstick was her trademark. Cissy was also much thinner than Debbie even by Hollywood standards; she usually wore long beaded sheaths with fringe, and swathed scarves around her swan-like neck. Not today.

Her mint green summer skirt flared out, Doris Day style, with a tulle peek-a-boo underskirt. Her top had a colorful pattern of watermelon slices. I lusted after that shirt. How cute would that look on me for the picnic tomorrow? Too bad I couldn't do a snatch and go.

I'd bought a floral top to wear with blue capris, plus silver and blue flower earrings. And as I would be so busy with names, games, and the supply of beverages and teddy bear cookies, no one would notice anyway. Sigh. My one chance to overshadow

Maddie with that adorable watermelon print. . . . Damn. I marched past the store.

By the time I reached home, my feet ached. Rosie barked, giving me what-for about leaving her so long. I let her out into the yard. Unstrapped my heels, rubbed my arches and toes. Onyx also voiced her opinion. That reminded me to clean her litter box. By the time I padded upstairs from the basement, I saw the blinking button on the answering machine. Where was my cell? I dug in my purse for it. Dead again.

Once I plugged it into the charger, chased down Rosie outside, scooped her poop, and then fed her, I sat down. Maddie sounded exhausted in her message.

"Hey, Sash. I'm coming home tonight. Flight arrives around nine. Wanna bet you forgot your cell if you're out and about? Or else it's dead, ha. Dad's a lot better, so I'm coming home to help you at the picnic. Gotta run!"

I'd started dialing her number before the message finished. Her cell rang a half-dozen times before a quavering voice answered. The speakerphone crackled a little, so I bent an ear closer to hear.

"Mom, is that you? Where's Mads?"

"Resting at the hotel." She sounded half-asleep, too. "Maddie figured you'd call, so she left her phone with me. I'm sitting here beside Dad. Alex, it's Sasha. Let me talk to her a little bit first. Relax, that's what the doctor said. How are things there?"

I had no idea how to answer that. "Fine. I guess."

"Maddie mentioned a picnic tomorrow, and how you need help."

Her resentment rang loud and clear. I worried my bottom lip with my teeth while I came up with something to say. "We have twenty families attending—"

"If the police closed the shop, you ought to have canceled."

"We didn't want to disappoint the kids."

"I wanted your sister to help me get Dad home and settled," Mom continued as if I'd never said anything. She placed her hand over the receiver and scolded him for being impatient. "They should be releasing him tomorrow."

"That's great," I said. "Dad must have improved a lot."

"If you call paying for an expensive breathing machine as being improved. I'm hiring a nurse to help out back home. I can't lift him with my sciatica pain." She hissed something else to him and then raised her voice again. "Do you want to talk to him?"

I jumped to my feet. "Yes!"

"Don't upset your father, though. We haven't told him." That last bit also came through in a whisper, although I heard Dad mumble. "Never mind, Alex. You always say that Sasha can handle things, so for heaven's sake let her. I'm not telling you anything until you get back on your feet."

At last Mom gave Dad the phone. "Hi, how are you feeling?" I began. His strong tone reassured me. "So they're releasing you tomorrow?"

"Get to the point, sweetheart. Tell me what happened—is it Ross? Did someone get in trouble? What's going on—" His deep coughing bout scared me. I could hear Mom struggling to grab the phone from him, although Dad finally wheezed out a few more words. "Tell me what happened, Sasha. Please. I can handle it."

"It's Will Taylor. He's dead."

"What?"

His half croak, half shout took me aback. "Mads and I found him in the factory Thursday night. Murdered—"

All hell broke loose in the hospital room. Although I wasn't there to see the actual mayhem, I heard Dad cursing up a storm in a hoarse voice. Demanding why Mom had failed to tell him and saying how she'd left us dangling in a crisis without his help. Then a string of loud beeps, a crash, and a loud clattering in my ear. Pain shot through my head. Ow. Dad must have dropped the phone. Mom's angry voice in the background came through loud and clear, yelling for help.

"Dad, are you okay? Dad?" My heart in my throat, I held my breath. "Mom?"

"Just a minute!"

A long silence followed. Guilt hammered me. My stomach's growling for lunch had vanished. I fidgeted, flexing my feet and ankles. Shouldn't have worn heels on a hot day. I shimmied out of my skirt and raced upstairs, polka-dot fabric and heels in hand, the phone still clutched to one ear—which didn't help the horrible twisting in my gut. Had I caused a setback? Me and my big mouth. I should have resisted his questions.

When Mom's voice finally floated over the line, she kept it short. "Well. That didn't help matters one bit."

"What happened? Is Dad okay?"

"The nurse is giving him a sedative right now."

"Mom. You know I can't keep anything from him." I gulped back tears. One escaped and slid down my cheek. "Besides, he has to know what happened—"

"Why can't Ross help you? He practically runs the whole place anyway."

"Because the police think he's the prime suspect. Not that he's been arrested yet."

Another prolonged silence, which killed me inside. "I'll talk to Maddie when she wakes up," Mom said at last. "This whole murder business is crazy. Your father's health is far more important than a silly teddy bear shop, too."

"Silly?"

"You heard me. I never wanted to start that business."

"Wait—"

She must have punched the off button, because my reply fell into dead air. Boy, was I steamed at that. The least Mom could do was give me a chance to ask questions, or explain herself. But no, her impatience was legendary.

My anger rose further. Clearly Mom blamed me for Dad getting all worked up, setting off another coughing jag, and needing a sedative to calm down. Nothing else mattered. I fumed while I hung my skirt and tossed my shoes in the closet. I'd never heard any discord between them over starting the shop or about the business's early days. They made it sound like they both had worked together to make it a success. How could they keep such a secret for so long?

Then again, Dad brushed things like that aside. And Mom didn't like to face conflict head-on. Until something drastic cropped up, like his pneumonia.

Maybe I shouldn't be so shocked. I also knew that she'd never give me credit. No matter what I did or how hard I'd struggled to keep tempers in check during weekly battles between Will and Uncle Ross. Mom would blame me if Dad ended up back in the CCU. But given the strength of his voice, I sensed he was on the mend.

"As stubborn as Uncle Ross," I muttered. "A family trait."

I had to face one more thing after tonight's chat. While Dad treated Maddie like a child and relied on me, Mom ignored me. Ever since she'd returned to work soon after I was born and let her sister-in-law raise me; I'd often called Aunt Marie Mom, in fact. Had that angered my mother? Probably, since she chose to stay home after Maddie was born. Lavishing attention on her second baby, dressing her like a living doll— my sister was her favorite, hands down. I'd barely noticed.

Until now.

We'd always appeared to be a normal, happy family. Free of

major crises, except when Grandpa T. R. died, when a few cracks appeared in the fragile veneer of our family life. Perhaps they'd been there all along. Or was it a single crack, with me and Dad against Mom and Mads? Did it take shape when Dad opened the Silver Bear Shop & Factory? I wondered how much Uncle Ross knew about that time.

Right now, I didn't want to find out. Everyone had to overcome troubles in their past to survive. I wondered if marrying Flynn was a way of getting the attention I'd lacked from my mother—but it only set me up for failure. Hmm.

By this time, I'd donned a pair of blue jean shorts and changed into a silk top with an orange swirly design. That seemed to match the chaos in my life right now. I slipped on Chaco sandals. With a floppy hat and sunglasses, I was ready to go.

Rosie circled me, leash in her mouth, so I grabbed her harness and a bottle of water. I had to find Dave Fox and ask him about his son's possible drug use. This time I avoided the Holly Jolly shop and headed in the opposite direction. The Walshes' sweet cottage stood serene, its white picket fence bright in the sunshine; Flambé was around the curve. The restaurant kept long hours Friday and Saturday and only offered Sunday brunch. Usually a line snaked out the door, but people were leaving. That meant they'd be closing soon. I checked my watch. Way past noon.

I skirted a small grove of birches to reach the picnic tables and a wooden playscape, right before the narrow gravel path ended at Main Street. I noticed Detective Mason's Dexter County SUV in the parking lot beside Quinn's Pub.

"Aha. Must be checking with Brian and his wife about Thursday night."

A good thing, too. I'd watched enough TV cop shows to know that checking up on stories and verifying alibis was vital. Before I could sneak past, however, Mason emerged from the pub and hailed me from across the street.

"Ms. Silverman? Hang on a minute."

I fidgeted on the sidewalk, watching while he retrieved something from his vehicle. When he crossed the street, Rosie lunged toward Mason even though I'd kept her leash tight in one fist. He clapped his hands sharply and woofed in her face. Rosie dropped back. He pointed at the ground.

"Sit." Her haunches immediately hit the cement. "Good girl." When Mason lowered his hand, Rosie lay down. She even gazed up at him in adoration.

"How did you do that?" I asked, amazed.

"Your dog was trained at some point. You're not the alpha, apparently."

"Far from it."

Mason retrieved a small treat from his pocket and waited for Rosie to sit again. Then he ruffled her curly head. "You're the one needing obedience lessons."

"Gee, thanks." I flashed him a sour look. "Did the forensics techs find any fingerprints? Or anything to help the case?"

"We matched the glass found in your parking lot to a car whose front end damage included a broken headlight. The one you saw leaving that night after trashing your mailbox. It's at a police impound lot."

"Where did they find it?"

Mason scratched his nose. "A police officer in Detroit saw it on a side street and ran the plate. After they had it towed, he contacted the local station here."

"So whose car is it?"

"Alan Grant's."

I bit my lower lip, thinking hard. "Alan, huh? I talked to Ben Blake, the local pharmacist. Did you know his store had a break-in?" Although he nodded, I continued before Mason could interrupt. "Ben told me he thinks Alan or Pete might have been behind it. Or both. He saw them smoking pot in public. And I've seen Alan smoking pot behind the bakery a few times."

"You're aware Pete Fox was arrested. He's in serious trouble. A Wayne County Sheriff's Department deputy caught him red-handed with drugs."

"Any heroin?"

"Only enough for personal use," Mason said, and hesitated before he added, "but Alan Grant is missing."

Chapter 18

"Missing?"

"His mother filed a report. Hasn't seen or heard from him since Thursday." Mason tapped a finger against his stubbly jaw. "Police tracked down the VIN, figured Alan must have abandoned his car. Probably knew we'd match it somehow to what happened in your parking lot."

"I wonder why he was at the factory." I unfolded my collapsible canvas cup and slowly poured water into it. Rosie lapped almost all of it. "Gosh, it's getting hotter. There's shade over there under the trees."

"Okay."

Mason followed us to the birch grove, where I perched on a picnic table's top. "So do you think Alan Grant killed Will Taylor?"

"Not sure yet. Either he did it and left town, hoping to beat the rap. Or he's involved with Pete Fox in buying and selling drugs."

"Or both—that might explain the teddy bear we found at the factory. I've been thinking why a seam had been opened and stuffing was spilled out. Will wouldn't bother fixing it. He'd leave it near a sewing machine for one of the staff. So I think someone was using teddy bears to hide drugs. Has the lab tested it?"

"Haven't gotten the results yet."

"So if it comes back positive, does that mean Will was involved?"

"Whoa, don't get ahead of yourself," Mason said. "All of the above is possible. But until we know for certain, better not jump to conclusions."

"But it's possible." After speaking with Ben, I could not hide my disgust. "It's sacrilege. A teddy bear is for little kids, to comfort them and make them feel safe. How dare they use our bears to hide drugs and sell them to school-age kids!"

"It wouldn't be a first."

"What do you mean?"

"Friend of mine is DEA. He's found all kinds of things addicts and pushers use to store drugs. Fake soup cans with the brand labels still on them. Sealed boxes of frozen fish with bags of crack inside, even bottles of cleaning supplies washed out to store heroin." Mason shrugged. "People will do whatever it takes."

I shook my head. "Unbelievable."

"You don't think like a criminal. And I did read the report of the pharmacy break-in. Two suspects fled and Officer Sykes lost them. Apparently they knew the village's back alleys better than he expected."

"Can't you ask Pete if Alan was with him Thursday night?"

"We did. He's lawyered up, not cooperating."

I frowned, elbows on my knees, chin cupped in one hand. "Maybe I could get him to talk. He does work for us, after all."

"Let's worry about that later."

"At least my uncle isn't the only suspect now," I said, and

watched for his reaction. "You haven't arrested him, I mean. You don't plan to, right?"

"Nothing on him so far for that." Mason started past me toward the street.

"Wait. What time was Will Taylor killed, and how? Like, strangled? Or was he hit first, with a tool? Maybe the wrench Jack Cullen had, or something else? And who was the last person who saw him alive?"

The detective rolled on the balls of his feet, back and forth, hands in his jeans pockets, clearly contemplating whether he should share that information. Mason's resemblance to a roly-poly Teddy Roosevelt bear, minus the uniform but in a short-sleeve beige polo shirt and with his gold wire-rimmed glasses, hit me again. His short brown hair had a bit of wave to it, and he had meat on those bones. Despite his pudgy build, I guessed he could chase down a fleeing suspect and catch him without breaking a sweat.

My ex-husband, Flynn Hanson, had been lean as an athlete, not an extra ounce of body fat, and yet panted hard after a brisk walk on a cold day. Not that it mattered what Detective Mason looked like, to be fair. But after disliking him, I had to admit we might be warming up to each other. Especially now that he'd shared some information.

Seeing a huge spider, I jumped off the picnic table. Rosie let out a quick yelp. "Oh. Sorry, baby! I didn't mean to step on your paw." Embarrassed, I floundered for words. "I'm surprised you don't have that notebook with you. You must go through a lot of them."

"It helps me remember things. I take notes, then write up my reports on the laptop. Burns all the details in the brain."

"That was my go-to method during college," I said. "So can you answer my questions? It had to be someone with enough strength to overpower him."

"Maybe."

"Then a woman could have murdered him?"

"Not certain." Mason folded his arms over his chest. "Okay, I'll give you what I got so far. Taylor didn't fight whoever was with him. That's obvious by a lack of bruises or scrapes on him anywhere. He may have had drugs in his system, but the autopsy results for that aren't complete. My guess is Taylor either took a pill or drank alcohol to mellow out after such a tense staff meeting. Asphyxiation was the likely cause of death, according to the ME."

"Asphyxiation? Meaning the fiber in his throat."

He nodded. "Looks like someone dragged him to the machine, either groggy or unconscious, then made sure Taylor had no chance to survive. Like I said, the official results and a full report won't be in for a while yet. But the estimated time of death was between eight and midnight. That's a wide range, but it's all we got for now."

"My sister and I arrived home right before midnight. So if Alan drove that fast out of the parking lot and knocked down our mailbox, he might be the killer."

"It's still early in the investigation," Mason said. "It's not like we have an hour to wrap things up like on TV. Even if they show things happening over a few days, it takes time. This case could drag on for weeks."

"Oh, man." Rosie crunched something, so I quickly snatched the broken acorn from her jaws. "Tell me we can open the shop tomorrow. Remember, we have our annual sale. Parents who bring their kids to our teddy bear picnic event always want to take advantage of our discount coupon. And we have to get production started again at the factory, or we'll never get orders filled on time."

"You can open, but no tours." He watched a car speed past, its engine revving hard. "The evidence is in order and processed. Make sure your uncle doesn't vanish, like Alan Grant. It's kind of odd he interviewed Devonna Walsh for a job, as if he knew Taylor's fate."

"Coincidence—"

"I don't believe in it. My cell number's on the bottom of this card." Mason handed it to me. "If you learn anything new, call."

"Did you find out how Will got in?" I asked. "Was the lock broken on the back door? Any windows broken around the factory?"

"Your uncle had a fit about that, but we didn't find any marks of a forced entry. Must have used a key."

"So what's next in the investigation?"

"Another round of interviews. It's a slow process, but we're always looking for any new information or changes in people's stories. You never know."

I nodded. "Must be hard, though, catching people in a lie."

"Lies are easy," he said, grim. "It's the information they forget to tell you, or how they remember it in a new way, or if they change certain things. They left ten minutes earlier than they first said, or perhaps later. Like I said, it's not an easy process. Be patient. Stick to your shop."

The detective crossed Main Street and unlocked his car. I slid his business card into a pocket while Rosie pulled me in the opposite direction, toward the lake. No, no, no—I tugged her back to the course I'd chosen for today. First things first, and that was finding Dave Fox. I brushed off my shorts and stopped to pick a few burrs caught in Rosie's curly coat. I'd have to get her groomed next week, plus contact our housekeeping crew. The windows needed washing, the cobwebs swept away outside, the wood floors inside given an extra polish. Fall meant a busier sales season. At least I hoped so, given the latest developments.

Fresh Grounds closed early on Sundays. Garrett and Mary Kate staffed the day with local kids and spent time with fam-

ily; their one day off was usually for rest, but I wondered if
Mary Kate might be baking the teddy bear cookies for tomorrow. Rosie half-ran along the sidewalk and across Kermit. I
nearly bowled over an older couple, Isabel French's parents.

"I'm so sorry!"

"No problem at all. Henry, dear, this way."

Suzanne French gently guided her husband, who was in the
later stages of Alzheimer's. They walked around us and down the
sidewalk. I tied Rosie's leash to the bike stand, hating to leave her
outside in the shade, but I'd caught sight of Dave Fox's trademark ponytail. He snapped a lid on his coffee cup at the back
counter.

"Dave! Do you have a minute?"

I knew it was him by the ratty sneakers, jeans, and plaid
cotton shirt that looked like he'd slept in it. He dodged out the
side door before I had the chance to weave through the line of
people. I followed, calling his name again. Dave rushed to a car
waiting on the street. After climbing into the passenger side, he
slammed the door and raised the cardboard cup in my direction with a grin. As the car sped away, I noted the woman behind the wheel.

"She looks familiar—"

"Hey, Sasha!" Devonna Walsh smiled when I turned her
way. "Wasn't that Holly Parker with Dave Fox? I hear she's
gonna open a business somewhere in the village. But I never
seen Dave rush off without stopping for a jaw fest."

"I'd say he was avoiding me."

"He dropped off these, anyhow." She pointed to a table
near the back door.

I snatched a copy of the flimsy newspaper from the stack.
The prime story was a missing woman from the next county,
whose car was found on the side of the local highway a week
ago. Ads filled the two-page edition for the most part.

"Not much about the factory in here."

"You mean the murder? I read about it in the *Ann Arbor News*," she said. "Come on, sit with me. I wanna ask you a few questions."

I had some for her, too, so I didn't protest. Devonna led the way to the painted wooden bench near the bike rack. Surrounded by petunias overflowing cement planters, the small space was tucked between the coffee shop and the hair salon. Rosie curled up behind my feet in a patch of cool grass. Devonna first swiped the wood with a wad of paper napkins, dumped them in the trash bin near the door, and then sat me down.

"Tell me what happened," she said in the same no-nonsense tone as Mary Walsh. "My brother wouldn't. Said he didn't know nothing, only that can't be true."

"First tell me why you met Deon and Uncle Ross at the pub Thursday night."

"Sugar, a girl's gotta eat. Your uncle offered me a burger, so I accepted."

"Okay, but why? Is it true he wanted to hire you as a sales rep? And how long were you at the pub? Long enough to see Carolyn Taylor with her friends?"

Devonna glanced around. Her huge luminous brown eyes were flecked with amber, and her coffee-hued skin glowed. The bright turquoise dress and laced tall wedge sandals enhanced her long legs and generous curves. I knew she modeled as a side job along with her younger sister, Deanna. Devonna had graduated with Maddie.

"Carolyn guzzled booze like she didn't have a care in the world. Ha, when everyone knows her marriage is in the toilet." She fluttered her thick eyelashes. "Not my biz-ness, though. Once my brother left with your uncle, I hung around with a friend. Carolyn sure acted like a fool."

"Did you see her leaving at any point?"

"Yeah, once, with a hand over her mouth like she was

gonna puke. If you party up, though, you gotta pay the consequences."

"But Carolyn was never gone for longer than five minutes, was she?" I'd been savoring a theory that the "pity party" attendees might not have noticed, being too drunk.

"I didn't pay much attention 'cept when they screamed out loud. They looked like they were having the time of their life."

"When did you leave?"

"Midnight-ish." Devonna inspected her long sparkling nails and then tapped them on the bench surface. "As for the sales rep job? Deon talked your uncle into offering me the chance. Didn't tell me first or even ask. No offense, but I got plans. Didn't your sister Maddie ever tell you?"

I blinked. "She mentioned how you sell lingerie."

"On the side, you interested? Lots of fun for the ladies!" Devonna flashed a knowing wink. "Gotta keep your man interested. Women can be sweet as pie in the public eye, but naughty in the bedroom. Too bad Carolyn never took me up on it."

"Yeah, I heard about Will's affair."

"No lingerie party would've stopped that bad boy," she said with a laugh. "What I hear, he roamed under any skirt. Short, long, middlin'. Will Taylor was trouble, just like your ex, Mr. Flynn Hanson, the big shot lawyer. But it isn't too late to invite some friends for a good time, Sasha. Or a catalog party. Lots more than lingerie, too. All kinds of—"

"No thanks," I said quickly. "I'm not interested in anyone right now."

"That's no excuse! Girl, you gotta live a little!"

Cheeks burning, I steered the conversation back to the real subject. Murder. "So you weren't interested at all in being hired as a sales rep?"

Devonna shrugged. "If it was the right time, but they sure

didn't think of that. Will Taylor wasn't gonna be pushed out, especially by a black woman. Don't go pokin' the bear."

"I don't think Uncle Ross—"

"Oh, he said right out he wanted Will to look bad. No way was I gonna be involved in that. Now that he's dead, though, I'll think about it. Unless your sister has something else in mind like we always wanted." Devonna must have noticed my confused look. "What? Maddie never tell you our big plans?"

I shook my head, confused. "Uh, no." Here I thought my sister was happy working for Mom and Dad. "What did you two have in mind?"

Devonna smiled. "We dreamed up an idea back in high school. She's gotta good eye for unique things. All we need is a little shop to rent, only not here—too much competition! Ann Arbor neither, the rents are sky-high. We thought maybe Plymouth. Or even moving over to South Haven, or Holland. I haven't checked yet into rents."

"Mads never said a word about running a boutique."

"Well, don't you worry, Sasha. I won't steal her from your shop yet!"

If Devonna meant to reassure me, she did the opposite. I watched her saunter toward the street, hips swaying, definitely girly-girl and proud of it. I rubbed Rosie's fur, thinking over all that Devonna had told me, and then scanned the *Silver Hollow Herald* once again. Except for a standard shot of our shop from the street, there was only a brief summary about the murder under Dave Fox's byline. Resident Will Taylor found dead, a police investigation under way, but nothing else. There was far more speculation on the Internet.

Maybe Dave knew his son was linked to Alan Grant, who was also a suspect. If he'd paid for a lawyer and bailed Pete out, that must have hurt his wallet. And now that we knew Pete's history with drugs, we'd have to fire him. Uncle Ross would never trust him again. I let out a long breath, wondering how we could find someone to take his place, train them, and recover the days we'd lost.

Good thing Maddie would be home tonight. We could talk about Mom and Dad, the factory and shop, plus the murder. I'd have to ask her about this boutique idea, too. Plymouth would be a great location, since they held an annual winter ice festival, plus Art in the Park in summer. The foot traffic was also bigger than here. South Haven and Holland were hours away. Was Mads serious about moving away from Silver Hollow? The thought boggled my mind.

Chapter 19

"Sasha! You look a world away." I glanced up, startled. Mary Kate stood at the coffee shop's back door, cheeks flushed, blue eyes sparkling. "I finished packaging the teddy bear cookies ahead of schedule. What time do you want them tomorrow?"

"No later than eleven."

"Here, take this. Let's hope Maddie approves this time."

She handed me a clear plastic package. The darling tan bear, outlined with white icing, had Kelly green sunglasses perched on the nose. I'd already opened it, slid the bear out, and taken a bite of one leg before I stopped. Mortified. My sister needed to see this.

"I love it! It's adorable."

Mary Kate walked over and sat beside me on the bench. "Okay, what's wrong? Besides everything else that's piled on top of your shoulders, that is." She squeezed my arm. "Come on, spill. That's what best friends are for."

"Gosh, what isn't wrong?" I hated sounding so down and devoured the rest of the cookie. Maddie would have to see them on Monday. "Two days lost in production, and a huge order that we haven't even started for the Teddy Roosevelt bear. My uncle's a murder suspect. Pete Fox is in jail for drug possession. Alan Grant is missing. And my dad's in the hospital for pneumonia. Thank God Mads will be home soon, because I can't take much more."

"Things will turn around soon." She cocked her head. "Wait a minute. Alan Grant is missing?"

"Yeah. And now Devonna Walsh told me Maddie might want to open her own boutique." I smacked a fist on the bench. Ow! The sharp pain in my hand lingered, too. "But I shouldn't complain, because why would she want to be stuck in an office, doing grunt work, when she's so creative? It's not fair to make her stay."

"What about you?"

"What about me?" I stared at Mary Kate, who just smiled. "Meaning I'm not creative?"

"You are, Sasha. Look at all these special events you've managed. And you're a better sales rep than Will Taylor. I've seen you in action, how you make it all so fun."

"But I'm so disorganized. I need Mads to keep things in order."

"Yes, but she's detail oriented. You're the big-picture expert."

I thought about that and smiled. Mary Kate was right—I did feel better about my part in managing the shop. I'd come up with selling accessories and clothes; I'd talked my dad into giving tours to school groups and seniors. And I'd been the one to insist on producing the rainbow colors for our smallest bears, which we sold like hotcakes.

"Managing a business is never easy," Mary Kate said. "Things aren't always rosy behind the counter. Sorry, Rosie, not you! You're always rosy."

I watched Mary Kate smooch my dog's muzzle. We both laughed when Rosie licked her face and neck in return. "I bet it's tough running this coffee shop," I said. "And Garrett's uncle keeps an eagle eye on things, too. But you've made it work."

"Family comes first. That includes their opinions."

"True enough. I thought Mads and I were a team," I said haltingly. "Mom and Dad have pretty much left things up to us. Uncle Ross keeps to the factory, thank goodness. He's never butted into how we run the shop since Dad retired."

Mary Kate nodded. "Okay. So what's the problem?"

"I don't know if it's the career Maddie wants."

"Ask her. She'll tell you if she's restless and wants a change. Maddie wasn't afraid to ask for a better cookie design, was she? I have to admit, this one is way better than the first one. But find out where she stands about the business. Never assume."

"Yeah. She's coming home tonight," I said, and stood. "Thanks. See you tomorrow at the picnic. Things might be crazy, but you know how much I appreciate all you've done. Oh—" It took me a minute to dig in my pocket. Mason's card fell out. I had to snatch it away from Rosie, who left a few teeth marks on it. "Here's the check. For Thursday's muffin and scone order."

Mary Kate hugged me, always impulsive. "Rest up tonight."

I headed for home. Rosie trotted, tail wagging, ready for supper and her favorite window seat. What a simple life, a happy attitude.

If only I'd been born a dog.

An electric blue Chevy Cruze slowed to a stop by the curb. Jenny Woodley rolled her window down and smiled. "Hi, Sasha. Anything new about the investigation?"

"I don't know much." I didn't want to be rude, but I wished I'd walked faster.

"I saw Jack Cullen last week," she said, and shut the engine off. "He was snooping around the factory around dusk. A few days in a row, in fact. I sent Glen over to chase him down and ask him what he was doing over there."

"What did he find out?" I asked. Rosie strained against the leash.

"Cullen wouldn't talk. Told Glen to mind his own business." Jenny gathered her hair off her neck in an effort to cool off. "I saw the old man late Thursday afternoon, too, with a big wrench. I wonder what he was up to?"

"You're not the first person who saw him."

"Oh?"

"Carolyn Taylor did, too."

"Did you know Jack Cullen steals things?" Jenny nodded. "Yep. Sugar packets and jelly from the diner, toilet paper from the public restrooms, and he even pocketed an ornament from Carolyn's store. She saw him do it. He denied it, of course, and claimed he dropped it on the floor. And then Jack gave her a hard time about the blinking lights on the shop. Says it drives him nuts. I doubt if he can see them from his apartment."

Rosie jumped up against Jenny's car, trying to sniff her hand. She reached over to scratch behind my dog's ears and was rewarded by a wagging tail. I pulled Rosie away, though, to avoid claw marks on the car's paint.

"He's probably complained about the village bells, too."

"Gosh, yes. Glen goes to the council meetings, and Cullen always sits right by the front so he can go first when they open the floor for discussion. He's complained about us, too, that our guests trample the reeds along the shoreline and disturb the birds."

"My uncle told me about that meeting."

"Did he?" Jenny laughed. "Cullen complained about the Sunshine Café, too, that the police chief's wife won't top up his coffee more than twice. He'll sit there all day long for free refills."

I didn't mention how Uncle Ross had an agreement with Tom Russell about helping to pay for any veteran who couldn't afford a cheap meal or coffee. Jack Cullen had served in Vietnam; he might also be one of Silver Hollow's poorer residents. I wondered if he suffered from postwar trauma and gave up on living a normal life, let his house deteriorate, and blamed the government for his problems. My uncle Ross had chosen differently, despite going through similar experiences.

"—always got a beef about something," Jenny rambled on. "Either there's litter on the streets or in the park. Or kids are knocking into him while riding their skateboards. He always complains about dog poop on the village green, too."

"I carry a bag or two when we go for walks, but I know some people don't. They must not be aware of the village ordinance."

She blinked. "I never meant your sweet dog."

"Well, thanks for the information."

Rosie pulled me toward home. I wondered if I should have asked Jenny about having an affair with Will Taylor. I bet she would have denied it. Maybe the rumor that she'd had dinner with him had been just that—rumor. Or perfectly innocent. But I also knew Glen Woodley had a violent temper.

I was curious if he'd suspected any funny business between Will and Jenny. Had Glen gone to the factory Thursday night after seeing the Camry in the parking lot? He'd mentioned asking Will for business advice last month. Mason must have questioned the two of them and established their alibis. Maybe that was Glen last night in his car, running an errand for Jenny. She often sent him at the last minute for milk, eggs, or fruit to serve the following morning. My stomach growled at the thought of food. Somehow I'd forgotten to eat lunch.

By the time Rosie and I made it home at half past four, I was starving. My skin felt like a wet dishrag from the steamy heat. I couldn't wait for my favorite season, autumn. Feeling the chilly crispness of the air, smelling the fragrant scents of wood smoke, hearing the crunch of dead leaves underfoot, and seeing the pumpkins, gourds, bales of hay, and Indian corn on stoops, doors, and porches. Heavenly.

The house felt stuffy, so I cranked up the air-conditioning. After filling Rosie's dish with kibble, I ate the leftover pizza from last night. Then I dumped a packet of meat and gravy into the cat's bowl on the window seat.

"Nyx! Here, kitty, kitty!"

Nothing. I searched downstairs in vain. Then I headed upstairs to check every closet. Had she gotten out? Onyx enjoyed a little time in the garden on a harness and leash, which allowed her to explore on her own terms. Not on hot summer days like today, though. And she didn't have front claws to defend herself.

I caught a streak of black fur escaping from under Maddie's bed and out the door, which saved me from having to crawl on hands and knees. "Okay, already! You could have meowed or something."

When I returned to the kitchen, I found the cat's dish sparkling clean. Rosie slunk under the table in the window nook, clearly guilty. I had to laugh. This time, I put Onyx's refilled dish up on the cat tower where I knew the dog couldn't reach.

Next I decided to get organized for the teddy bear picnic. I collected the list of attendees, a package of black markers and name tags, plus two cans of spray paint. I'd learned the hard way to separate the kids, after a near catastrophe the second year when an older group knocked down the younger ones during games. Luckily, Maddie had printed the booklets that welcomed our guests each year, which included a brief history of our teddy bear shop and a sweet cartoon of bears. She drew a new one every summer, in color, which helped bring locals to see her newest creation. This year's offering had a conga line of teddy bears dancing with tropical fruit on their fuzzy heads.

Red and white gingham napkins, check. Maddie had wanted blue ones, but I stood firm. Red was a summer color. Water, check. I'd bought enough small bottles, six per family; if or when we ran out of lemonade or juice, they could have something besides the odd-tasting water from the park's drinking fountains. As a kid, I'd hated to drink that. Lemonade cups, check. I'd opted for five-ounce paper ones instead of the eight-ounce plastic, which would have depleted our beverages at a faster pace.

Ten clean and empty jugs for the lemonade, check. Ten cans of frozen lemonade, plus three bags of lemons, check. Three bags of sugar, check. Tonight I'd mix the concentrate with water and sugar; then I'd add the lemon slices at the park. I texted Uncle Ross to remind him to bring five bags of ice to the park. He texted back. *Yup.*

"Orange and apple juice boxes, check."

Mary Kate had suggested having both on hand in case pickier kids didn't like the lemonade. Garbage bags to recycle the cups and boxes, check. The village was eco-friendly, and I didn't want to get in hot water over litter in Silver Park. That meant the two trustworthy teens I'd hired for the afternoon, who had the energy to help chase errant kids or keep them happy with the games, also had to collect trash afterward.

"What am I missing?" I grumbled. "I know there's something. Oh, tablecloths."

I rooted in the kitchen pantry and found the white plastic roll. Whew. I wasn't in the mood for a late run to the store. In a drawer, I found leftover stickers with honeybees. Maddie had bought them on sale several years ago to spruce up the tables. She was always on the prowl for cheap items, discounted below cost.

I collected the new fliers I'd made explaining the Okto-bear Tea Party and stashed them with the stickers, napkins, and tablecloth packages in the wicker picnic hamper. That, along with the juice, water, and jugs of lemonade—I'd need a wagon to get it all to the park. In the past I'd relied on Uncle Ross, Pete, or Deon, but they often didn't show until the last minute. Despite text reminders. I'd have to deal with it.

"Oh yeah. Teddy bears and their disguises. Plus the song. Where's that crate?"

In an upstairs storage room, I hunted for the large wooden box we used exclusively for the teddy bear picnic. Pushing aside bolts of plastic-wrapped fur stored on their ends in the corner, I stubbed a toe on the hidden crate and let out a howl. And a curse. Pain pulsed through my foot.

A figure on the street outside the window caught my attention. Jack Cullen—I could tell by that shuffling gait. He ducked beneath the arbor's trailing foliage, but I knew he was making his way toward the factory. Despite my throbbing toe, I rushed downstairs to the kitchen. Rosie stretched out on the window seat, enjoying the sunshine, snoring. I had taken her out for a long walk, and in the heat. She deserved the nap.

By the time I raced through the garden to the factory, I didn't see or hear anything. The sun beat down on my bare head. I dodged around the building to the back and then turned the corner to check the far side. Nothing. No one, and no prints in the dirt. Where had Cullen gone?

Had I imagined it? I didn't think so. Discouraged, I walked to the hedge and followed it. There was a gap, half-hidden, that led to the woods behind. Clever, the way the branches had been trimmed to allow for someone to turn sideways and fit through; beyond, I glimpsed a shimmer of Silver Lake's surface. I sighed and returned to the house. Seemed foolish to hang about and wait for Jack Cullen to materialize again.

I had better things to do than worry about his snooping.

Back upstairs, I drew out the crate of stuffed bears my sister and I had rescued from resale shops or friends. Paddington Bear, Pooh, Corduroy, Baloo, Yogi Bear, you name it. We'd sent them all through at least three dryer cycles to kill off any bugs or germs and stored them in a waterproof bag. We only used them for the parade, since some kids didn't have a teddy bear of their own. They loved seeing their photo, bear in arms, posted on our shop's Facebook timeline.

I lugged the large bag and set it near the rest of the supplies. No way could Maddie and I get all this to the park without help. I dialed my cell.

"Hey, Ben. Got a minute?"

"Sure, Sasha, what's up?"

"I was wondering if you were working tomorrow."

"Nope, the drugstore's closed. I plan on sleeping in until the blaring fire truck and police sirens wake me up during the last part of the parade," he said with a laugh.

"If you're willing, would you mind helping me take stuff to the park?" I asked.

"Sure. I like kids, even if they do get rambunctious. Whatever you need me to do. I'd volunteer Wendy, but Vivian wouldn't let her have the day off."

"I'm surprised the bakery's open on the holiday."

"Hoping to entice people coming for the parade. So what time?"

"Right around noon," I said, and then groaned. "I forgot we needed a new boom box. We play Bing Crosby's 'Teddy Bear's Picnic' song while marching around."

"I'll bring mine. The speakers are great," he added.

"Thanks so much. I'll let you lead the parade with Dad's special hat and whistle. So come at noon or half past. Then we can pack my SUV."

I was so grateful. Not every guy wanted to be a part of a kids' event, and few dads came to the picnic. My cousin Matt was an exception.

I toasted a bagel and spread a thick layer of cream cheese on for supper and then sat down to watch some mindless television. Not that I paid attention. My brain whirled. The past few days had been so stressful. I was exhausted and must have dozed off, because a loud bang startled me up from the sofa. I raced to the kitchen. Maddie had dragged her wheeled overnight bag inside and swatted a few mosquitos near her head. She looked frazzled, her linen floral sundress limp from the lingering humidity.

"Glad you made it home," I said. "Was it a good flight?"

"The plane sat for almost two hours on the tarmac in Newark. Gaah."

"I know you're exhausted, but can you fill me in on Dad?"

"They'll release him tomorrow. Mom wanted me to stay and help, and she's mad because I refused." Maddie kicked off her sandals. "They'll be fine without me. Plus all their bickering got old, fast."

"Bickering about what?"

"The business. Apparently Mom wants Dad to sell everything. Says it's too much for us to handle. She thinks Will's murder means there's bad juju, and that Uncle Ross should retire, and we ought to get other jobs, yadda yadda. Drove me crazy. I bet Dad thought moving away from here would make her quit bugging him. Guess not."

"I still don't understand all that," I said. "I thought they both wanted to start the teddy bear factory."

"You wanna know what I think?" She leaned against the wall. "Mom's jealous of all the time Dad 'wastes' when he's supposed to be retired. His mind is constantly on sales numbers, and what new products we might offer. He told me over and over that we need to participate in Toys for Tots at Christmas as charity involvement. At least five times. I was ready to scream."

"We do that already. So he *is* worried about sales being down?"

My sister groaned. "Sash, please. I'm toast, and I can't think straight. We'll talk everything over in the morning. Okay?"

"Let me ask you this first," I said, refusing to cave. "Devonna Walsh mentioned how you two might want to open a boutique. Maybe in Plymouth. Or over in Holland or South Haven."

"Long time ago," Maddie said, although I noticed her eyebrows had risen in surprise. "We talked about it, yeah. That's all."

"Okay, but—"

"I'm done for, Sash. I'm so tired and crabby. Good night."

She dragged her bag up the stairs behind her, *bump, bumpety, bump*. Mom would have had a fit seeing the scratches on the wooden risers, but I didn't say a word. Instead I wondered if Mads deliberately wanted to avoid discussing her future plans.

Plans that might already be in the works.

Chapter 20

I stood on the corner of Kermit Street and Main, watching the parade. Scores of Scout troops, both girls and boys, walked by and waved to parents and siblings. A group of veterans slowly marched past, followed by a group of volunteers leading dogs on leashes; two carried a sign for Wags and Whiskers, the pet rescue located on the village's edge. Three cars rolled past, all decorated to showcase small businesses. The Legal Eagles had a large stuffed bird atop the hood. One had garlands stretched over the hood, roof, and trunk with a banner for Mary's Flowers. The Quick Mix factory float, trimmed with paper streamers, carried huge boxes of their products.

Debbie Davison walked by and waved, so I waved back. She pulled a large wagon packed with crates and a large teddy bear on top, holding a yellow plastic jar. I knew the crates held real jars of honey nestled in straw to keep them from breaking.

A few siren blasts from the village fire truck sounded far down the street. I finally caught sight of my uncle's blue and white Thunderbird. Maddie had made the sign that mounted on the hood, with glittery letters spelling out "Silver Bear Shop & Factory." Our largest teddy bears hung out the side windows, and more bears filled the backseat to the roof. Uncle Ross didn't wave, however; the rattling tin cans only half drowned out the oohs and aahs of the children admiring the car—or the bears. I was never sure. But then I caught sight of someone passing out fliers—I almost shouted in protest. Teddy Hartman? What was he doing? He forced parents and kids alike to take the papers while he trailed after my uncle's car. Teddy Hartman, of Bears of the Heart.

Fists clenched, I sprinted into the street. Two skateboarders almost ran into me and yelled an obscenity. I ignored them. Thank goodness I'd left Rosie home due to the noise and all the people. I raced to catch up with Hartman.

"Hey, what do you think you're doing?"

Hartman glanced at me in surprise. Short, pudgy, he reminded me of Billy Crystal with his receding hairline and boyish face, but he wore a cheap plaid suit and scuffed wing tip shoes. A large button with a bear holding a string of hearts was pinned to one coat lapel.

"What? It's a free country."

"What are you passing out?" I snatched a flier and scanned it. "This is advertising for your Bears of the Heart company. You can't do that!"

"And why not?"

"You're following the Silver Bear Shop and Factory float—"

"So? A little competition never hurt anyone."

"But this isn't the time or the place."

"What do you know about promotion?" Hartman tore half the flier out of my hands. "Who are you, anyway?"

"Sasha Silverman. My parents own the business and I manage it. And my uncle who's driving our float has no idea you're undermining us!"

"I don't give a fig what Ross Silverman thinks."

Stunned momentarily, I tried grabbing the rest of the stack from him. He dropped half, and the papers whirled away in the stiff breeze. "You idiot! Look what you've done. I'll report you to the cops."

"Fine, go ahead. They want to talk to you anyway."

Hartman snorted in disgust. "What for? I haven't done anything wrong."

"I'm sure you're one of the suspects in Will Taylor's murder," I said.

He stopped walking. "What? Taylor's dead?" His skin paled to a pasty hue.

"Yeah, murdered."

"When was this?" Hartman barked that at me, but I only shrugged. "I just saw him the other day. How could he be dead?"

I gauged his tone. He didn't look as surprised as I'd expected. "Where were you last Thursday night? We know you met with him for lunch."

The businessman flushed red and then turned pale again. "I didn't kill him. Why would I?" Hartman's small eyes darted past me. "We only talked business, for a few hours. At that pub over there."

"What kind of business?"

"Trade shows, the usual stuff."

"Like our bear pattern?"

"What pattern?" He shrugged. "What do I need a pattern for?"

I didn't believe that for a minute. "Will Taylor offered to sell you the Silver Bear pattern, didn't he? Tell me the truth."

"I'm missing half the parade—oh, forget it." He started walking fast down a side street, although I hustled to overtake him.

"What were you two discussing? Negotiations of some kind?" I asked, persisting.

Hartman stopped so fast I stumbled into him and knocked the rest of the fliers out of his hands. Right in front of Cissy Davison's Time Turner shop, which wouldn't please her. Many of them scuttled toward the alley.

"Listen, we just talked. Simple business chitchat, nothing set in stone."

"You'd better explain. Especially now that he's dead."

He kicked the scattered fliers with a curse. "Nothing important. I swear on my father's grave! Who would want to kill Taylor?"

"A county detective is trying to figure that out, but don't change the subject," I said. "So what exactly was this lunch discussion about?"

"Taylor bragged that he was taking over your shop," Hartman said reluctantly.

"Really?" I couldn't help sounding sour. "What else?"

"Once he forced Ross to retire, Taylor was planning to send production overseas. Our production is half and half right now and I've seen a bigger profit." Hartman puffed out his chest. "Best decision I ever made."

I folded my arms over my chest. "I suppose you two discussed a possible merger in the future? To benefit you both."

He shrugged. "Maybe. So I had no reason to kill Taylor. Not when we planned to do business together."

"So why did you return to Silver Hollow Thursday evening?" That was a guess on my part, and his pasty face burned red again.

"I didn't. I met him for lunch, and we split afterward. Then I went fishing with my friends." He turned whiny. "Listen, I've been on vacation the past few weeks. I only met Taylor because he called me! I didn't care what he was doing here at your company. I'm heading back to New England. Tomorrow morning."

"I'd drop in and make a statement to the police, then, before you leave. Or they might get the idea you're leaving town to avoid the detective working the case."

Hartman wiped his hands on his cheap suit jacket, clearly nervous. "I didn't kill Will Taylor. I can prove I was out fishing Thursday with my friends."

"Like I said, you'd better call on Detective Mason. Need his number?" I fished out the card. "Write this down."

He scrounged for a pen and then grabbed a flier before it blew away. "Okay, what is it?"

I rattled off the number, triumphant. "So Will Taylor really did want to sell you our bear pattern? How much did he want for it?"

"Too much, but I didn't need it." Hartman grinned. "He was smart, but not that smart. Sure, I was interested to see if he could pry Ross out of that factory, especially since Alex is retired now. Business is business, after all. Cutthroat, too."

"It's our business. Not Taylor's—"

"I didn't hold my breath about his chances, Ms. Silverman. Figured Taylor would blow it at some point. Guess someone blew it for him if he's dead."

Hartman stalked down the street. I ignored his callous remark, wondering if he was lying about going fishing after lunch on Thursday. I didn't care what he and Will Taylor talked about any longer, because our Silver Bear Shop & Factory was safe from both of them. I breathed a sigh of relief and rushed back to Main Street. The parade was almost over, the shrill blasts of the fire truck echoing between the village buildings. Digger Sykes waved at me from the patrol car, which followed the fire truck, blue and red lights flashing. He hit the siren as well, and then leaned out the window after the noise died.

"Hey, Sasha! Tell Mads I'll call her, okay?"

I gave him a thumbs-up, wondering what that was about.

They'd dated back in high school, from what little I recalled, but I doubted she'd agreed to rekindle any romance. Friends, yes. But Maddie hadn't been forthcoming about a lot lately. Hmm.

As for Teddy Hartman and his fishing trip, Mason would have to figure out whether his alibi held water.

Chapter 21

Ben slapped his chest and eyed the bright blue sky. "What a great day for a picnic!"

I glanced over at him, less enamored. "Try doing these events every summer, sometimes twice, for five years straight. You might come to think differently."

"Aw, come on. We're here. The lemonade's ready. The water bottles and juice are in tubs of ice—where did your uncle go? He ought to park his car in the lot. It looked great in the parade stuffed to the gills with teddy bears."

"You're kidding, right? The first thing he does is dump the bears back into the shop. I'm still not sure how Dad talked him into being in the parade in the first place. That car is more precious to my uncle than anything. It's the biggest reason his wife divorced him, in fact," I said airily. "Aunt Eve lives in Chicago. Do you remember her? Always wore fifties dresses, the poufy ones with the crinolines, those shiny patent-leather handbags, and stiletto heels."

Ben nodded with a wide grin. "Yeah. Hard to miss her."

"Uncle Ross is covering the shop until my sister can take

over. She got in late last night from New Jersey. Dad's doing great. They'll release him today and head home."

"With a bag of drugs, I hope. Planes are notorious breeding grounds."

"Maddie didn't tell me much last night." I surveyed the picnic tables we'd reserved early that morning to set up our supplies. The dense grove on the park's edge would help keep us cooler than closer to the blacktop lot. "Thanks for choosing this spot. We would have ended up in the sun all afternoon like last year."

"Shade should start within the hour."

Ben sounded cheerful, which I needed right now given all the work we'd done. What a great sport. A light breeze drifted our way. The grassy lawn spread toward the bank of the narrow Huron River, which bordered the village, and ended at the line of tall, thick evergreens. A wire fence beyond that kept people from trudging into a cornfield.

"See that group of picnic tables?" Ben pointed to where several families had laid out cloths, baskets, and bottles of pop on the sturdy wooden structures. "Your cousin Matt built them as his Eagle Scout project. Our troop helped him."

"I remember. My sister and I collected bottles and cans to help pay for materials." I swiped my damp forehead. "I'm surprised they're still in good shape."

"Annual coat of varnish, that's why. Okay, what's next? The plastic cloths are on the tables. We've taped them down—"

"Time to decorate." I handed him the honeybee stickers. "Put them wherever, in rows, or scattered all over. Be creative. I've got lemons to slice."

I wished now I'd done that before the parade instead of cooking a huge breakfast for my sister. Eggs, bacon, and a batch of banana nut muffins. I must have gained a few pounds inhaling all those wonderful smells, plus chowing down half the eggs, several muffins, and the blacker bacon strips. Despite my multiple calls from the bottom of the stairs, Maddie slept through. I heard her shower running after Ben arrived at half past noon; the two of us lugged everything to the SUV and rushed to the park. So much for talking to my sister about Mom and Dad, the Silver Bear Shop & Factory's future, and Maddie's dreams of owning a boutique. All that would have to wait.

I checked my watch. Time to get the games started. I grabbed a blue spray paint can and then marked off space for Toddlers to Kindergarteners. Ben took the red paint and crossed the field to the opposite corner. The two teen girls I'd hired—okay, bribed with a decent gift certificate from our shop—helped control the crowd. Megan checked off names against the list of attendees, while Bridgette wrote name tags and stuck them on the kids' shirts.

The two sisters, granddaughters of Gil Thompson, had plenty of babysitting experience. I spotted Elle with Matt and their kids. "Hey, over here!"

"Sash, how's it going?" Matt gave me a quick squeeze. "Sorry about what happened at the factory. Been so busy at work. Need anything?"

"Yeah." I handed him a roll of twine. "Stretch this across the grass. That will keep the older kids away from the younger ones."

Not quite six foot, with a stocky build and rugged looks, my cousin tied one end of the twine to a sapling and then headed across the field. Matt took out his jackknife after measuring off enough to fasten the other end around a birch bole. Elle led the kids toward Megan, who gathered the under-six crowd together. They had a blast playing Duck, Duck, Goose, a beanbag toss, and a race where moms pulled their kids and teddy bears on blankets across the field to the finish line. Older children tired themselves out with a far more competitive gunnysack race—holding their teddy bears in one hand, the sacks in the other—and then a balloon stomp.

Uncle Ross had inflated all the balloons last night and tied strings on them, then brought them in huge bags. Megan and Bridgette played referee, making sure no one ended up with bruised ankles, cuts, or scrapes while the kids stomped hard to break the balloons. Then the children trooped back to their families to eat.

"Fun, huh?" I grinned at Elle, who held her youngest. Matt chased after their son, who bumped into another boy. Both burst into tears. "Uh-oh."

"You sure you want kids, Sash?" Matt winked and set the boys back on their feet. "You're all right. Come on, let's get a teddy bear cookie."

That ended their tears. Once Megan and Bridgette passed out the cookie packages, everyone admired Mary Kate's design. Ben plugged in an extension cord at the public restroom and dragged the line to the boom box. Maddie suddenly tapped my shoulder.

"Hey. I didn't expect so many people here, that's great." Dark circles showed under her eyes, but she looked cool and stylish in white shorts and a lacy mint top with spaghetti straps. I was sweating in my capris and had forgotten my hat. She slid on a pair of dark sunglasses and tipped her straw fedora back on her head. "How long will the picnic last?"

"You ought to know without me telling you."

"Geez, Sash. Bite my head off—"

"Four or five o'clock, depending on whether we run out of lemonade and water. Check out the cookies Mary Kate re-designed, too. Why aren't you at the shop? I had to ask Uncle Ross to cover for you until you were ready."

"Oh yeah." My sister sounded dazed. "I'm a basket case. You ought to know how crazy stressful it's been dealing with Mom and Dad."

"I do know. But go relieve Uncle Ross at the shop before

he has a fit. I have no idea if Lois showed up to help out. Did
you check?"

"No. I didn't think of it."

Maddie wandered toward the parking lot. I couldn't worry
about her now, with so much yet to do. Several women asked
about the cookies and complimented them. I was surprised
when Wendy Clark popped out of the crowd. Her spiked hair
was now tinged with pink, teal, and pale blue hues; the colors
stood out in contrast to her white crochet and linen romper.
She smiled when a group of moms praised the adorable icing
outline and sunglasses piped on each bear.

"Yes, the cookies are from Fresh Grounds," Wendy said. "I
was only following Sasha's directions. Gave them a little more
'oomph' in the decoration. I hope to make cookies for the
Cran-beary Tea Party. Isn't that what you're calling it, Sasha?"

"Yes," I said. "Wendy and Mary Kate are so talented."

"What a wonderful idea. You girls might like a tea party with
your teddy bears," one woman said to her daughters. "We'll be
sure to sign up."

When she herded the kids back to their blanket, I turned
to Wendy. "Thanks so much for coming. I thought you had to
work at Pretty in Pink."

"Vivian got mad because we weren't getting any customers. She wanted me to stand outside with a plate of broken
cookies, but I refused. I quit before she could fire me." Wendy
laughed. "I was tired of her drama queen antics."

"I heard a lot about that from Mary Kate."

"She quit, too, a few years ago. Tradition! Vivian had hired
another decorator two weeks ago, and we didn't get along. I
showed her up, so it's been nasty to work there." She shaded
her eyes. "Where's Ben?"

"Over there handing out lemonade."

"Thanks. I'll go help him."

Wendy meandered over to the table where a steady stream

of parents and grandparents accepted water bottles, cups, or juice boxes for their kids. When I whistled for everyone's attention, girls and boys clutched their teddy bears in excitement and lined up around the picnic area.

"Is everyone ready for the parade?" Once a chorus of cheers erupted, my finger hit the button. No music sounded. "Oops. We'll check on the power. Hang tight!"

Ben rushed off to fix it, so Wendy took over filling cups with lemonade. I noted our sewing ladies—Flora Zimmerman with her young granddaughter, and Harriet Amato, who tried in vain to control three little boys batting one another with their teddy bears and shrieking with laughter. Despite her scolding, they didn't stop. Joan Kendall had taken over handing out the last of the juice boxes to the waiting kids.

"Yoo-hoo! Sasha," Mary Kate called out. She held her toddler daughter by one hand. "Sorry I'm late, but someone napped too long. How were the cookies?"

"Fabulous. Everyone loved them." I squinted at Ben, hoping he'd fixed the power problem. The kids' restlessness increased. "We need to get the parade going, and then we're done after cleanup. I am so ready to go home."

"I stopped at the shop before we came here," Mary Kate said in a low voice. "Boy, did I hear major fireworks between your uncle and Lois Nichols. She was taking forever at the cash register."

"Oh, great." I turned to Joan, who'd emptied the last large tub of water bottles. "What do you know about Lois's past work experience?"

"Um, I think she worked as a school secretary."

"I thought Flora had a job like that."

Joan tossed her dark red ponytail over her shoulder. "Yeah. They worked together in the office at that school. I was in the library until they cut staff. That's when Flora told us both about the bear factory sewing jobs."

She dumped the icy water out of the empty tub and set it to dry upside down. Stunned, I didn't know how to answer that. I wished I'd taken lessons from Dad about dealing with people. He'd been far more in touch with workers and treated everyone like close family. At least I knew that Flora could tell me more about Lois.

"Give me that bear!"

Harriet's two grandsons fought and kicked, fighting over one of the toys they'd found in the crate. I glanced around but didn't see her anywhere. Flora left her granddaughter reading to her bear on a blanket and rushed over; she parted the two boys, took the bear away with a firm command, and gave them a stern warning.

"Your grandma will not be happy when she returns from the bathroom."

Cowed, the two joined their third brother to play with his dinosaurs. If Ben was having trouble getting power, we might have to skip the parade. That would disappoint the kids, but it couldn't be helped. I walked over to Flora, who always looked so together, her hair frosted, her jewelry matching her outfits.

"Thanks for controlling the situation."

"Harriet's a softie," she said with a laugh. "I'm a drill sergeant. Kids know they'd better listen to me, or else."

"I have a question. Has Lois ever been in trouble with the police?"

Flora hesitated for a long moment. "What kind of trouble?"

Uneasy, I chose my words with care. "I overheard something about Huron Valley, and wondered if she'd spent time there. In the women's prison."

"Prison? How can that be true?"

"Ms. Silverman! I'm so glad to catch you." Harriet Amato hurried over to join us, ignoring her grandsons who'd started wrestling on the grass. "I meant to call you, but I figured it was better to tell you in person." She patted her silver cap of curls and then turned to yell at the boys. "Stop that, this instant! Right now, boys. Or you'll be sorry."

"Tell me what?" I asked, curious now.

"Well, what with the factory being closed the last few days, I had the chance to think." Her eyes shifted from the boys to Flora and then beyond me. As if she didn't want to meet my gaze. "I mean, it's horrible. My sewing machine is right near it."

"Near—"

"That stuffing machine. I know I'm supposed to give a two-week notice," Harriet said, clearly nervous. She yelled again at the boys. "That's it! We're leaving."

"But—"

"I'm sorry. I can't walk past that machine. I quit."

She hurried off to gather her blanket and picnic basket. The boys followed her like rambunctious cubs after a mother bear. Flora cleared her throat while I stood, speechless. Even Joan looked shocked by Harriet's news.

"You do understand, things have changed," Flora said slowly. "A murder—well, it changes everything. I told your sister a month ago that I'm going to retire at the end of the year. I'd like to move that up to now. But I'm willing to train any replacement workers, though. To help you out."

A double hit. I reeled from that news, although I tried to change her mind. "This is a bad time for us to lose three of our sewing staff. We'll never fill the order for the Teddy Roosevelt bear without you and Harriet. We can't put all the work on Joan."

"Yeah," Joan said with a scowl. "I'm not Wonder Woman."

Flora glared back. "Only Harriet is quitting."

"There's Lois, too," I said with impatience. "If we confirm she hid a criminal conviction, we have no choice but to let her go."

"I doubt that Lois would deliberately lie," Flora said.

"Our policy is stated right on our employment application—"

"Sounds like a legal argument's in the making."

I whirled around at that familiar voice. Flynn Hanson—my ex-husband—grinned at me. His sun-kissed blond hair, crowned with Ray-Ban aviators, glowed above his tanned face. He looked beach ready in a pale blue shirt that matched his eyes, plus white shorts and tennis shoes. Sexy as hell, as usual.

And all of the surrounding moms glued their eyes on his every move.

Chapter 22

"What are you doing here?"

Flynn raised an eyebrow, hands on his hips. "What kind of greeting is that? I'm here to help. You ought to be grateful."

"Since when have you ever—oh, never mind." I turned back to Flora. "Look, if we lose more than half from our staff, we'll never fill our orders. Can't you wait until after Christmas? We can't train anyone before the holidays—"

"Nonsense. Lots of people need jobs," she said.

"We used to have a revolving door of people before you came. They couldn't keep up with either quality or the pace." I blew out a breath. Gaah. Everything bad was happening at once. "If I'd known we'd lose half our staff, I would have let Will Taylor send production overseas."

"Well," Flora said, biting her lower lip. "I suppose I could wait till January."

"We appreciate your offer to train new people, but please. We need more time."

"You could make an exception for Lois if you're that desperate," Flynn suggested. "Maybe it was only a misdemeanor. Easy to overlook."

I glared at him. "Who asked for your professional opinion?"

Suddenly Bing Crosby's smooth voice blared from the boom box. The kids all squealed in delight. Ben rushed over but stopped in surprise to see Flynn—who had moved to chat with Wendy by the lemonade table. I shoved a teddy bear into Ben's arms, plus the special hat with attached ears and the silver whistle. He must have seen the pleading look in my eyes; without a word, Ben headed off to begin the parade. Kids, parents, and grandparents all followed him around the picnic area, holding their teddy bears with pride or waving them. Many kids and their bears wore eye masks for the disguise part of the song.

I looked around, but Flora had disappeared. Joan Kendall joined Wendy and Flynn, whose deep, sonorous voice was powerful enough to cast a spell over an entire courtroom—judge and jury included. Let him entertain them and stay out of my hair.

Turning back to the parade, I snapped photos of the kids and their bears with my cell phone. Totally adorable. Maddie usually posted pictures on Facebook and Twitter, so I made sure we had plenty to upload for promotion. The song repeated before parents dragged their kids home. I was swamped with people thanking us for a wonderful picnic. Many begged us to host another before the weather turned cold.

I handed out fliers for the Cran-beary Tea Party instead. "This is our next event. I'm still scouting around for a location, but please sign up before it sells out. Adults and kids are both welcome, and bring your favorite teddy bear. Who doesn't love a tea party?"

"It sounds wonderful," one mom gushed.

"We'll have fun." I turned and ran smack dab into Flynn's

hard chest. He planted firm hands on my shoulders, but I shook myself free. "What are you doing in Silver Hollow, anyway?"

"When you called, you sounded so panicked that I flew up to check on things. Won't you give me a little credit for being concerned?"

"Your credit's been in the red since seven years ago. New Year's Eve."

"Oh, come on—"

"You wasted airline miles." I stared at him, my fists clenched. "I asked a favor, to find out whether my parents had gotten home from New Jersey. You never called."

"Au contraire." Flynn touched the tip of my nose. I pulled back, embarrassed by his condescending manner. "I did track them down and explained how you'd called me, that you were worried sick about them. That you might have notified the FBI and the CIA. Your mom agreed that she'd better answer the phone next time you called."

"She told you about Dad's pneumonia?"

He blinked. "Yeah. She also told me how you haven't dated anyone since our divorce. Kind of surprised me, actually."

"So?" I folded my arms over my chest.

"So I thought that was interesting."

My ex loped off, the hint of a sly smile on his face, before I could reply. Fuming, I walked over to help Megan and Bridgette collect the trash. Ben and Wendy lugged things to the SUV; they looked like they were arguing, so I hated to butt in. I noticed Flynn trudging toward a rented car, where he met Joan Kendall. They climbed into the small rental sedan and left. Joan didn't live far from the park, and her eagerness seemed odd. Oh, who cared? I focused on the task at hand. My back ached by the time we finished packing everything.

"I'm so glad everything turned out well," I said to Ben and Wendy.

"Yeah. It was great."

He sounded morose. Wendy poked him. "Oh, stop it. You have no reason to be jealous of Flynn Hanson. He only said hi, trying to be nice."

"He's a snake."

"I owe you both big-time," I said, and then yawned. "Thanks—"

"What was that?" Wendy turned around. I'd heard a shrill sound, too.

"Sounded like a scream."

"Probably a kid who doesn't want to go home," Ben said with a shrug.

But I'd caught sight of Megan waving her arms frantically by the restrooms and pointed. "Help," she yelled. "We need help over here."

We raced over to investigate. Passing the low block building, I saw Megan pull Bridgette up the riverbank's steep slope. Her clothes were soaked. She tugged off her wet sneakers and wrung out her hair, then turned to point wildly at the river behind her.

"Call the cops!"

"What happened? What is it?" I asked, my heart in my throat. "Did someone fall in? Are you okay?"

"I'm fine." Bridgette twisted the bottom hem of her sopping T-shirt, which sent a stream of water onto the ground. Her wet hair dripped into her eyes. "I slipped and fell into the river, but lucky for me it's not that deep right here. But I saw something caught under a log."

"Something? Like what?" I asked.

"I think it's a dead body."

Ben whistled low. "You're not kidding?"

He grabbed the branches of a tree on the riverbank and made his way carefully down a less steep slope. The rest of us waited, peering through the foliage, trying to see where he was and what he'd find. Bridgette moved to a sunny patch. She billowed her shirt out several times, trying to dry it, but it didn't help. Ben scrambled back to rejoin us and brushed dirt and bits of broken branches from his clothing.

"Did you see what it is?"

"Can't tell much except it does have clothing on, so call 9-1-1."

"Already did," Wendy said, and turned to speak into her cell phone.

"We saw that old guy hurrying away into the woods," Megan piped up, "the one who used to own the house where your parking lot is now."

"Jack Cullen?" Surprised, I glanced at Ben. He shrugged.

"I didn't see anyone on the path or the pedestrian bridge."

"—at Silver Park . . . Yes, send the police," Wendy told the dispatcher. "We may have found a drowning victim in the river. Thank you."

"We found this, too." Bridgette held up a vinyl gym bag. "Mr. Cullen was trying to pull it out from under a bush."

"Yeah," Megan said. "We saw him snooping around."

"That's why we were so curious. So after he rushed off, Megan crawled under the bush to see what he was trying to get. I followed Mr. Cullen, but slipped on the grass and fell down the riverbank. That's when I saw . . . the body."

"Let's hope it's something else and not a body." I examined the camouflage print oblong bag, noting the scuff marks and lack of a logo. "Is that why you screamed?"

"Yeah. That was freaky, seeing something in the water. No way was I gonna touch it." Bridgette shivered. "I hope it's a bundle of clothes someone threw away. One of my friends said he finds lots of junk around here. Old tires, all kinds of stuff."

"Look at this—" I'd unzipped the bag and pulled out a teddy bear. Bits of stuffing spilled out from a hole. With my fingers, I searched inside. "There are five more bears in this bag. And guess what's hiding in them."

Ben held the bear near his nose and whiffed. "Definitely pot."

"And look, there's a bunch of pills in the bag, too," Wendy said.

"Don't touch it. I'm guessing it's narcotics."

"And these teddy bears have our company logo tags on the ears." I turned to Megan. "Which bush did you find this bag under?"

"Over there."

She led the way to one of the scrubby bushes close to a large stand of evergreens. Given how close in color the bag was to the dark foliage, it wouldn't be easy to find unless you knew where it was hidden. But I found something else on a patch of bare ground, between two of the closest evergreens. Several cigar stubs. I recognized that type. The kind Jack Cullen smoked, with the same silver band.

I wondered what he'd been doing here and for how long, given the number of stubs. Carolyn Taylor had mentioned how Jack had asked about Will's return from New Jersey. So did that mean Jack Cullen was somehow involved in drug dealing? Had he killed Will Taylor? And what about the body in the water? If it was a body. I doubted it, though. Bridgette was right. I'd heard plenty of stories about people dumping things off the bridge into the river.

I pulled out Detective Mason's card and punched the numbers into my cell. He'd wanted to know if I came up with anything new. This was definitely worth reporting.

"Call me back," I said after the voice mail beep. "We found hidden teddy bears in the park with drugs. We called the cops already."

And now we had proof that Jack Cullen wasn't just snooping around. He'd been here in the park, near the bag. Either he'd put it there and waited to see who would retrieve it—or he knew who put it there and was watching to see who would come and get it. I couldn't think of any other reason. The county lab should be able to match his DNA on the cigar stubs, too. It gave Mason a good reason to question Cullen about what he knew and who was involved.

Ben and Wendy agreed to wait in the parking lot and direct the police when they arrived. I rejoined the girls near the restroom. Sirens soon blared. Once again, blue and red flashing lights made my head spin. Ben and Wendy followed Digger Sykes, who was in full uniform and must be roasting—dark blue shirt, twill pants, and a navy tie with official patches on each upper sleeve. Keys jangled at his hip while he walked. He wore his blond hair in a buzz cut.

"Hey, Sasha. How come Mads isn't here?"

"She's at the shop." I explained what the girls had found.

"Whoa. First a dead body at the factory, and now one in the river?" His grin faded at my frown. "What? It's not like murders happen every day around here."

"We're not sure it's a body," Wendy retorted. "And who said it's murder?"

"The way things are going nowadays . . . Never figured Sasha would be party to one of those ambulance chasing lawyers. Wait, isn't your ex-husband one?"

I resented that. "Flynn and I divorced, remember?"

"Don't get all hot under the collar." Digger took out his small notebook. "Okay, who found this so-called body and when?"

"I did," Bridgette said. "I can't tell what it is, because I only saw it stuck under a big log. Over that way."

Megan slid an arm around her sister for emotional support. "Can we go home? Our first day of school is tomorrow."

"Yeah, sure. I'll call you in if I need anything more."

"We also found this." I showed him the camouflage gym bag holding the bears, the pot, and the bottle of pills. "I called Detective Mason, since he's investigating Will Taylor's murder."

"Okay, but—Hey, girls. Wait a minute!" When Digger beckoned, Megan and Bridgette trudged back over the grass. "Any of your friends selling dope? Or maybe one of you might be involved. Or both of you."

"They only found it," Ben said, and Wendy agreed.

"Why would we tell someone if we're the ones who put it there?" Bridgette huffed in disgust. "That doesn't make sense."

"I can vouch for the girls," I said to Digger. "I hired them to help me at the teddy bear picnic, and they're Gil Thompson's granddaughters."

"I'd better take all your fingerprints, just in case," he said.

A voice rumbled behind us. "That won't be necessary."

I'd been so intent on convincing Digger, I hadn't heard Detective Mason until he joined us, wearing blue jeans and a Red Wings shirt. Talk about casual—he must be off duty. He'd arrived in record time after getting my voice mail message.

"So what's this about finding teddy bears?"

"And a dead body," Digger said. "Only they can't tell if it is a body."

Mason looked skeptical, so Ben, Wendy, and I all tried to explain at one time. He held up a hand to stop us. "Contact the coroner's office, Officer Sykes, just in case."

"But he's not back from vacation—"

"Just do it." He waited until Digger stalked toward the patrol car in the parking lot. "Where exactly did you find the object or body in the river?"

"This way."

Bridgette led him toward the evergreen trees and pointed down the dirt-streaked slope. Taking it slow, the detective slid to the bottom and found a narrow track along the marshy edge. He soon vanished out of sight. The sisters whispered to each other while Ben and Wendy huddled behind me. Hot, sweaty, exhausted, and yearning for a cool shower, I waited with growing impatience. Was it a body? And who could it be?

Ben looked frazzled. "Finding that gym bag was an eye-opener," he said. "I'm guessing Alan Grant and Pete Fox might have used this spot. Pretty remote. Hard to find anything hidden unless you know where to look, too. They both live at home, so I bet they had to find a place where the stuff would be easy to store and quick to reclaim."

"What if it rained? Wouldn't that ruin the drugs?" I asked.

"That bag is fairly waterproof. And I doubt they left it out long."

"I doubt if anyone noticed either of them coming and going," Wendy said. "Not with the playscape area so far away and the soccer and baseball fields across the river. But people come to walk here all the time, too."

"Bet Alan and Pete would come at night to store the bag or pick it up," Ben said. "There's no gate. And no one ever pays any attention to the sign about the park being closed after dark."

"Everyone in school knows Pete and Alan sell drugs." Megan brushed a stray hair from her eyes. "I've seen them in the school parking lot meeting kids after school. I heard that Alan really hated Mr. Taylor, too. The man who was killed at the factory."

"Oh? Why is that?" I asked.

"Because he was dating his mom. We heard Alan say he'd kill Mr. Taylor—that was after the big food fight at Pretty in Pink."

Bridgette nodded. "Yeah, he was pretty mad. His mom's bakery was trashed, and Mrs. Taylor caused all the damage. And even after she took down all the crazy photos on Facebook, everyone made fun of what happened. And him."

"Yeah, it wasn't cool. Trust me, I was there," Wendy said.

"So did Alan kill Mr. Taylor?" Megan asked.

"We don't know that yet," I said. "Go on home. I'm sure

the police will want you to keep all this to yourselves. Thanks for all your help today, both of you. Stop by later this week. I'll have the gift certificates ready."

"We're getting two bears in wedding clothes as a twenty-year anniversary present for Mom and Dad," Bridgette said. "They can't get off work to take a trip. Thanks, see you later." They both raced toward the bike rack near the parking lot.

I turned to Ben and Wendy. "So Alan Grant threatened to kill Taylor. Wow. You'd think more people would have heard about that. Instead they jumped to blame Uncle Ross."

"Yeah, it's a good thing Digger Sykes didn't arrest him."

"Arrest him? Was he going to?"

"Last Friday. That's what I'd heard anyway," Ben said, "at The Sunshine Café. The chief's wife told me, but then I found out the county detective was taking over. Your uncle was pretty steamed. Told Digger he'd better get the facts straight, or he'd straighten him out but good."

I had to laugh. "Sounds like Uncle Ross, all right."

Detective Mason climbed back up the slope, his jeans muddy, his wet tennis shoes squeaking. He brushed past us all without a word and headed over to confer with Digger Sykes; the young officer ducked into his car and grabbed his radio from the dashboard. I didn't know what to think, and Ben and Wendy looked puzzled as well. Mason walked off to his own vehicle. He soon rejoined us in battered and scuffed deck shoes, without his wet socks.

"Where are the drugs?"

"In here," Ben said, and nudged the gym bag with his foot.

"All right, we'll take it in as evidence."

"So can you tell whether it is a body in the river?" Wendy asked.

"If it is, we always notify next of kin first." Mason sounded impatient. "It could be totally unrelated to Will Taylor's murder. We have several open cases in the county of missing persons, and in neighboring counties as well."

"So it is a body," I said.

"I didn't verify that. Thanks again for the heads-up."

"Wait, Detective." I beckoned him over to the cigar butts on the ground. "These are the same kind that Jack Cullen smokes, so it proves he knew about the drugs being here. If he wasn't involved, he must have been watching for who left the bag. Or maybe whether they'd come back to claim it."

"Or he was out for an innocent walk in the park by the river." Mason patted his pockets and used a clean handkerchief to gather up the cigar butts. He pocketed them. "I'll get these submitted to the lab, though."

"If Jack Cullen found out about the drug deals, he might have wanted a cut of the profits. Blackmail is more his game," Ben said.

The detective shrugged. "Maybe. I'll look into it."

"We all touched the bag, but can they detect fingerprints on that type of canvas material?" I asked.

"My kit isn't advanced enough. Tile, glass, metal, porcelain—that's easy for me. Maybe the lab can, though." Mason pulled two bears out of the bag and opened the holes wider. "Pot in this one, all right. Poor quality. The pills look like Percocet, but I'll have 'em tested."

"Did you know Alan threatened to kill Will Taylor?"

"First I heard it. And Mrs. Grant insisted her son doesn't use drugs."

"He always keeps a joint in his pocket," Wendy said. "I work at the bakery—well, I used to, that is. Vivian knows he smokes pot, but Alan promised he wouldn't during his shifts. I've seen him plenty of times after deliveries, though."

"And his car smashed our mailbox," I said. "Have they finished processing the forensics evidence from the factory yet?"

"Takes a lot more time than on TV, remember."

"At least you can question Jack Cullen." I struggled to hide my annoyance, although Mason seemed aware of it. "And what about Teddy Hartman? I saw him today at the parade. He did meet Will Taylor on Thursday for lunch. Maybe he came back to the village later—"

"How about letting me investigate, and you sell teddy bears?"

"I'm only trying to help."

"Hartman knows how to dodge questions," Mason said, growing impatient. "He did say he's on vacation when I asked why he's here. He only met Will Taylor as a courtesy, or so he claims. To compare business strategies, I suppose. Brian Quinn verified seeing them together Thursday at his pub."

"Hartman claimed he was out fishing with friends that night."

"I'll check on that." Mason sounded annoyed. "It's only been a few days since the murder. Things don't work out so cut-and-dried like on *CSI*."

"I watch *NCIS*."

"Just leave reality to the professionals."

The detective stalked back to the parking lot, the nylon gym bag in hand. His advice burned me. While it had been only four days since we found Will stuffed to death in the factory, it seemed like a month ago and the detective was taking forever to solve the case. I'd read enough stories in the newspapers about unsolved murders lasting years before evidence came to light, or a witness finally came forward. Sometimes the killer bragged about it in prison, or confessed.

I hoped that wouldn't be the case this time.

Thank goodness the teddy bear picnic had been a success—for the most part. If word did get out about the drowning victim, people might associate it with Will's murder at the factory and our teddy bear shop. I sighed.

"I wonder why Flynn Hanson showed up," Ben said. Wendy groaned, but he sounded cross. "I'm just curious. He arrived out of the blue."

"His parents have a cottage on Gull Lake," I said. "It's possible he came up from Florida to visit them for vacation."

Wendy shrugged. "Who cares? I'm starving. How about we get some Chinese and bring it over? That way we can help you unpack and put things away."

"Gosh, thanks. I really dread unpacking."

"I'll call in an order at China Palace," Ben said.

They headed out in their separate cars. I drove home, listening to my grumbling stomach. Twilight had set, although a few people—couples, mostly—still wandered the village streets. With school starting tomorrow and parents heading back to work after the holiday break, summer was officially over. September meant the football season would be underway in earnest at the high school and in Ann Arbor. We always got a flurry of school tours in between the senior groups who'd booked earlier in the year.

All leading up to the busiest season right before Christmas.

I left the SUV in the driveway. I had no energy to unpack everything, no idea where Maddie was, and whether the spat between Lois and Uncle Ross had been resolved. I was sure I'd hear the details. We could commiserate over Chinese takeout with Ben and Wendy. I dragged my feet while walking around to the side of the house. Rosie wasn't in the yard. That was odd.

So was seeing a rental car, larger than the one Flynn used, in the parking lot. Who could be visiting? I heard loud voices inside the house, too. Rosie barked, hearing my footsteps before I wearily climbed to the porch.

I stopped in shock at a tall figure looming in the doorway. "Wha—"

Smiling, Dad held out his arms. "Surprise!"

Chapter 23

I hugged my father, so glad to see him looking no worse for wear. Alex Silverman resembled a less rugged version of Harrison Ford without the crooked nose. He did have graying hair, a rock-like chin, and mischievous charm oozing from every pore. Instead of his usual business suit, he was Mr. Casual in a red cotton golf shirt, cargo shorts, and sandals on his bare feet. Compared to my mother, who always looked fashionable like Maddie, Dad could have passed as an aging beach bum.

I followed him into the kitchen. "You look great, Dad—"

My tight bear hug must have set off a coughing spell. Maddie rushed to the sink to fill a glass with water, and I gently patted Dad on the back. Mom rummaged inside her huge Dolce & Gabbana pink tiger lily tote bag and took out a zipped bag of prescription bottles.

"Time for your antibiotic," she said in a threatening voice. "You don't want to end up back in the hospital, do you?"

"No, no." He sat heavily on a stool.

Maddie handed him the glass. "Must have been a good picnic. You look wiped, Sash. Sit before you fall down."

"Of course it was a success." Dad sipped water. "Sasha would never fail."

His voice sounded strong. Mom leaned against the granite island, arms crossed over her chest, lips pursed. She wore a blue floral top and white jeans, her short reddish-blond hair highlighted to perfection, makeup flawless, long nails manicured pink with swirls of glitter.

"Why aren't you two in Florida?" I couldn't hide my wonder. "I mean, I assumed you were heading home. To the condo."

"We decided to help settle things down here," Dad said, and coughed a few more times. "So what happened at the picnic? Maddie said tons of people showed up. I'm assuming you held the teddy bear parade, as usual."

I waited until he popped a fat pill into his mouth and gulped water. "Yes, it's tradition. We had great attendance. But don't you think it would be better to recover at home? Not that you can't here, but—I didn't expect you two until Thanksgiving."

"Will Taylor's dead. Isn't that reason enough?"

"Now, Alex. I didn't think you needed us," Mom told me. "Ross is here. And there's nothing we can do while the police are investigating."

"My brother's still a prime suspect." Dad cleared his throat. "I called the local police, but they won't tell me anything. I'm going to track down Chief Russell tomorrow and find out what's going on. There's no way Ross would kill anyone."

"I've been telling Detective Mason that since Friday morning," I said. "And I'm glad the county detective took over. Ben Blake told me just a few minutes ago that Digger Sykes would have arrested Uncle Ross last Friday."

"You're joking!"

"Nope," Maddie piped up. "Digger admitted the whole thing is over his head. He doesn't have experience investigating a murder, and neither does anyone else in town. He did say

Detective Mason is top in his field. Digger's doing all he can to help."

Everyone looked at me for verification. "I guess so. They both came out to the park after I sent a text about the dead body in the river."

"What?"

"A dead body?"

Chaos broke out. Everyone asked rapid-fire questions at the same time until Maddie whistled shrilly. "Hey, shut up! What's this about another body, Sash?"

I explained the whole thing, but Mom kept interrupting me as if she didn't believe her ears. "I didn't see it, so I can't tell you much. And Mason took the gym bag with the teddy bears, the pot, and pills. But I know for certain the cigar butts are the same kind Jack Cullen smokes."

"So are you saying he might have something to do with all this?" Dad asked.

"No, I'm not saying anything. I have no idea."

"What about Lois Nichols?" my sister asked. "She acted so nervous at the shop, especially after Uncle Ross lost his temper about being so slow to make change. I talked to her about serving time at the Huron Valley Correctional Facility, but she denied it. Rushed off before I could say anything more, so I'll have to do an Internet search. Maybe even call the county records department."

"If she does have a felony conviction, then we'll have to let her go."

Dad held up a hand. "But it doesn't mean Lois killed Will—"

"She threatened to, though," I said, "Thursday night at the meeting. You should have heard her. If only you'd squashed Will's idea about cutting jobs and sending production overseas! What a mess."

"Are you saying it's your dad's fault, Sasha?" Mom asked, her tone sharp.

"Stop, Judith. She's right," he admitted. "I should have told Will flat out the idea was bad. Ross is mad at me, too. They both have good reason to be upset that I let things get out of hand."

"Ross's mouth gets him in trouble."

"That may be true, but he isn't a killer." Dad turned to me again. "Did you know Flynn Hanson is back in Silver Hollow?"

"Back?" I stared at both of my parents in shock. "What do you mean?"

"He's left Florida for good."

"He's moving back to Michigan?" I rubbed my eyes, feeling stupid and slow. "That can't be right."

"Sold his condo, so he told your mother. And he put an offer on a house west of Ann Arbor, about eight miles from here."

"Six thousand square feet," Mom confirmed. "Gorgeous place."

"Uh, I think I need some sunburn lotion."

Stunned by the news, I stumbled toward the half bath. It couldn't be true. Flynn living in Ann Arbor? A huge house, three times the size of his Florida condo? I had to wonder why. Unless the woman I'd seen in his latest Facebook posts was involved—maybe as his fiancée. More power to her, if so. She was welcome to him. Along with his cheating ways.

I wanted to drop from exhaustion. My face felt hot to the touch; my reflection in the mirror showed lobster red cheeks, chin, and nose. I remembered applying sunscreen early in the morning but forgot to reapply it by midafternoon, when the sun was at its highest point. Everything had zipped by in a blur: the games, the parade, Harriet's announcement of quitting, Flora's decision to retire earlier, plus finding the teddy bears, pot, and pills in the gym bag. And the drowning victim in the river. Jack Cullen's cigar butts, too . . . It was all too much.

"Here, you forgot this." Maddie appeared at my shoulder

and handed over the aloe vera gel. "Take some aspirin, too. You look as bad as I did this morning. Everything worked out? Things looked pretty wild to me when I was there."

"Yeah, I'd never have handled it all without Ben and Wendy. Why are Mom and Dad here, really?" I whispered. "I never expected that."

"Mom said it was easier coming here than battling to get him home. She's got him under control." My sister had shut the door behind us, although the bathroom was so small Maddie had to stand in the corner. "We had loads of customers at the shop, plus a few online orders. But Uncle Ross put his foot down on giving tours. At least until we're caught up with production."

"That might be a problem."

"Not doing tours?"

"No, filling orders," I said. "Pete's been arrested. Harriet quit outright—"

"What?" Eyes wide, she fell back against the sink.

"Wait, let me finish." I smeared lotion over my face. "And I'm sorry I snapped about you not doing a background check on Lois. It must be true, though."

"I should have been more careful." Maddie sighed. "I didn't expect her to have a criminal background. Plus all her references checked out, and Flora's the one who sent her to us in the first place. But why did Harriet quit?"

"Apparently she can't walk past the stuffing machine. It's creepy, which is true, but what can we do about it? Except move it into a corner. We're losing Lois, and Flora wants to retire, although she promised to train new staff. But who will we find with the right experience? We'll never fill that Teddy Roosevelt bear order."

"Yeah. That's a bigger problem than I thought."

The gel cooled and soothed the pain on my face, neck, and

forearms. "So it's true about Flynn? He's actually moving to Michigan."

"Yep. Even Mrs. Davison heard about it, and told Mom last week. She'd talked to her a dozen times, even though she wouldn't take our calls." Maddie sounded as mad about that as I'd been. "I guess Flynn got through to her and told her his plans."

"Unbelievable. Did he explain why?"

"Mom said Flynn was bored down in Florida with all the old people. Not his thing, dealing with senior citizens. Not enough women his age, either."

"I thought he has a girlfriend." I relayed seeing the Facebook photos and then shared how Ben had looked jealous over Flynn chatting with Wendy. "How odd that Joan Kendall latched on to him."

The doorbell rang. When Maddie banged the door into my shin, I howled in pain. She raced out of the bathroom—too late. Mom had already answered the door. That gave me a sick feeling; I'd forgotten Ben and Wendy were bringing over Chinese food. They stood just inside the door, brown bags in hand, eyebrows raised in surprise.

"Hey, everyone," Wendy said brightly. "We brought dinner."

"Come in, come in! Ben Blake, good to see you again," Dad said, and shook hands with him. "Haven't seen much of you since you opened the pharmacy. Of course, we moved to Florida shortly after that. How are things with you?"

"Very well, sir."

"Aw, you're not a high school senior anymore." He turned to Wendy. "We've never met, have we? Alex Silverman. And this is my wife, Judith."

"So nice to meet you. I'm a cake decorator, formerly at the Pretty in Pink bakery." She glanced at me and winked. "Here's hoping Mary Kate hires me tomorrow."

"She will in a heartbeat," Maddie said. "And thanks for helping with the picnic today." My sister took the bags from Wendy and beckoned them both to follow her. "Let's get it dished out."

"I'll make extra rice," I said weakly.

Still numb from my parents' sudden arrival, I groped through the pantry shelves. Dad had sidetracked Ben into the dining room to catch up on the latest news, politics, and no doubt the stock market. Mom grabbed Wendy and led her out of the kitchen as well.

"You're a guest. Plus you've already helped enough at the picnic."

Since I wasn't thinking clearly, Maddie reached past me to grab the rice behind a red box of crackers. She fetched a pot, its lid, and a measuring cup. I sank on a stool at the island. I was so tired. Beyond tired. But that didn't stop me from puzzling over the latest developments. Plus my parents' sudden arrival.

"Did Mom say how long they're staying?" I asked.

"Probably until Uncle Ross is in the clear, but who knows. Dad refused to go home, even though Mom had already rented a car. You know how she hates to fly."

"Only with a drink or two, and a Xanax."

"Yeah. She wasn't a happy camper about taking a plane to Metro Airport." Maddie turned the faucet on. "Dad insisted on coming here. He said it wasn't fair to us that Mom wouldn't take our calls, and that she kept him in the dark about what happened to Will Taylor."

"You're not telling me everything. Spill it."

She set the pot of water on the stove burner and adjusted the flame beneath it. "First off, Dad's really mad about Will talking to Teddy Hartman. He called the guy, but Hartman refused to tell him anything. He said what was done is done, now that Will's dead. Water under the bridge."

"That doesn't surprise me. Wait till I tell him about all the fliers Hartman was passing out during the parade. Anything else?"

"Dad talked about filing a lawsuit against Bears of the Heart, although there probably isn't much to go on." Maddie measured out three cups of rice next and set it aside, waiting for the water to boil. "Of course, that doesn't mean he ever will."

"I take it Flynn offered his services. I still don't get why he's moving here, of all places. I can see Chicago or even one of the Detroit suburbs. But here?"

"I guess Dad put him on retainer."

"A personal injury lawyer?" I shook my head. "Oh, brother."

"Oh, sister, it gets worse," Maddie said.

"How? I mean, Flynn does have criminal experience in court, but not in murder trials. Unless he's branched out." I waited for her to explain, but she was busy pouring rice into the boiling water. Maddie stirred, turned down the heat a little, clapped a lid on, and set the timer. "You could have used the microwave, you know. Faster and easier."

"Fluffier this way. Twenty minutes, so keep an eye on the clock. We'll have to warm up all the Chinese food, too." She ran a hand through her short dark hair. "Okay. Mom heard from Mrs. Davison that Flynn is joining the Legal Eagles."

My jaw dropped. "You're not kidding."

"Nope."

Knowing my ex-husband was hundreds of miles away in Florida had helped me recover from his betrayal. Now his move to Michigan—to Ann Arbor, no less—meant seeing him more often. That was certain, not even a remote possibility. And now he'd be working in Silver Hollow and billing my dad for high-priced hours of legal advice. My gut twisted. What a day this was turning out to be, and far worse than last Thursday night after finding Will dead.

Maddie transferred the cashew chicken into a bowl and set

it in the microwave. "So tell me about the drowning victim at the park."

"Detective Mason said they had to notify next of kin first." I slowly rose to my feet and gathered plates and flatware. "I'm more angry that someone, either Will or Alan or Pete—or maybe all three of them—used our teddy bears to hide drugs."

"Sick, isn't it? I hope people don't blame us for that."

"Mason doubts the lab can get fingerprints off the gym bag's fabric. So we're back to theories about who's selling the drugs, and who killed Will, and why."

"Let me tell you what I heard at the store today," Maddie said, although first she put the bowl of pepper steak in the microwave. "Uncle Ross was staffing the counter until I fetched some aspirin. So he's ringing up a few sales, mostly people with our coupons, when I got back. Guess who came waltzing into the shop? Vivian Grant! She wanted a teddy bear for a friend's baby."

I shrugged. "Okay, then what?"

"She was all up in arms about her missing son." Maddie put the pork fried rice in to reheat next. "Vivian swore that Alan didn't run over our mailbox. She said Pete Fox had borrowed her son's car—"

"Wait, he was arrested Thursday night."

"Yeah, but supposedly he had the car before his arrest. I guess that's what she meant. That Pete crashed into the mailbox."

"Hmm. I wonder where the cops found Alan's car, and if it was anywhere near the spot the cops picked up Pete. It's possible, I suppose. I also heard that Alan once threatened to kill Will for dating his mom. I wonder if that's true."

Wendy poked her head into the kitchen. "I overheard Vivian a few times on the phone, just last week, telling people that Will was planning to divorce Carolyn. She said he promised to marry her."

"Whoa." Maddie retrieved the last bowl of sweet-and-sour

chicken from the microwave. "The rice is done. Let's eat in the kitchen. Maybe one day I'll get Will sitting at the dining room table out of my head, and arguing with us."

I groaned. "Don't remind me."

Wendy helped set out plates, flatware, napkins, and glasses, buffet-style, on the granite counter. I set down a huge pitcher of iced tea floating with lemons. Mom didn't say a word about not using the dining room, but I could tell she wasn't pleased. She hadn't mellowed one bit. But she did take a normal-size helping of pepper steak instead of a tiny spoonful.

Silence surrounded us while we ate, along with rising tension. "This is great after that hospital stuff they called food," Dad finally said. He coughed, another long bout. "Pass the rice, please."

"You'll need a breathing treatment in an hour." Mom's tone sounded flat. "You're not out of the woods yet."

"And a good night's sleep. Now, about Will Taylor—"

"We're eating, Alex," she interrupted, but he sailed on.

"I trusted the man since I first hired him. Treated him like a son. How could he pull the wool over my eyes like that? Steamroll over us all like the business was his to do as he pleased? And then trying to sell our bear pattern."

"Ben didn't tell me what happened at the factory, about how Will was murdered," Wendy said, so Maddie gave her a brief summary. "Wow. I wonder if Will gave Alan and Pete the bears to use?"

"I can tell you this." Dad wiped his mouth. "Will never said he was unhappy working as our sales rep. I raised his salary twice. But I know well enough he resented Ross. Why, I don't know, but they didn't get along. It's amazing that he had the nerve to take steps and force my brother out the door."

"That surprised us, too. Will made it sound like you supported his plans."

The screen door banged open. Rosie rose up from her spot

under the table, but she wagged her tail instead of barking. Uncle Ross stomped into the kitchen, his Hawaiian shirt damp under the arms. He raised both hands like a martyr.

"I heard that last bit on the porch. That really got me, Alex—the whole idea that you were on board with a blowhard like Will Taylor!"

"It wasn't true," Dad said. "I told you it was my mistake. I should have been clearer to him that I disagreed."

That didn't seem to pacify Uncle Ross. "I'm gonna say it, even if it makes me look bad. I'm not sorry Taylor's dead. In fact, I wish I had killed him."

Chapter 24

"Helluva thing to say, Ross." Dad rose and shook hands with his brother. "Glad you stopped by, but how'd you know we were here?"

"I didn't. Heard there was trouble at the picnic." He looked at me. "Someone drowned in the river? I didn't think you used the area near it."

"No one drowned," I said, "from our group anyway. I read that a woman was reported missing last week. Her car was found by the side of U.S.-23. I'm hopin it's not her, but it's possible."

Ben nodded to Wendy. "Well, we'd better get home."

"No need to eat and run," Dad said, but they both insisted. "Then let me pay for the food you brought. That was really kind of you to bring it."

"My treat, Mr. Silverman," Ben said. "Thanks again."

We all thanked them both before they departed. Maybe Ben sensed the family needed to talk without non-family members listening. Wendy had squeezed my hand and whispered, "Text me if you need anything," on the way out. I was so grateful for that.

Uncle Ross sat with an exaggerated sigh at the island. Mom fetched him a beer from the refrigerator, popped the top, and set the frosted bottle before him. I glanced at Maddie, who hadn't been paying attention. She scooped the last of her pepper steak and washed it down with iced tea. When Mom reached over and pushed a strand of hair behind Maddie's ear, my stomach twisted.

Uncle Ross swigged his beer. "Nothing but fortune cookies left? I didn't get a chance to grab a burger at the diner."

"Plenty of leftovers." Maddie hurried to make him a plate.

"So explain to me again, Bro, why you let Will Taylor think he was running the show around here," my uncle said.

"I'm sorry, Ross, really sorry," Dad said. "The last few months, I've been feeling lousy. The trade show was supposed to be easy, so I went. Then, wham, next thing I know I'm in the hospital with pneumonia. Judith didn't want me to go in the first place."

Mom shook a finger at him. "Good thing I came along, or you'd be six feet under by now from not getting antibiotics in time. And I was there at the hotel when he met with Will Taylor, Ross. The man was relentless. Alex tried to put him off, but Will kept pushing for an answer about how Chinese workers would be cheaper, faster, and give us more profit, et cetera."

Dad frowned. "He convinced you it was a good idea."

Uncle Ross crushed a fortune cookie in his fist. "You believed him, Judith? Why the hell would you?"

The underlying tension rose to the surface in a heated exchange. "Because Alex is supposed to be retired," she shot back. "He promised we'd do so much together, but he hasn't. So far, I've had to visit the Tiffany museum, Busch Gardens, and even Harry Potter World by myself."

"You're busy ten to twelve hours a day," Dad said, waving a hand in dismissal. "Whenever I do suggest a trip, you have a book club meeting planned, or lunch with the girls, or a shopping trip."

"How about playing golf? You promised we'd take lessons!"

"And we will. The only reason you came with me to New Jersey was to shop for tax-free clothing and shoes."

"Can we get back to Will Taylor?" I asked, impatient, and explained about seeing Teddy Hartman at the parade. "He said business is business. And it's a cutthroat one, so he and Will planned to merge eventually."

Dad took a deep breath. "Will never once said anything to me about talking to Hartman. Which is why I'm going to sue the living daylights out of that blackguard. He should have realized Will didn't have a leg to stand on, sending production to China without my approval."

"Hartman's a sneaky bast—devil," Uncle Ross amended after a glare from Mom. "Will wanted to control the business by getting rid of me. I bet he figured he'd roll over Sasha easy when that happened and do whatever he wanted."

"That wasn't going to happen," I said.

"Yeah," Maddie said in support. "You should have seen and heard her Thursday night at the meeting! Flat out told Will that no one would lose their jobs, and that nothing would change until we talked to you first."

Dad smiled. "Sasha's doing a fine job."

"Given what I heard about the picnic, I'd agree," Uncle Ross said.

"Dad, did you hear about the teddy bear we found beside Will in the factory Thursday night?" I explained the possibility of drug residue being found inside the cavity, and the gym bag we'd found at the park with more bears and drugs. "Things are far more complicated than we first thought."

"But we don't know for sure if Will was involved," Maddie said.

"Okay, but what if he discovered that Alan and Pete sold drugs to the high school kids? Maybe they struck a deal. Will would supply the bears, and they'd split the profits."

"Until Pete Fox was arrested in Detroit," Uncle Ross said.

"And Will was murdered. Did you know Alan Grant is missing?" Everyone looked at me. "I think they must have been working together."

"It's a good theory," Dad said. "But we'll have to let the police handle it."

"Alan or Pete met Will Thursday night," I said. "Or both of them. And the police did link Alan's car to the damaged mailbox."

Mom sighed. "I'm so tired of all this talk about drugs and dead bodies."

"I hired Jay Kirby to create a new mailbox," Maddie said suddenly. "I forgot to tell you, Sash, that I saw him today in the village. I can't wait to see his design."

"That woodsman who calls himself an artist?" Uncle Ross snorted with laughter. "Wears sandals in the winter, and shorts? Lives in some barn beyond Richardson's Farms and uses a chain saw for most of his work."

"You're the last one who should talk, wearing that silly cap all the time." Dad grinned. "We should have hired Kirby when we had that tree in front cut down. He could have carved it into a teddy bear and put the mailbox on top. So, Maddie. How much is he charging?"

"I don't know yet. But I told him we wanted the box for mail inside the teddy bear's open mouth. How cute is that?"

The men groaned, although Mom brightened at the news. "Adorable!"

Good thing I didn't mention that I'd come up with the

idea. Mom wouldn't have been as thrilled. Uncle Ross cleaned his plate and wiped sauce with one of the huge rolls China Palace sent with the food. Dad pushed his half-eaten egg roll aside.

"So, let's get back to the theories about Will's murder."

"Must we talk about it?" Mom sighed.

Dad ignored that. "Let's say he was involved in selling the pot. And found out Pete and Alan were skimming the profits."

"Or dipping in the stash for their personal use," Uncle Ross said. "That might have led to an argument. And murder, if things went south."

"But Detective Mason told me Will didn't fight being dragged over to the stuffing machine," I said. "There wasn't any trauma or injuries on him, anywhere. And what killed him was all the fiber crammed in his throat. That was deliberate."

"Alexandra!" Mom pushed up from her stool with a frown. "How horrible, to tell us exactly how it happened. I'm done listening to any more talk of murder."

"It *is* horrible. Whoever killed him wanted to make sure he was dead."

Dad cleared his throat. "Will did mention something odd at the trade show. How people he trusted were backstabbing him. Kind of went over my head at the time, but it might have some bearing on all these drug deals."

"He was the one backstabbing you," Uncle Ross said, "especially if he planned to merge the company with Teddy Hartman's. Probably thought nothing of it, too."

"Will's ego was huge," I said. "And he always passed the blame to others for his mistakes."

"It's psychological. People rarely believe they're at fault," Dad said. "More so if they get involved in wrongdoing. 'So-and-so cheats me, so I'll cheat them.' Or 'I deserve to take the office supplies because my boss won't give me a raise.'"

I tapped the table. "I'm wondering if Will wanted to send production overseas, not to make the bears cheaper, but without joints. That way it would be easier to hold the hidden drugs."

"His phone calls and texts might be one way we could track how far back he and Teddy Hartman were talking," my sister suggested.

"Mason might have done that already, but I can check."

"I think if Vivian Grant is so desperate to convince everyone Alan isn't using drugs, chances are high he is." Mom stood in the doorway. "Denial is a classic defense."

"Hey," Maddie said. "Remember Vivian got that text during the movie Thursday night, and left early? I wonder if she showed up at the factory to meet Alan."

"But we didn't see any other cars except for Will's and Alan's."

My sister shrugged. "Well, remember Vivian expected Will to get a divorce and marry her. I wonder if that plan soured, so she took her revenge and killed him."

"Mads, are you saying Vivian could be the murderer?" Uncle Ross asked. "You'd think Mason would have figured that out by now."

Dad held up a finger. "What about Carolyn Taylor? Mason must have questioned her at some point."

"Yes, several times. I was there once," I replied. "And Uncle Ross saw her at the pub the night of the murder with a group of her friends."

"I bet Carolyn would strangle Vivian Grant instead of her husband," Maddie said. "They had that huge food fight at the bakery. I'm still seeing people reposting photos Carolyn put on Facebook. Once they're out there, you can never delete them."

"Well, it's late. Your dad needs sleep." Mom started clearing the plates.

"I could fall asleep right here," I said, and carried the empty glasses to the sink. "Plus we're open tomorrow. Come on, Rosie. Outside."

My sister followed us to the porch. "Should we follow up with Detective Mason?"

"I'm texting him now about whether he plans to trace phone records between Will, Alan, and even Teddy Hartman."

"Don't forget about how Vivian left early from the cinema."

"Yeah. I never thought about telling him that."

Maddie nodded and returned inside. I finished the text and then whistled for Rosie. "Come on, girl! Bedtime."

"Sasha, Sasha."

I whirled around, my breath catching in my chest. Flynn had emerged from the shadows of the porch and now leaned against the railing, his blond hair mussed. He grinned wide. I was so tempted to snap at him for scaring me half to death.

"So where's that lover boy I saw you with at the picnic?"

"I don't know what or who you're talking about. I don't have any lover boy."

"The pharmacist."

"Ben? His girlfriend was there, Wendy Clark. You talked to her."

"So, still pining after me."

I sputtered while he climbed the steps and entered the house. The door thwacked behind him. Damn. Flustered, I checked the *ping* from my cell and pressed the side button. An incoming text from Detective Mason.

On it, records on the way. Thanks for tip re VG, but stick to selling teddy bears. Some cases go cold. Remember that.

I sank onto the porch swing. Rosie jumped into my lap, which helped my sagging mood and sent us both rocking back and forth. A mosquito buzzed near my ear. I wondered who could be cold enough to stuff Will Taylor's throat with fiber.

Carolyn had a prenup, but she'd been with friends the whole time. That left Alan Grant and Pete Fox. Could they have killed Will and then fled the scene? And then gone to Detroit—where Pete was arrested.

Then there was Lois Nichols. She had threatened Will, but where was she on Thursday night? Her husband would claim she was home, even if she had gone to the factory. Same with Vivian. Unless someone came forward who saw either of the women arriving here.

And who knew how Jack Cullen really fit into all this.

I dreaded going inside. Flynn must be talking to Dad about his legal options. Why couldn't he have asked Ben's brother, or Mary Kate's? Reluctantly I set my dog on the floor and opened the door. Mom and Maddie looked up from the island.

"What do you think about selling Debbie Davison's honey in the shop?" I asked. "You know, bears and honey? She was in the parade today, pulling a wagon full of her products."

"It's a wonderful idea!" Mom sounded pleased. "Barbara would love it. Debbie needs a boost for her business, or so she told me yesterday."

"Makes sense to me," Maddie said. "Go get some rest, Sash. You look all out."

Dad was nowhere in sight, so I tiptoed down the hall and peeked through the study's French doors. Flynn sat opposite Uncle Ross, leaning back in a chair, one foot hooked across a knee. Aha. They must be discussing what would happen if Mason actually did arrest my uncle. He didn't have an alibi, after all. Wearily, I walked upstairs and rapped on the door to my parents' suite. It creaked open. Dad hadn't even undressed. He lay on the bed, snoring.

Double dang. I headed to my room. At least the shop was open once again and factory production could be resumed. We needed to bring in extra help to tackle the latest order from South Dakota. Experienced help—but I couldn't think of anyone to contact. Tomorrow. My brain was fried. I stripped off my clothes, took a quick shower, and fell into bed.

Mason's typed words on my cell phone echoed in my brain. *Some cases grow cold. . . .* That definitely wouldn't be good for business.

Chapter 25

By Friday, I knew we were in trouble. Labor Day's picnic may have been successful, but after that our business dropped off the cliff. I had little reason to wonder why. Mary Kate, Elle, and Uncle Ross had all updated me on the gossip running rampant during the week. I wasn't surprised that talk had spread, of course, but the latest hurt.

First a rumor started that a child at the teddy bear picnic had spotted the body in the river and was traumatized for life. Another rumor had Ben Blake rescuing a teen from the water, who died shortly after, choking and spluttering, because no one knew CPR. And everyone in the village was now calling me a dead body magnet. Uncle Ross grumbled about having to defend me over breakfast at the café each morning. But Elle's bookstore? More than half of people stopping by were visitors from other areas, wanting to discuss the murder and asking questions.

A few wondered if I'd drowned the person we found in the river. I wasn't happy. Me, drowning people? Ludicrous.

Today things were far worse given the lack of customers.

"We've never had zero sales four days in a row. Ever, not since I started managing," I said aloud. "Not even one from the Internet."

My voice echoed through the front room. The bears on the shelves remained mute, although I swore one winked at me. I turned away. We hadn't gotten any applications for new staff, either. At this rate, I'd have to get Mom and Dad sewing at the machines. I checked for any updates about Will's murder on my cell's News and Facebook apps. Nothing.

Flynn's timeline hadn't changed, either, to my surprise. I thought for sure he'd post pictures of his new house. Or new woman. Was I jealous? I shut the phone down. No way. Not possible. I was so over him.

Resting my elbows on the counter, I faced the truth. Maybe I was a little jealous. Sure, it was wonderful managing my parents' dream business and shop—but it wasn't my dream. Or my shop. I didn't make a huge salary. My car wasn't new, just serviceable. So was I happy? Or just satisfied to coast along?

Yes. I was happy. I wasn't coasting. Having a huge Mc-Mansion couldn't compare to seeing kids walk into the Silver Bear Shop, their eyes lighting up, their arms reaching to hug a bear. I loved that. Far more than having a new car, a career independent of my family, owning a gorgeous home, and being arm candy for a crack lawyer. Even managing a career—all the while wondering what my cheating husband was up to next. Sure, I could have had kids. I'd have invested more time in their lives than in my marriage to Flynn.

My gut instinct, to bail before our first anniversary, had been the right decision. I was more confident living in Silver Hollow and investing my time in the family business. I wasn't too old to find someone else worthy to be the father of my future kids.

One day.

I watched the birds at the multiple feeder out front. Maddie had filled it earlier before she headed to her office. My sister, loaded with a twenty-ounce cup of coffee, a toasted bagel spread with cream cheese, had reluctantly accepted the task of contacting vendors. Trying to explain the situation about Will's death and mend fences was tough, but she did succeed.

The phone rang. "Hey, we're working with a skeleton crew here," Uncle Ross grumbled over the line. "Me, Deon, Flora, and Joan. Doesn't Maddie have anyone new coming in?"

"I doubt it, but I'll ask and call you back."

Lois must have known the jig was up, since she hadn't shown up for work on Tuesday. I'd called her house, but her husband chewed me out royally. Claimed his wife was now at the Quick Mix factory, making a ton more money, and that we owed her two weeks' severance pay. Harriet had stuck to her guns, refusing to return; Pete's dad had bailed him out, but Dad wouldn't hear of him returning. There'd be no second chance, whether or not the murder was solved.

I watched a car drive along Theodore Lane and then slow while passing the Christmas shop. Carolyn's business hadn't suffered like ours. Not that swarms of people descended on it, but given the echoes in our shop, she was doing okay.

Sure, I'd fielded a few calls about the Cran-beary Tea Party, but I couldn't answer questions yet about where it would be held. Mary Kate and Garrett's shop was too small, we'd decided. The few venues I'd checked were booked. I figured if push came to shove, I could rent a hall. I didn't have any other options.

The shop was so quiet, I heard each tick of the wall clock. That drove me to pace the front rooms back and forth. Rearrange the shelves. Pace. Doodle on a notepad. Break open my cozy mystery, which I finished in record time. Pace again, around and around the rooms.

"Hey, I've contacted our vendors," Maddie said, her heels

clacking on the floor. "All the agreements are renewed and on file."

"Thanks for doing that. Any problems?"

"Nope. I even got an application from a woman with German citizenship." My sister handed me a piece of paper. "After she gets a work permit, I'll hire her."

"Visiting relatives in Chelsea," I said, reading off the application. "Hilda Schulte. Will she have trouble getting it?"

"No idea. But she's coming next week, so that she can watch Flora during the entire process of cutting and sewing a bear from start to finish. Just in case."

"What a difference a week can make," I said, and propped an elbow on the counter. "Last Friday we were being questioned by Detective Mason all day."

"Yeah. And nothing much has happened since the Labor Day picnic." Maddie marched back to the office with a wave of her hand. "Have fun."

"Fun, huh."

I walked around the circular stairs to the loft and then back down to burn off some frustration. Where was Mason? I hadn't seen the detective around the village all week, and he hadn't texted me. Except for the initial reports of the body in the river at the park, nothing else had appeared in the newspapers or on television—not even a brief report identifying the gender or age. That was odd, unless the police had reason to keep quiet.

I locked the front door at noon. Might as well take my lunch hour, although if I'd left the shop wide open no one would know it. And the house. I headed back to the office.

"Might as well get this over with," I said aloud. "Long past due."

Maddie glanced up when I entered her cubicle, the phone glued to her ear, but she held up a finger. She looked adorable in gladiator sandals, a white shirt, and red floral shorts. The toenails on one foot were painted red, the other left undone; the bottle of polish remained on her desk. I didn't see any evidence of food, not even a wrapper in the trash.

"Yes. Yes, of course we understand," she said into the phone. "But our staff is short right now—we just cannot fill a rush order. I'm sorry." Maddie hemmed and hawed for another few minutes and finally hung up. "I want to scream! Why can't people understand that we're at a disadvantage right now?"

"I know."

"They want our silver bears, which is great. I mean, I'd love to send them a hundred out of our stock. We have them, but the size! Oh, they don't want the eight-inch. Not the twelve- or the sixteen- either. They have to be *ten-inch,* because it's their company's tenth anniversary."

"They want a hundred, and they have to be silver?" I pushed a strand of blond hair out of my eyes. "How long will it take to get Hilda on staff?"

Maddie held up a hand, as if stopping me. "I can't promise a hundred bears in that size, not when our Teddy Roosevelt bear order comes first. Hilda applied for a nonimmigrant work visa, but it might be two weeks to two months."

"Whoa."

"That's better than if she wanted to apply for U.S. citizenship and then work for us. That would take years to process. So keep your fingers crossed." Maddie filed a few papers into slots with an angry frown. "I have had four other applications. Most never finished high school, have never worked at all, or else missed too many work days. Oh, and showed up late half the time."

"That means they want to be trained for a few months and then rush off to work at the Quick Mix factory." I shrugged. "I'm surprised they took Lois with her prison record."

Maddie shrugged. "Me, too. Turns out Lois was convicted

of felony assault, which means she used a weapon. In her case a knife, against a coworker at a factory. So yeah, I'm shocked they hired her at all."

"Maybe she lied again on their employment application," I said. "Or 'forgot to mention it' like she did with us."

"That's their business. After I saw her record, that was enough for me. Lois is officially terminated. I calculated her back wages, cut the check, and sent it off."

I perched on her desk's edge, thinking of how to change the subject. "Listen, why don't you take over Will's office? You're the main cog in the wheel here, and you do more than he ever did. Even more than me. We can redecorate it, however you want. It's got a fabulous view of the garden—"

"I can't think of that right now, Sash. Okay? I'm too busy."

I watched Maddie tidy up her papers. Something was up. I could tell by her sharp tone, her tight body movements. She was upset, and I had no idea why. Was it due to worry about the shop and the factory? Or something I said? Maybe she didn't want Will's office. But that wasn't the vibe I was getting.

"What's going on, Mads?" I followed her to the low file cabinet in the corner. "Are you angry at me for some reason?"

"No."

"Come on. Tell me what's wrong."

She blew out a deep breath. "Mom's pressuring me. You know how she gets," Maddie added. "She thinks if I quit my job here, then the business will fold on its own and Dad will be forced to sell. Then he can spend all his time on her instead. Like that would matter. Nothing will get Dad to give her what she wants. Why don't they just divorce?"

"Because Mom thinks failure is worse than putting up with a tepid marriage." I noticed her surprise and grinned. "You should have heard her after I left Flynn. She ranted on and on about how much money they'd spent on the reception, my dress, their clothes, your maid of honor dress, et cetera. Apparently that was far more important. My feelings didn't matter one bit."

"I don't remember much of that. I was so busy with school."

"Mom didn't think his cheating was grounds for divorce," I added. "She even believed him when he promised he'd never do it again."

"You're not kidding?"

I rubbed my eyes. "Nope. And now Mom seems delighted that Flynn bought a big house and will be working in Silver Hollow."

"Yeah, that does seem strange."

"Whatever. I'm not impressed and don't want anything to do with him. As for the business, maybe it's time for me to get a loan and buy Dad out. That's bound to make Mom happy. I'm not giving up the last seven years I've invested by seeing the business sold to someone else."

"This is all my fault," Maddie said.

"How?"

"I've been complaining, about how much work it all is. Let me talk to Mom. Don't worry, because Dad's never going to sell. To anyone but you, I suppose. I think Will's death and the way he tried to undermine everything scared Dad. I bet he feels threatened, and won't let go that easily. No matter what Mom wants."

She dashed off before I could stop her. Great. Once Maddie laid things out on the table, things would no doubt heat up again between my parents. The last thing we needed was more fireworks right now. I headed to the kitchen for yogurt and some fruit and then returned to the shop. It didn't take long to eat lunch.

Bored, I checked through all the sales slips from the past weekend. Not that there was a huge amount compared to previous years, of course, but decent enough. I rearranged the displays again in each room and switched the wall calendar with the battery-operated clock. I couldn't see the hands from where I stood or perched on a stool. Then I checked the time every ten minutes.

I looked up Debbie Davison's number, but my call went to voice mail. "Hey, it's Sasha Silverman. We'd love to sell your honey in our shop. Give us a call, thanks."

Too bad I hadn't yet received replies to the texts I'd sent this morning. First Wendy Clark—although I wasn't sure I had the right cell phone number. I hoped she could tell me what time Vivian Grant had left the movie theater. Then I'd texted Jenny Woodley, asking if she or Glen had seen any cars Thursday night at any point in our parking lot. I sent a similar message out to Mary Walsh. If either she or Tyler saw another car besides Will's and Alan Grant's from their house across the street, maybe we'd be getting somewhere.

I wasn't going to let this case string out forever. The murder hung like an unlucky albatross around our necks. Something had to give. But it wasn't going to be our shop and factory.

Maddie returned around three o'clock. "I talked to Mom before she went shopping with Barbara Davison. She said she wasn't going to worry about anything more than Dad's health. And she's over the moon about us selling Debbie's honey."

"What's Dad up to today? Helping out at the factory?"

"More like hindering, but Flora offered to train him on a sewing machine."

"Better than the cutting press," I said.

Maddie laughed. "I told Mom to be subtle and ask Barbara about the 'pity party' for Carolyn. It was Cissy and Debbie's idea, from what I heard."

"I sure hope we get Internet orders. Anything, because we're totally dead."

"Why are you so worried? People are busy getting their kids off to school this week. We usually get a few calls from moms wanting our teddy bear backpacks or key chains—"

When the tiny bells twinkled over the front door, we glanced around in surprise. Vivian Grant stepped inside, her dark eyes darting between us, frizzy black hair surrounding her like a cloud. She wore a hot pink shirtdress with black opaque tights, plus pink leather ankle boots. She ignored our greeting, swung her pink shoulder bag in front of her, and reached inside. After rummaging a bit, Vivian slapped a receipt on the counter.

"I bought a silver teddy bear for a baby shower on Labor Day."

Maddie glanced at me. "Yeah, I remember."

"You didn't tell me there was a sale. I never got the discount."

"People usually bring in the coupon from the newspaper—"

Vivian cut her off. "You're kidding, right? I'm a fellow business owner in Silver Hollow and you require a coupon?"

"Of course not," I said, hoping to defuse the situation. "We'll refund twenty percent of the purchase price."

"Sasha, it was only a ten-dollar bear." Maddie faced Vivian. "If you want two bucks, then we'll give it to you. But this week's been pretty tough on us. We've taken a hit due to Will Taylor's death. Surely you understand that."

"You think my business hasn't suffered? I haven't sold more than a dozen items since last weekend. And why is it you're always ordering baked goods from Fresh Grounds?" Her dark eyes narrowed. "Fresh Grounds is killing my business. Mary Kate Thompson stole Wendy Clark away from me, all because of those silly teddy bear cookies!"

So that was what really fueled this diva moment. I debated

repeating what Wendy had said about Vivian's bad moods, but held up a hand.

"We're hosting a Cran-beary Tea Party next month, and I planned on ordering cupcakes from Pretty in Pink."

"Just cupcakes? What about pastries?"

I stood my ground against Vivian's demanding tone. "I want to divide the work between your bakery and Fresh Grounds. They'll be doing scones."

"So that's supposed to make me feel better? When—"

The bells jangled this time over the door when Detective Mason lumbered in, his coat rumpled, his tie askew. He straightened it and tugged his coat down, although it didn't help neaten his appearance much. Vivian tried dodging around him, but he blocked her access to the door.

"Morning—er, afternoon. Mrs. Grant, I've been looking for you."

"I was just leaving," she said, her tone sour. "I have to get back to my bakery, so if you'll excuse me. Unless you have news of my son. Who's still missing."

"I have a few questions." Mason ignored us, flipped open his notebook, and then looked at Vivian, who stiffened in anger. "I know you said Alan isn't a drug user, but we have proof otherwise. Are you sure you didn't know Alan was selling drugs? Marijuana and narcotics?"

"That's a lie!" She stabbed a finger in my direction. "Pete Fox bought them in Detroit for Deon Walsh, who's selling all the drugs in this town."

"No, he is not," Maddie said. Vivian sniffed in disdain.

"Your son was seen smoking joints with Pete Fox, on several occasions, by several witnesses," Mason said calmly. "We also have his fingerprints on plastic bags of pot for sale."

"I never saw Alan smoking pot. And why would he need to sell drugs? I give him whatever money he needs. Deon

Walsh scrambles all the time for money to pay off his college loans, even though his parents own that diner! Apparently they aren't as generous with their children."

"I checked Deon's record. He's clean, and we found no sign of drug use. His girlfriend claims he was with her Thursday night, too. Alan's car showed damage to the front end, which matched the damage to the Silver Bear Shop's mailbox."

Vivian huffed, her tasseled pink purse swinging. "I've heard from plenty of people—Ross Silverman swore he'd gut Will like a fish."

"A threat is no proof of a crime. Witnesses also saw Pete and Alan together at the junior high school, holding backpacks or gym bags similar to the one that was found at the park. It held teddy bears with marijuana stashed inside, along with a bottle of narcotics."

"Maybe, but my son's not a killer! You've got to find him—"

"We did. That's why I'm here."

She blanched. "Then where is he? In jail?"

"I think we'd better find somewhere private to talk. Come with me," Mason said, and reached for her elbow.

"Tell me where you found him!" Vivian twisted away. "Alan texted me Thursday night. I called him, and he sounded scared to death. But he wouldn't tell me why."

"What time was that?"

"Let me check." She retrieved her phone from her purse. "Here, I'm not lying. This is the text Alan sent me, at 11:20 p.m. I left the movie and called him, calmed him down, but he refused to tell me where he was. Then he said Pete needed to borrow his car. Alan had to go pick him up, and then said he'd be home late. You can see all that on my phone."

Mason scrolled through the messages. "Yes, it all checks out. But Alan never came home that night."

"No. I never heard another thing from him. Pete promised to return the car, but he never did," Vivian added. "I got the call about the police impounding his car. I'm worried sick about Alan. Where is he? He must have his phone."

"We did find one, yes." Mason looked wooden, in fact, grim and forbidding. "I'm sorry to have to tell you, ma'am, but your son is dead."

Chapter 26

"No!"

"I'm sorry—"

Vivian staggered sideways as if from a blow to the head. The detective gripped her by the waist and steadied her. "It can't be true. He can't be dead. I would know! Where did you find him, tell me!"

"Please, come with me," Mason said in a low voice.

"Where has Alan been all this time?"

He glanced at me and Maddie. "Your son drowned in the river. We believe it was an accident, since he had barbiturates in his system."

Mason drew Vivian outside the shop. The door clicked shut. My vision blurred and I groped for tissue to wipe my tears. That was Alan's body in the river? Maddie sat behind the counter, wiping her wet cheeks and blowing her nose.

"Alan wasn't that bad of a kid," she said.

"I can't bear to think that was him in the water during the picnic."

"I had classes with him in high school." My sister buried

her face in her arms, crying harder. "He's only twenty-four. Was. Alan was a champion swimmer, too. How could he have fallen into the river?"

"I don't know—"

"What if he was murdered, Sasha? He must have been at the factory—what if Alan saw whoever killed Will?" Maddie cried out. "What if they caught up to him and murdered him, too?"

She rushed to her office. The door slammed behind her, but I didn't follow. What could I say to comfort her? All this sadness and bad news had multiplied. It had to end. I knew Detective Mason must have found out from the autopsy report how Alan died, and whether he'd questioned Teddy Hartman, but I didn't feel right tracking him down in the village.

I didn't want to sit here, either, in an empty shop. I could picture Alan finding Will's dead body and then panicking. Maybe Alan had been the one to drop the teddy bear on the floor. Maybe he'd gone there to pick up another gym bag or get money for the drugs he and Pete were supposed to buy in Detroit—and discovered Will's body. Alan had definitely left in a hurry, destroying our mailbox in the process. He must have texted his mother afterward.

And then what happened? Had he picked up Pete Fox, who wanted to use the car? Did Pete drop him off somewhere? Where would Alan go besides home? And how did he end up at the park? Why there and not the cinema, or anywhere else in the village?

I retrieved my phone and texted my sister. *Appointment for Rosie. Closing shop early.*

That was a bold-faced lie, of course, but a handy excuse to cover my absence. I rushed to collect Rosie's leash and harness. She jumped up, eager and ready for a walk. I didn't bother changing out of my silver T-shirt and black pants. Lying turns into a bad habit, so I decided to make an appointment at Mark Fox's vet clinic and assuage my guilt. Maybe he would know where his younger brother had dropped Alan after midnight a week ago.

The vet tech informed me that Dr. Fox had an opening in half an hour. Lucky me. Not so lucky for Rosie, who remained oblivious when I bundled her into my car. Glen and Jenny Woodley waved as they walked down the street. I waved back and rolled the window down halfway so Rosie could sniff the fresh air and bark at a few squirrels. Together we drove down Theodore Lane and past Kermit Street.

Mark Fox had graduated a few years before me, and all those years in college and vet school paid off for him. While his office was small, the nearest competition was all the way in Ann Arbor; he definitely kept busy most of the time. In fact, I was shocked they had an opening today. I had no doubt that Mark heard plenty from his dad about Pete's drug use and arrest. And Dave Fox had bailed his son out of jail. Perhaps Mark could update me on that, too.

I turned right on Alice Street and parked in front of the vet's cement block building. Rosie cowered in the seat—she'd recognized the longer drive and the turn and now sat shaking on the passenger's side.

"Poor baby. We're only here to visit."

I still had to drag her out of the car and into the office. Cold air blasted my face from a vent above the door. Clearly they loved cranking up the AC, even though today's temperature hadn't reached the mid 80s. A strong scent of antiseptic tingled in my nose. Two other clients waited, one holding a cat carrier, the other standing near the reception desk with a pit bull mix. The tech called the cat's name for their appointment while I signed in. That reminded me to give an excuse for our visit.

Rosie seemed frisky, exchanging happy sniffs with the pit bull and wagging her tail. The other dog's haunches landed with a thump on the tile floor after the owner dragged him away. Rosie whined a little, now that she wasn't having fun. The pit bull struggled to his feet and coughed hard.

"Swallowed a toy," the man said, and leaned down to pet his dog.

"Poor thing! I hope they won't have to operate." I scratched under the pit bull's chin. "Aw, I hope you feel better soon."

"I'm hoping it's just a Lego or something small enough to pass."

I glanced down at Rosie. "Yep, been there with her. She was lucky."

"Roger Dodger—you poor thing! Come on, let's go straight to X-ray," the tech said. The pit bull and owner followed down the hallway.

Rosie started whining louder, so I rubbed her ears. She didn't like being poked and prodded, but she was up-to-date on her shots. Framed pet photos hung on the near wall behind a single row of white plastic chairs. Shelves of dog and cat food, plus an oblong fish aquarium stood opposite the reception desk. At last the tech returned, her sunburn nearly as red as her hair.

"Rosie, what's wrong? You look so sad right now."

"She hasn't been eating. Threw up a few times. Maybe it's a stomach bug?" I hated the deception, but at least the young woman showed us to a back room. "Thanks so much."

"No problem. Dr. Fox will be in shortly."

I kept the door open and peered out every now and then. I thought I'd heard Pete Fox's voice in the back hallway. I hadn't expected to see him here. Great, I could get the information from him instead of secondhand. My patience was rewarded when I glimpsed Pete from behind, heaving a mop back and forth on the floor where the pit bull must have left a puddle. He slouched, as usual. I'd always considered him shy. Perhaps it was a defense to hide his drug habit.

Keeping Rosie close, I tiptoed down the hallway and

cleared my throat. Pete whirled, his shock evident. "Damn! Scared the crap out of me."

"I'm sorry—I didn't mean to do that, Pete. But I have a few questions," I said. "You never called me back. I heard you were arrested Thursday night."

He looked shamefaced. "My dad and brother are really mad. They both said I've ruined my life. I needed the money, more than I can make working for you. But Dad bailed me out. Only he said it would be the last time."

"If you cooperate with the police about what happened, the judge might take that into consideration." I kept my voice low. "Were you using our teddy bears to hide pot, and then selling them to kids who wanted to buy drugs?"

"Yeah." Pete leaned against the wall, avoiding my gaze. "The cops got me with about fifty pounds of hash. A few pills, a little heroin. That was for Alan. Now I'm lookin' at a felony charge."

"Please, tell me everything. Who all was involved with you in buying and selling? Just Alan Grant, or was Will Taylor as well? And what about Jack Cullen?"

"That old coot?" Pete snorted. "He saw us stashing the bags at the park. Damned snoop. Decided to blackmail us, and promised he'd keep his mouth shut. Me and Alan, we told him no way, so he swore he'd tell Will Taylor. That didn't bother us, though. He was in on it."

"Weren't you afraid he'd rat you out to the police?" I asked.

"Nah, Taylor said he'd take care of old Jack."

That puzzled me. Did Pete mean Will and Jack had gotten into a spat? Or more than a spat, given the wrench Carolyn Taylor and Jenny Woodley had seen in Jack's hand? But Will didn't have any head or body wounds from a weapon.

"So Will gave you and Alan the teddy bears to use?"

"Yeah, ever since spring. He and Alan's mom were dating,

so Alan thought it would help if people thought they didn't get along. Like a feud, you know? So we cut Will a share of the profits. Things worked out great. Even with summer, the kids still wanted the stuff."

"What about the heroin?"

"That was just for Alan. Told him to quit the big H. Bad stuff, man. But he wouldn't listen." Pete rubbed his jaw. I didn't say anything, figuring he'd continue without prompting. He did seem relieved to tell the story in full. "So Thursday night, Alan called me around eleven thirty. Said he was at the factory to pick up the bears but found Will on the floor. Dead. He totally freaked. Didn't know what to do."

"Why didn't you tell him to call the police?"

"Hell, no. Taylor was dead and gone. Nothin' he could do. Alan had to get out or else the cops might think he did it."

I heard Mark Fox down the hall and lowered my voice. "Did Alan see anyone else there at the factory?"

"Nope. Said he ran like his tail was on fire." Pete smirked. "Told me he smashed the car against your mailbox out front. After he picked me up, he wouldn't go with me to get the drugs that night. I could tell Alan needed his fix. So I dropped him off at the park and told him I'd be back with his stash."

"Did you know the police found his body in the river?"

His jaw dropped. "No way! Like, he was half out of his mind. Couldn't walk straight, couldn't hardly open the car door. Damn."

"Why didn't you take him home instead?"

"He didn't wanna go. Said he'd wait by the spot where we hid the bags. But he didn't have a flashlight. Bet he couldn't see a damned thing, it was so dark. Must have slid down the bank into the river." Pete shook his head. "I gave him a little codeine, to take the edge off. I doubt it worked."

I'd heard enough. Alan may have fallen into the river and been so out of it he couldn't save himself. How tragic. I fished out the business card Mason had given me from my purse and pressed it into Pete's hand.

"Please, call this number. Explain exactly what you told me to Detective Mason. Cooperating might help your case."

Pete didn't look happy, but he nodded. A minor victory. I rushed back to the waiting room with Rosie. The tech waved me down, but I flashed a big smile.

"She's fine now. Look at her," I said, and lifted Rosie into my arms. "She threw up before I brought her in, so that might have solved the problem. Thanks!"

I headed out the door. Rosie was ecstatic in the car. I slowed near the apartment complex where Jack Cullen lived. Had he met Will Taylor Thursday night—and then what? Gotten ridiculed? Possibly, knowing Will's ego. Perhaps Jack had grown angry. But Will could have easily overpowered the older man, even after a few beers or a joint, if that's what he'd used to relax after the stressful staff meeting.

I parked a block from the complex. Rosie nearly escaped; I caught her leash at the last second. Whew. Especially since a woman with two large dogs was walking sedately across the street, headed to the village green. Lovely dogs, a black mountain cur and a beige mix of Labrador and bulldog. Rosie strained at the leather tight in my fist. She considered all breeds and sizes fair game for playing.

I scanned the mailboxes located to the left of the front door. J. Cullen, 205. Although I pressed the bell several times, no one answered. Where was Jack if not at home? Anywhere, from Fresh Grounds or the diner, or walking around the village. The ultimate snoop, as my dad and uncle called him. Rightly so, given what people witnessed lately.

I pressed the neighboring buttons—203, 207, 204, 206—until a woman replied in a quavering voice, "Yes? Who is it?"

"I'm sorry to bother you, but have you seen Jack Cullen? Is he at home?"

"I don't know," she said. "I didn't hear him at all this morning."

"Would you mind buzzing me in? I'm Sasha Silverman, of the Silver Bear Shop and Factory," I added. "I'm worried about Mr. Cullen. Perhaps he's ill."

"Oh, do you think so? I bought a bear from you earlier this spring. I'll let you in, but we're not supposed to do that."

"Thank you. I really appreciate it."

Once I heard the buzz, I raced up the steps with Rosie in tow. An inkling of unease had prompted me. My instincts had never failed before. The frail elderly woman, Mrs. Irwin, met me at the top, one spotted and trembling hand leaning on a cane. She wore a faded housedress, and her white hair was pulled back in a tight bun. Rosie whined and scratched at Jack Cullen's door. I twisted the knob—locked.

"I think we better call the police." I ignored her gasp. "Something is wrong. Rosie can tell. Look at the way she's acting."

"What do you think happened?"

"It's possible he passed out, either from the heat or from not eating."

I refrained from adding *or something worse*. I didn't want to voice that aloud. And if Jack Cullen was lying dead inside, God forbid, the moniker "dead body magnet" would be written on my forehead with invisible ink but readable by everyone in Silver Hollow.

I told the dispatcher our location and hoped that Digger Sykes wouldn't respond to the call. The police should be here within a few minutes, given the station was a few blocks down the street. Within five minutes, six-foot Bill Hillerman tramped up the stairs, sweating in his navy blue uniform. I was, too, given the stuffy corridor. Once Mrs. Irwin and I explained our reasons for suspecting Cullen might be in trouble, Officer

Hillerman waved us both aside from the door. He rapped first, however, with his meaty fist.

"Mr. Cullen? Mr. Cullen, I'm coming in!" His voice echoed around us. "Stand back, ladies. And keep that dog secure."

He heaved his bulk against the door several times. At last it gave way, the doorjamb splintering with a *crack;* the policeman motioned us to remain in the hallway. He slowly entered the apartment. Hillerman's handheld radio crackled with voices, in between the buzz of static. When I heard him request an ambulance, I tied Rosie to the stairway's iron railing and then entered the stifling hot front room.

Mrs. Irwin followed. "Oh, my," she said. "His air conditioning isn't on."

Jack Cullen was lying on one side near the sofa, an arm outstretched, as if he'd rolled off the seat. "He's breathing," Hillerman reported, "but dehydrated. Do either of you know if he has a blood sugar problem or diabetes?"

We both shook our heads. Hillerman listened to a garbled message on his radio and then replied with a code. He turned to us. "I won't move him in case he broke a bone. The EMS team should be here any minute."

Hillerman turned to answer another message from the dispatcher. The cluttered apartment smelled of rotten bananas and sour milk. Musty, too, as if Cullen never opened a window. I did that and turned on a fan, since the tiny window air conditioning unit wouldn't do much to clear the smells. Dirty dishes filled the sink. Jack Cullen certainly needed help. The garbage overflowed with foam containers, cardboard coffee cups, blackened fruit skins, and crumpled fast-food bags. Curious, I checked the refrigerator. Almost empty. The door held a small carton of milk and a single bottle of cheap beer.

Mrs. Irwin had returned to her apartment. Since Hillerman remained beside Cullen's side and hadn't noticed me, I checked a few kitchen cupboards and found moldy bread and two empty peanut butter jars. Tiny restaurant tubs of jam or preserves, and packets of plastic utensils, which also held salt, pepper, and folded napkins, filled another cupboard. Jenny Woodley had been right about Jack Cullen taking things from the diner.

"But he didn't have to be such a crank," I muttered, and tossed the bread. "He should have asked the church pastor for help. We keep a pantry for seniors."

I tied up the trash bag and headed outside. Mrs. Irwin stood in the corridor, looking startled, as if she wondered how she could twist the doorknob while holding a box of cereal and a loaf of bread. I dropped the bag and relieved her of the items.

"I'll take those. I'm sure Mr. Cullen will be grateful."

"No, he won't, but that's neither here nor there," she said cheerfully.

"I'm calling the church in the morning. They'll send over groceries," I said, "because their pantry has been restocked for the coming winter."

I also planned to call the local market and have them send both Mrs. Irwin and Jack Cullen plenty of perishables as well as canned, boxed, and bagged food. They both must have little money from pensions or Social Security. When the EMS crew arrived, we moved out of their way. They immediately clustered around the old man and set to work, checking his pulse and blood pressure, his pupils, and starting an IV drip. Hillerman joined us in the doorway.

"You're not taking me to the hospital," Cullen said, his voice raspy. "I'm fine!"

"Please hold still, sir. Calm down—"

"How the hell can I calm down with that woman here?" The paramedics held him down, but Cullen fought them to sit up. "Get her out of my place!"

Mrs. Irwin blanched, but I stepped around her into the corridor. "He means me, not you."

"Alex Silverman ruined me! He's the reason I'm—Ahh!" Jack Cullen started moaning and lolling back in a prone position.

"I'm leaving. It's okay."

My cheeks burned. Bill Hillerman looked sympathetic as he guided Mrs. Irwin back to her own apartment. I retrieved Rosie, who sniffed the trash bag while I untied her leash from the iron railing. She'd sat quietly despite the EMS team rushing up the stairs but now whined in the back of her throat; the hubbub inside Cullen's apartment bothered her. I ruffled her ears, reassuring her, until she calmed down. I didn't blame her one bit. My instinct was to get as far away as possible.

Despite Cullen's bad attitude, he had to realize at some point that neighbors did care. Once we deposited the garbage in the alley Dumpster, I called in the order to Jackson's Market, rattling off a list, and then pocketed my phone. Rosie led the way to the drinking fountain near the library. My sweet dog lapped water from my hand, which I wiped dry on my jeans.

I realized now that Jack Cullen could never have dragged Will Taylor, either drowsy or unconscious, over to the stuffing machine. Our former neighbor was no doubt ornery, complaining, and petty in hanging on to the grudge against my dad. But a killer?

Impossible.

Chapter 27

I retrieved my car and drove back to the shop. Rosie hung out of the window, sniffing hard, and almost jumped out when I opened the car door. I caught her in time. She'd hurt her leg the last time she managed to evade my hands.

Seeing my uncle's Thunderbird, I battled a wave of guilt. I could have spent a more productive day at Harriet's sewing machine. Right now, Uncle Ross was no doubt cursing at the cutting press. Flora and Joan might be bent over their machines, listening to the *zing* of the needle. Maybe we should have made an exception with Lois. We desperately needed more staff to finish the Teddy Roosevelt bear order. But Dad was strong on honesty.

Tomorrow I would ask Flora to help me review how to operate the sewing machine. I wasn't sure any bear I sewed would be up to snuff, but I could try. Maddie had to find someone besides Hilda Schulte, and fast. We'd be in deep trouble if we couldn't deliver on time.

Ross and Deon had already moved the stuffing machine to a corner of the factory. I'd tried so hard to rid myself of the image of Will Taylor beneath it. A few of my dreams this past week had revisited the eerie darkness, the haunting sight of more than one teddy bear and fiber strewn across the floor, the shadow of a body lying still. We ought to set up a partition around the machine and keep it hidden. Future visitors during tours might ask too many questions.

I walked over the lawn, watching Rosie sniff among the Shasta daisies. So Ben guessed right; Jack Cullen had tried to blackmail Pete and Alan. Jack had probably been overjoyed, knowing what was happening in secret behind our backs. The company's sales rep, stealing teddy bears and helping two kids to hide drugs in the body cavities. Oh yeah. Jack would have milked that for as long as possible.

The murderer must have been someone capable of over-powering Will—who was tall, fairly fit, and close to forty years old. As much as I'd wanted to point the finger at Jack Cullen for his mean and nasty attitude, I crossed the old coot off my list. Who was left? I thought that over, picking a flower from the clematis vine off the covered walkway's post on the way back to the garden gate.

Lois Nichols had a felony assault conviction. Was losing her health insurance a strong enough motive? Harry hadn't seemed all that worried. He'd even urged her to quit and work at the Quick Mix factory. Was she physically capable of killing Will Taylor? I doubted it. And I had a feeling she'd have fallen back on a simpler method, like a knife or pistol.

Teddy Hartman was next. He'd been scheming with Will Taylor, hoping for a merger in the future. But why resort to murder? And I had no idea yet if Hartman's alibi was sound.

Carolyn Taylor had been at the pub, drunk. What about Glen or Jenny Woodley? Glen had a temper, although I couldn't see Jenny having an affair—she wasn't Will's type. It might be pos-sible; stranger things had happened. What if Glen's jealousy led to him seeing Will's car in the parking lot? Maybe he walked over to confront him. But would Will have allowed him inside the factory that late at night? Unless he'd left the door unlocked. . . .

Or was there something I'd missed?

I breathed in the fresh air, grateful the sun was heading west. Watched Rosie chase a squirrel up a tree near the house, barking like crazy, her tail wagging. She tore off toward the fence lining the parking lot. Still barking. I followed her and then let out a deep sigh. My ex, Flynn Hanson, climbed out of a shiny brand-new blue Mercedes, its sticker still in the back window, and sporty enough to overshadow Uncle Ross's Thunderbird.

When Flynn retrieved an oblong florist box from the car, I almost choked. No way. Who would he be giving a dozen roses to, and why? Flynn strolled toward me, grinning like a fool. Rosie sniffed his legs and then headed back to the lawn, clearly disinterested. I folded my arms across my chest.

"What are you doing here?" he drawled.

"This is where I live, or have you forgotten?"

"I meant shouldn't you be inside the shop? Working?"

"What do you want, Flynn?"

"I'm here to thank your mom. Judith helped me find my new house, and I got it at a fantastic price. I brought her flowers. Is she at home?"

"Nope. Off shopping."

"Better get these in water for her, then."

He held out the box. I snatched it from him and marched up the porch steps, refusing to peek inside the box until I reached the kitchen sink. The pale pink roses nestled in tissue would delight Mom, for certain. Flynn had followed me. He pulled off his sunglasses and stashed them in the pocket of his blue and white Hawaiian silk shirt. Silent, I searched the drawer for the pruning snips. Rosie's claws clicked on the tile behind me; she jumped to the window seat and then barked when Onyx gave

her a nasty swat to the nose. I wondered what Dad would
think about this gift of a dozen roses from an ex-son-in-law.

He watched while I fetched a glass vase. "So. How come
you're not dating?"

"Why do you care? And how's the bimbo with linguini
sauce on her chin? Saw that photo on Facebook."

I checked for thorns, although Mary at the flower shop always snapped them before boxing up roses for customers. The
roses were lovely, pale and closed up, meaning they'd last a long
time. Flynn had often brought me flowers—tulips, iris, gladio-
lus, mixed bouquets. He did have a good eye for color. But
he'd never given me a dozen roses.

"You mean Darlene?" Flynn shrugged. "She's still deciding
which white beach she likes better. Sarasota, De Soto, Naples,
or Siesta Key."

"Tough choice."

I didn't bother to hide the sarcasm in my tone. After
adding a splash of bleach and the packet of flower food to the
vase's water, I trimmed the stems at an angle and then placed
each rose artfully until I was satisfied with the arrangement.

"You sound jealous, Sasha. I invited you plenty of times
down to the Gulf. Lots of room on the beaches in Florida."

"I'm not into *sharing,* as you ought to know."

Ignoring my insinuation, he retrieved his phone from his
pocket and juggled the iPhone's boxy case. Flynn punched up
a photo. His easy grin hadn't changed, and he nudged his
shaggy blond locks from his eyes. He smelled the same, with
the musky aftershave I once loved. Now it only brought back
painful memories.

"Wanna see my new office furniture at the Legal Eagles office?"

He held his phone out. Shrugging, I noted his prideful
post on Facebook, showing him sitting at a massive desk with

a burled-oak finish, inlaid with leather and edged in gold. Behind him, a tall bookcase was filled with huge legal tomes.

"See my chair? Black leather, higher back than normal. Sweet."

"Sure."

"Wait. There's more." Flynn scrolled through his timeline. "These are the chairs where my clients will sit. Premium burgundy Cordova leather."

"With brass studs." I liked the chairs. Who wouldn't? But over-the-top excess, along with his superior attitude, turned my stomach. "Isn't it a bit much?"

"No way! And the leather matches the red in the Persian rug. Wait, here's another. Mike and Mark already put my name on the sign out front. See? Hanson, Branson, and Blake."

"Top billing, huh." I took his phone in hand, admiring the professional carving job. "Who did the work?"

"Jay Kirby."

The same artist Maddie contacted to carve our new teddy bear mailbox. "Good choice. So your partnership deal with the Legal Eagles must have been in the works for a while."

"A few months, maybe. As for top billing, I've got more experience than the two of them combined," Flynn said. "Made a killing in Florida. But I'm tired of medical malpractice, though. I could retire, you know, but decided to keep a finger in the pie. I'll go in a week or two a month. I started doing estate planning down in Sarasota, too."

His words washed over me while I stared at his phone. He'd posted over twenty photos on his timeline. Some people loved selfies. Why did that bother me? A niggle of something fluttered just out of my mind's eye. But what? I bit my lower lip, trying to concentrate while Flynn droned on. Blurry. Blond curls. I suddenly shoved the device back at him.

"See you later, and thanks from Mom."

"What? Hey, where are you going?"

I raced upstairs to my bedroom's wide window nook. I loved sitting here in the evenings whenever I needed to relax. I'd brought my laptop up to bed last night but was too tired to catch up on e-mail. I sank on the seat, ignoring Flynn—he'd followed me into the bedroom without invitation—and waited for Facebook to load. Then I started searching. That same blurry photo popped up, along with the few I'd already seen. But nothing else.

Odd. Especially since my ex wasn't the only person who loved putting everything out on display for the world to admire. Flynn plunked down on the cushion beside me with an easy grin, but I shoved him off. He fell on the hardwood floor with a *thunk*.

"What gives?"

"I didn't invite you up here."

"So? Is this your private nunnery?"

I didn't answer, since I was already halfway down the stairs. Grabbing my purse and keys, I retrieved a bottle of water from the fridge and headed to the door. Rosie raised her head from the window seat but then stretched her legs out and arched her back. Flynn clattered down the steps, clearly puzzled, but I didn't wait for him. I raced outside, through the back garden, and across the street.

I should have asked Maddie for her opinion, but that would have taken time. The whole thing might be silly. I'd rather shoot this theory down myself before sharing the details.

Debbie Davison waited on customers inside the Holly Jolly Christmas shop. I halted inside the doorway, wondering if Carolyn was working in back, and then wandered around the decorated Christmas trees. A shelf held jars of honey with adorable round sticker labels, showing a bear dressed in a yellow and black sweater with white wings. I'd seen that similar design in Maddie's office. Had she made these labels for Debbie? My sister never mentioned it.

Did it matter? Maddie was talented, so why not do a little freelance work for extra pocket change? Given how cute the design was, I hoped Maddie charged Debbie a decent fee. One customer dawdled, unable to decide between ornaments, so I perused the entire shop. After fifteen minutes, Carolyn hadn't shown her face at all. I wondered why she hadn't closed her business until after Will's funeral. People would understand if she wasn't up to working.

Since Debbie was busy, I peeked around the almost closed door to the back room. It was empty except for boxes, some opened, some strapped shut, and the usual miscellaneous items to tag or send back, stored on shelves. A messy desk was piled with orders and files. Had Detective Mason taken Carolyn in for questioning?

"I'll be right with you," Debbie called out.

Feeling guilty, I moved away from the back room. The customer seemed to get the message and narrowed down her choices. I tapped a finger on one of the glass display counters while Debbie wrapped the woman's purchases in tissue and placed them in a green and red bag. Once all the customers departed, Debbie turned to me with an exaggerated sigh.

"Hey, Sasha. Gosh, I wish things were slower. By the way, I gave Maddie a whole box of my honey jars this morning."

"Great. Uh, is Carolyn around?"

"She popped home a while ago. I'd given her a box of honey, too, but she didn't have room to store it in back. She's getting more Christmas items in for the holiday season," Debbie added, and then pointed to a low shelf. "But she put your bears with my jars of honey."

"Okay, thanks. Have you heard when Will's visitation and funeral will be?"

Debbie shrugged a shoulder. "Funny you should ask, because a whole bunch of people called about that. Carolyn said the autopsy results aren't back from the lab. They screwed up, so they're redoing the toxicology part, to see if he took any drugs. She's really mad."

"That's terrible."

"Yeah. Carolyn said she could tell Will had a few drinks that day. Probably a joint or two by the time she closed for the day. She told us he tried pressuring her into smoking pot with him. Claimed it would calm her down. He always got on her about nagging."

"Really?" Not that I was surprised, of course.

"Oh, you know it," Debbie said with a laugh. "Carolyn bugged him on the phone, at home, and while he was off on his trips. She had good reason!"

"Because of his affair with Vivian Grant?"

"So now you know. There's rumors he was sneaking around with another woman or two since that broke up."

"You must mean Jenny Woodley."

"You heard that, too?" She leaned over the counter. "What do you know?"

"Not much," I admitted. "Did they really have an affair?"

"Cissy saw them having dinner over in Ann Arbor. Why else would Will Taylor take Jenny to the Gandy Dancer? That place is expensive."

My parents often celebrated their anniversary there, so I couldn't deny that. But Jenny Woodley? With her mousy hair, an apron around her waist, weeding in her garden? Will Taylor would be far more tempted by sultry Cissy Davison.

"Don't take this wrong, but did Will ever make a move on your sister?"

Debbie clapped a hand over her mouth. Giggling, or was she shocked? She kept her voice low, although we were the only ones in the shop. "Gosh, yes! Cissy refuses to date married men, though. It's against her personal code. Did you see her latest selfie?"

"No."

"Here, take a peek. The guy's a real hottie." Debbie retrieved her phone, swiped it several times, and then held it out for my perusal. "He's the new sous chef at Flambé. Gustavo Antonini. Sexy, and such a nice guy. Very sweet."

Whoa. I swiped through a dozen selfies of Cissy with her new boyfriend and a few photos showing only him. He had dark curling hair, deep brown eyes, and a smoking-hot body given his sculpted muscles. Gus wore his swim shorts low enough to show off rock-hard abs, while Cissy's red silk bikini also left nothing to the imagination. On that white sandy beach, I figured they had to be enjoying the Gulf side of Florida.

"Looks like Siesta Key. How long have they been dating?"

"About six months. We laughed so hard last Thursday, at Quinn's Pub. Some guy sent over the bottle of champagne to our table, hoping to pick up Cissy. I usually don't like the bubbly, but that stuff was great."

I decided to throw caution to the wind and pose a question. "Hey, while you ladies were all together that night, didn't you take a bunch of selfies? I saw one or two. Usually Carolyn posts a dozen or more on Facebook."

"Ha, we were all pretty wasted," Debbie said. "We got to talking, I guess. We all had a tough week."

"Talking about Will?"

"I don't remember much of it. I had a martini at first, then switched to a Mai Tai. Maybe I should have eaten before starting to booze it up," she said. "Then, out of the blue, Brian Quinn brought over that bottle of champagne. You should have seen how mad the guy was after we drank it all and then Cissy wouldn't leave with him. Claimed he had a Mercedes and was new to the area. She blew him off."

"A Mercedes?" My stomach knotted at the thought.

"Yeah. Never saw him before. Gray hair and glasses." She laughed. "Sometime before eleven o'clock, I felt really sick from mixing drinks."

Relieved that Flynn hadn't been the guy hitting on Cissy Davison, I nodded. While the Davisons had heard about my brief marital adventure and divorce, I had no idea if they ever met my ex. I steered our chat back to the real matter.

"If she was that drunk, Carolyn must have felt sick and spent a lot of time in the bathroom."

"I sure did. But I didn't see her come in while I was there for over an hour. On that bench, which wasn't comfortable at all. I was not gonna pass out. Otherwise, someone could have ripped off my purse." Debbie plucked it from behind the counter, showing off a Dooney & Bourke leather satchel in a lovely pink hydrangea print. "Cost me almost two hundred bucks."

"Nice." I had a purse fetish myself, and I could tell hers wasn't a knockoff. "But you didn't see her? What time was that again? Say, right before midnight?"

"Oh, it had to be eleven or right after when I went to the restroom. I was so woozy. Isabel French brought me some coffee around eleven thirty. I was supposed to be the designated driver, ya know? I always am. But I couldn't do it that night. Cissy had to drive us all home. Around one o'clock. But Carolyn was the worst I'd ever seen her. Bombed."

Huh. She'd been drunk, yet had never gone to the bathroom. My newest theory seemed to make sense—it might have been possible for Carolyn to slip out. Would anyone have noticed? Even for fifteen minutes. Isabel usually opened the Silver Scoop, so she'd be long gone—and lived in Chelsea. I couldn't take the time to drive all the way there to ask her.

I headed for the door. "Thanks. See you later."

"Sure thing," Debbie called out. The door banged shut behind me.

I walked back to the parking lot across the street. Flynn's Mercedes was gone. Thank goodness. I climbed behind the wheel of my car, wracking my brain. Someone *had* said that Carolyn went to the restroom. Not Debbie. I snapped my fingers. Devonna Walsh, that was who. She'd said Carolyn rushed off, holding a hand over her mouth, at some point. And Kristen Bloom's words floated back to me. Kristen, who'd joined the group later and taken a few selfies with her phone. She'd said something that hadn't hit me at first.

I thought maybe she'd fallen into the john. . . . That must have meant Carolyn was absent long enough to be noticed. Kristen thought she'd gone off to be sick. Yet Debbie Davison had not seen Carolyn between eleven and midnight.

The pub's restroom, the one place Carolyn should have been but wasn't. How long would it take her to run over to the factory? Had she known Will would be there? Had she planned to murder him and faked being smashed from the start? Did she have the strength to drag her woozy or unconscious husband under the stuffing machine? She must have wanted revenge for his affair. . . . And that prenup agreement would be another strong motive.

I pulled out my cell and checked Facebook again. Peered closer at the photos Kristen had uploaded. In one, Carolyn and Debbie sat together, their lips pouting for the camera. Nickie and Isabel laughed over their drinks in another. I went back to the first photo. Was that Carolyn with Debbie, or Cissy? Both had curly blond hair, unless Cissy straightened hers.

Both had curvy figures, similar facial features, and wore red lipstick. Maybe I was wrong. But maybe that photo had been taken after Carolyn snuck out of the pub. What had Kristen said again? *I'd have taken more photos, but my phone died.*

I called Detective Mason's number, but it went straight to voice mail. Dang. "Hi, it's Sasha Silverman. I found out a little more about that 'pity party' at Quinn's Pub. Last Thursday night. Call me as soon as you can."

After hanging up, I debated sending him a text. Mason could be juggling multiple cases. He might not check his voice mail for several days. I wondered if he'd escorted Vivian home or to her bakery, all while typing with my thumbs.

Carolyn Taylor may have left pub between 11 and 12 Thu night. Going to ask Qs at her house.

I set my phone in the car's vinyl cup holder. Mason wouldn't be happy if he saw my text. He'd warned me to let the police handle things. But he wasn't quick enough for my taste; he hadn't nailed down Teddy Hartman's alibi, and who knows when he'd get back to me. I couldn't wait until our business was dead and gone for him to solve the case. I had to find out from the source.

That meant talking to Carolyn, who might not answer my questions anyway. She might not be home. I might have missed her by now if she'd gone back to her shop.

But I had to take that chance.

Chapter 28

I drove slowly past Kermit Street and turned right on Archibald. Since I'd forgotten my sunglasses, I squinted past the Courthouse Square to Delano Street. Half a mile from the village proper, the Taylors' colonial residence stood in a row of newer homes set back from the road. The lush oaks before each house had leaves barely stippled with gold and orange. I parked next door at the curb. Carolyn's car had to be in the attached garage, since the blue compact car on the street in front of her house looked too new. And it didn't leak oil.

Delano Street was far from the high school and elementary. No kids played outside. Then again, they might be inside with their video games. One car sped past over the residential speed limit. Was Carolyn at home? Or had I missed her?

There was only way to find out.

A few dry leaves scudded over the sidewalk. The house with its black shutters had two shrubs near the foundation. It looked naked compared to the Holly Jolly Christmas shop with its twinkling lights, red and green sparkly sign, and the excess of merchandise inside. I was surprised by the lack of flowerpots. Not even a petunia or geranium to add color. And I heard loud voices closer to the porch. The door was half-open, and a man and a woman argued beyond the screen.

I crept alongside the garage. Glanced back at the street—that had to be Glen Woodley's car, given his voice. If Jenny and Will had an affair, then why would Glen be here talking to Carolyn? Unless . . . I flattened myself against the door's edge, mere steps from the front porch, and listened. Not that I had to listen hard.

"—know how much that cost me? Adding on half-price dinners at Flambé across the street, when we already give them a free gourmet breakfast!"

"You could have given them a ten percent discount instead."

"That wasn't the deal. I had to pay for every meal, even for kids. And I bet Will got a kickback from the owner. They were college friends, after all," Glen spat out. "I'm gonna lose the bed-and-breakfast due to his stupid advice."

"Don't expect me to save you." Carolyn's sour tone reverberated. "I listened to him, too. That was my biggest mistake."

"But we're in a bind—"

"Quit your whining. I paid you already."

"It's like this." Glen must have backed closer to the screen, since I saw his shoulder straining the mesh when I took a quick peek. "Sasha Silverman texted Jenny. She wants to know if we saw any cars that night. What if Tyler or Mary Walsh saw me on foot going into the factory?"

Carolyn snorted. "They could have seen me, too. Don't worry. They'd have said so by now. I'm not paying you any more, so get that out of your head."

"You're sitting on a huge inheritance! We just need a little more."

"No."

"I might have to call that detective. Drop a few hints about

the real story of what happened. Anonymously, of course."
Glen's threat got a quick reaction.

"You scheming son of a—" Carolyn spewed more curses in one string than Uncle Ross at his worst. "Get out!"

"You tricked me. I didn't think you wanted to kill him. Just scare him."

"I didn't think you'd chicken out at the last minute."

"I need five thousand. That's all, I won't ask for more—Hey!" Glen sounded surprised. "There's no need to get crazy."

I figured I'd better sneak off while the going was good. It wouldn't be easy, though. My SUV was too conspicuous on the wrong side of the house. I couldn't duck for cover behind any shrubs. If only Glen had parked in the driveway.

Unfortunately, an old station wagon cruising down the street turned into the driveway and screeched to a stop—hemming me against the garage. Jenny Woodley tossed her loose brown hair over a shoulder, climbed out of the car and slammed the driver's door.

"Why are you here, Sasha? What is Glen up to? That's his car in front."

"Shh!"

"He's having an affair, isn't he? With Carolyn," Jenny snapped. "Revenge doesn't do any good. I told him I never slept with Will. I swear it."

"It doesn't matter—"

"It does, too! Just because Will took me to Ann Arbor once for dinner," she said, and rolled her eyes. "I didn't know what he wanted. He asked about buying our bed-and-breakfast, and said that he wanted to control everything on Theodore Lane. I turned him down. Called a cab to get home—"

"Shut up, Jenny!" Before I could move, I heard a loud *click* behind me. I swiveled to see Glen beside Carolyn. "Damn."

"Come inside, both of you," Carolyn said. She pushed Glen forward, her other hand hidden by a draped newspaper, but I saw the pistol's muzzle sticking out beneath the pages. "Right now."

Jenny's jaw dropped. "What?"

"Are you that stupid?" Carolyn motioned again with the weapon. "Yeah, Glen said you were dense. Get up here and you won't get hurt."

"Is this a joke? What's going on?"

"She's got a gun, Jenny," I hissed. "Move."

"Get inside." Glen motioned toward the door. "Do what she says."

I shoved Jenny ahead of me. When she stumbled against her husband, I had an urge to run. But the risk of being shot in the back—it wasn't worth it. I'd bleed out before help could come, if anyone heard at all. Better to go along. Stay quiet, see if one of us could defuse the situation. Jenny and Glen had disappeared inside. I wiped my clammy palms on my shorts and passed Carolyn, ignoring her self-satisfied smirk.

"Not so smart, are you?"

"Look, it doesn't have to be this way—"

"Cut the crap and get inside."

Carolyn prodded me up the steps with a hard jab to my spine. How had this happened? I'd only planned on asking her a few questions. My hand lingered near my pocket, but no bulky cell was there. I'd left it in the car.

Inside, the stark white décor surprised me. Everything— walls, furniture, carpet—was all white except for a pale gold sofa and two patterned Queen Anne chairs beside the white-painted brick fireplace. Even the lamps were white. The box filled with honey jars from Debbie Davison stood open on a side table, next to a large eight-by-ten wedding photo of Will and Carolyn in a white resin frame. She'd worn a white dress and carried calla lilies. It masked her black heart. She had murdered her husband after all.

But she couldn't shoot us. The blood spatter would ruin all this purity.

Jenny stepped closer to Glen, shivering. "So are you having an affair?" She sounded timid. "Is that why you're here?"

"Please. Not even if he was the last man on earth," Carolyn said.

Glen looked affronted. "I wouldn't cheat on my wife."

"Good for you," Carolyn sneered. "I've had enough of men. My first husband was no prize, either. At least I got enough money to start my business, but Will was a genuine bastard. Besides cheating on me, he kept a secret bank account."

"For his drug money," I said. "We found out he was selling drugs to the kids in Silver Hollow, along with Alan Grant and Pete Fox."

Both Glen and Jenny gasped. Carolyn laughed. "Sick, isn't it? He didn't have a shred of remorse using your teddy bears in the scheme. Will deserved to die."

"No one deserves murder."

She didn't hear me, sailing on with her complaints. "He didn't think I knew what he was doing! I saw those gym bags in his car. Looked inside once. Even followed him to the park. He always came back empty-handed, though."

"Why didn't you report him to the police?" Jenny asked.

"I found out about the bank account while he was in New Jersey." Carolyn waved her gun at me. I deliberately bumped into Jenny, who stepped backward. "Will returned Tuesday, did you know? He shacked up with Vivian that night. Wednesday, too."

"And he met with Teddy Hartman," I said. "He offered to sell our bear pattern, send our production overseas, and then merge with Bears of the Heart, our biggest rival."

"Yeah, go figure! Hartman offered him half a million if he could get all that done. That's why he wanted to celebrate Thursday night, but not with me! He bragged that he was filing for divorce. All this time, I'd been talking with a marriage counselor and thinking we could salvage things. And for what? For him to go off with that bakery bimbo, and leave me behind in the dust! I'm glad he's dead."

I folded my arms over my chest. "So you did kill him."

"Once he got rid of me, he'd marry that tramp." Carolyn looked close to tears. "Will paid off a loan she'd taken out after she had to clean up the bakery from the food fight, too. He said it was all my fault. Yeah, right! She suckered him good."

"That prenup would prevent you from getting anything after a divorce."

"He forced me to sign that. I wasn't gonna go empty-handed, not after putting up with him that long—"

A blast from Carolyn's pistol deafened me. I'd jumped toward the side table in shock, hitting my knee. Pain shot through my leg. My heart pounded in my chest and ears. Jenny Woodley had fallen over a low ottoman. Glen pulled her to her feet and kicked aside shattered pieces of her cell. Carolyn cursed, but he drowned her out.

"What the hell, Jenny!"

"I was calling 9-1-1," she yelled back. I could barely hear either of them.

"The next one goes through your head," Carolyn warned. "I've gotten plenty of practice at the shooting range, so don't try anything else."

"You can't kill us," Glen said. "It was easy with Will. He was stoned."

"Yeah, yeah. Thanks for dragging him across the factory for me," she said. "But I had to manage that stuffing machine myself, since you chickened out."

"You helped her?" I stared at Glen, whose face flushed beet red. "So you thought he slept with Jenny. Is that why?"

"How was I supposed to know he was more interested in buying us out?"

"Bingo," Carolyn said. "Will wanted his finger in every pie around here."

I faced her. "But you took the biggest risk. Pretending all night you were drunk, and then sneaking out. Someone might have noticed—"

"No one paid attention. Except you, and you weren't even there."

I hoped someone in the neighborhood had heard the gunshot and not just dismissed it as a car backfiring. "I checked your Facebook timeline and all of your friends' posts. It was odd that only one or two photos showed up. You love selfies."

"Cissy didn't want photos taken. She hadn't straightened her hair that night." Carolyn sniffed. "You know how vain she is. Especially now that she's got a new man. He'll be just as bad as Will. Wait and see if I'm right."

"So that was her, not you, in the photo Kristen took late that night. I couldn't tell until today." My voice cracked and my knees shook. "Glen's right. You can't kill three people and get away with it."

"How about I make it look like Glen shot you both, and then killed himself." She smiled at the thought. "Yeah. He was deranged. So jealous, because Will wanted to seduce his wife and then get an easy deal when you sold him the Silver Leaf. Sounds believable. But how am I gonna explain that Sasha was here as a wit—"

Glen chose that moment to launch himself across the room. He landed on top of her; the second gunshot unnerved me as much as the first. I'd fallen against the side table. My ears rang. Jenny cowered before the sofa, whimpering.

My hand closed over a jar of Debbie's honey while Carolyn shoved Glen off. He groaned, one hand pressed against his belly. A red stain spread over his shirt.

As she raised the gun, aiming for me, I threw the jar. It smacked her right above the eye. Bounced off her skull and then shattered against the brick of the fireplace. Jenny screamed in terror. I seized a second jar, but Carolyn had collapsed. Scrambling on my knees, I snatched the pistol. Just in case she regained consciousness.

Then I rushed to the kitchen. Grabbed a white towel, raced back, and knelt by Glen's still body. By now his shirt was soaked with blood. I pressed the towel against his stomach anyway, while Jenny dropped to the floor beside him. She sobbed, hysterical.

"Glen, Glen! Don't you die on me, not now!"

I'd heard distant sirens but kept pressure on the gunshot wound. Until the door burst open and Detective Mason barged in, followed by Digger Sykes, Bill Hillerman, and two more police officers. I sagged backward. Thank God.

The next half hour was a blur. My head ached from Jenny's nonstop wailing. The paramedics worked over Glen until they loaded him onto a gurney, raised it, and wheeled him out the door, IV bottle and tube in hand. Mason had shunted me aside when Bill Hillerman offered to escort Jenny to the hospital. She begged to go with Glen in the ambulance, but the cops refused. I shook my head in sorrow, hoping and praying he would pull through.

"Maybe now you understand why I kept telling you to stick to your bears," Mason said. "Anyone who kills is likely to kill again."

I gave him a shaky grin. "Okay. I was wrong. But I told you from the start that my uncle was innocent."

In the living room, Digger Sykes placed handcuffs on Carolyn's wrists. She'd regained consciousness, although remained groggy from the huge egg-shaped swelling on her temple, and moaned while a second EMS unit placed her on a stretcher and wheeled her out. Digger walked beside them.

"—anything you say may be used against you in a court of law," he continued, but Carolyn cut him off.

"Shut up!"

"You have the right to consult an attorney—"

She drowned out the rest of his rote speech, screaming, cursing, and blaming me. "All because we didn't take enough selfies!"

Once Carolyn had been carted away, my nerves finally calmed. Mason waved me over to a dining room chair. I stared at the white padded cushion.

"I've gotta go."

"Bathroom's around here somewhere."

"No, that's—That's not what I meant. It's . . . too weird."

Dizzy, my hands and body shaking, I walked outside and sat on the porch's top step, head over my knees. I gulped in fresh air. Rested a cheek on one knee. Mason blocked my view of the street, although I could see the cars lined up by the dozen. Neighbors craned their necks, and kids rode back and forth on their bikes.

"Feeling any better?" Mason asked.

I had to answer honestly. "No. Not really."

The thought of coming that close to dying, at the hands of a woman I'd trusted, gave me the creeps. Watching Carolyn wave a pistol in our faces. Seeing Glen shot and all that bright red blood on his shirt. The red spatters on the immaculate carpet, the sticky honey oozing over the hearth, the shards of glass . . . Even the amber and red footprints the cops and paramedics tracked between the fireplace and the door.

"You need to go to the hospital, get checked out," Mason said.

A gravelly voice spoke above me. "I'll take her."

I raised my head and saw Uncle Ross standing there. "I'll be fine—"

"Like hell you will," my uncle said.

I didn't protest. Not when he pulled me to my feet and led me to his jazzy blue and white Thunderbird. Mason opened the back door. My uncle pushed me onto the white leather seat, which felt cool beneath my fingertips.

"It takes almost being killed to get a ride?" I asked weakly.

"Shut up." Uncle Ross slammed the door.

I had to laugh. He stood talking to Detective Mason, so I relaxed and closed my eyes. I had survived, but Mason was right. From now on, I'd stick to selling teddy bears.

Murder wasn't all fun and games.

Chapter 29

"I feel sorry for Jenny," I said, stroking Rosie's silky fur. "Everyone in the village thinks Glen's a hero for saving his wife and me, and paying with his life. Even though Carolyn talked him into helping her kill Will. Now she's up for double murder."

"She'll probably serve a prison term for the rest of her life," Maddie said.

We sat with Uncle Ross and my parents around the large kitchen island on Sunday morning. Mom had cooked bacon and eggs, and Maddie had brought coffee and scones from Fresh Grounds. Lenore Russell, the police chief's wife who ran the Sunshine Café, had sent over a basket of fresh lemon and blueberry muffins, too. A printed note read: "Thanks, from the Chief." Tom Russell was ecstatic that the case was solved. Silver Hollow could go back to normal, and that was good for everyone's business.

Glen Woodley had survived surgery but died from complications. Poor Jenny. She'd been betrayed by Will and now was a widow. Her kids also suffered. The whole village was supporting them, but rumors had started that Jenny would sell the Silver Leaf and move back to Wisconsin where her family lived. She didn't have the heart to keep it going alone. I hoped she would find some sense of peace.

Even my mother had been shocked by my brush with death. "Thank goodness you weren't killed by that madwoman." Mom had chosen to sit beside me that morning opposite Maddie. "That was too close, Sasha. Promise us you'll never do that again."

"Do what?" I tried to sound innocent, but everyone chimed in.

"No more sleuthing!"

"I'm surprised Detective Mason didn't mention that you helped solve the case," Dad said. "I watched the whole press conference on TV. He didn't say a word about the factory, our shop, or mention your name. At all."

"That's a good thing."

"There's no such thing as bad publicity. P. T. Barnum believed it, too."

Uncle Ross poked my shoulder. "Why did you run off without telling me or Maddie what you were up to? Good thing you texted Mason. He couldn't get you on the phone and then called me. Told me you'd gone to see Carolyn at her house."

"How was I supposed to know—"

"No excuses," Maddie interrupted. "I feel horrible enough for Jenny. But losing my only sister? I'd never forgive you, Sash."

"I feel bad for Vivian Grant," I said sadly. "Poor Alan. Hooked on heroin and then falling in the river. Pete Fox never came back with his fix Thursday night."

Dad sipped his coffee. "Any drug would affect Alan's judgment, for sure."

"How did you figure out that Carolyn pretended to be drunk?" Maddie asked.

"You know how she loves posting selfies on Facebook. Except there were only a few photos, and none of them were taken by her, either. That seemed odd to me. But I'd mistaken Cissy for Carolyn in that one posted photo."

"So Teddy Hartman didn't kill Will," Uncle Ross said.

"Mason checked on his alibi about fishing. Turns out Hartman left around eight to go back to his hotel," I said. "The manager saw him arrive, too. Who else had a good motive except Glen? His jealousy is what made him help Carolyn."

"Revenge often leads to more trouble," Uncle Ross said, and then changed the subject. "So what do we do next? How are we gonna find new sewing staff?"

"I've got three lined up so far," Maddie said, smiling broadly. "All of them with solid experience. I'll start interviewing tomorrow, and if we can get them started, along with Hilda Schulte, we'll be able to handle all the orders coming in."

"But what about opening a boutique? The grunt work in the office here bores you," I said, "and that's why you're doing some freelance artwork. No, don't give me that look. I saw those cute bears on the labels Debbie is using on her honey jars. You designed them. I know your style."

"I designed Carolyn's shop sign, too. The sparkly one, and the labels for the green and red bags she uses. Used, I mean. I bet the Holly Jolly will close for sure." Maddie shrugged. "I can't leave you all in the lurch without office help. I'm not ready to open a boutique, either. Maybe next year will be soon enough."

"That's what you said two years ago," Mom pointed out. "Madeline Ann Silverman, you're quitting the office. Your dad will find someone to keep the books. You're too talented to be stuck behind a desk unless it's a table for design work. We didn't pay for your art degree to let it go to waste."

"But I love working here in the shop!"

"I'm going to talk to Barbara Davison about renting the Holly Jolly once that's all cleared out. You can rename it, of course, whatever you want. Something cute and clever. Either a design studio or a boutique. I'll help you find all the inventory."

"We'd be up against Cissy Davison's The Time Turner." Maddie sounded doubtful.

"And I know she plans on closing it after she gets married. The corner building is a perfect spot. You can hire someone to manage it, like Sasha manages the Silver Bear, and then freelance, too. That would keep you happy."

"And we'll still need you to do our fliers, the picnic poems, and other stuff," Dad said. "Like that teddy party Sasha's got in the works."

"The Cran-beary Tea Party," I corrected him. "We'll pay you, Mads, instead of your working for free. I know exactly who to hire for doing the books. Guess who called yesterday morning? She read about all that's happened this past week here in the village, in the newspapers, and was worried sick."

My parents looked puzzled, although Uncle Ross grumbled under his breath. I knew Aunt Eve had called him first, but he hadn't given her enough details beyond what she'd read. She kept us on the phone for three hours.

"Aunt Evie wants to move back from Chicago," Maddie said with a huge grin. "I said we'd help find her a job. She's certainly qualified to work in the office."

Dad slapped the table. "Hired! She helped set up the books when we started."

"What's the story from back then?" I asked, curious. "We both thought you and Mom opened the Silver Bear Shop and Factory together."

"We did, but Eve got a little too pushy. In my opinion,"

Mom said. "And your father supported her ideas and never listened to me—"

"That's not true!"

"Yes, it was," Uncle Ross said. "Even I thought you two were a bit chummy. That's not why Eve and I split, though. She's too good for me. I'm a crotchety old skank. I know it. Eve refused to put up with me any longer."

"Water under the bridge," Mom said. "That was so long ago."

"After Eve and Ross divorced, I figured you girls could learn the ropes," Dad added. "After all, the business is our legacy to you both."

Maddie jumped up and hugged him. "We're grateful. Of course we are! I love the idea of hiring Aunt Eve. She's neat and a lot of fun. I hope she can do the books for my boutique whenever I get the chance to open it."

"And she's the one who urged the experienced sewers to call us." I held up my bandaged thumb. "Perfect timing. I can go back to selling and guiding tours. I'm not cut out to battle with a needle on those machines."

"You got that right," my uncle said sourly.

"So that's what happened?" Mom clucked her tongue. "I could have tried my hand at it these last few days. I am so tired of listening to Barbara Davison going on and on about poor Carolyn, and how badly Will treated her. As if that matters!"

My swollen thumb throbbed at the memory of Carolyn ranting about her dead husband. In fact, I had yet to recover from Friday's confrontation. We all needed to relax. Despite how the phone kept ringing and orders for bears had come pouring in over the Internet since the press conference; I'd let my father handle the shop for a few days, and customers new and old were delighted. Perhaps Dad was right. Even bad publicity could be good in the long run.

Rosie suddenly rushed to the door, barking like mad. My

sister slid off her chair. "Someone must be here. That's a car horn—"

We all trooped outside, although I shut the screen before Rosie could escape. My heart broke at her sorrowful face, but I didn't want her jumping on any guests. I also couldn't buckle on her harness and leash with my bandaged thumb. I hurried after the others to the drive. A truck had pulled in beside the house. Jay Kirby climbed out, his light brown hair mussed, a three days' growth on his face. He smiled at me and waved a hand, as if in recognition.

I vaguely remembered him from years ago, when I had signed up for high school woodshop. But I'd dropped the class halfway through the term, having clobbered my thumb with a hammer. The same one now clad in a thick bandage. He waggled his own thumb with a broad smile.

"Still having fun with tools, I see." Kirby's black T-shirt had sawdust clinging to it, and so did his ragged jeans. He wore hiking boots, though, not sandals. "I brought your new mailbox. Hope it's what you had in mind."

Maddie clapped her hands in excitement. "I can't wait to see it."

"James John Kirby. Been a long time," Dad said, and shook his outstretched hand with vigor. "Your dad had that small farm on Townhall Road, right? Heard you set up shop as a carpenter besides doing all these wood carvings."

Jay nodded. "Still on the farm out that way, except my parents retired. I'm using the barn as my studio. You need something?"

"A small room inside the factory to enclose our stuffing machine. With shelves for the cotton fiber we use. Name your price."

He lowered the truck bed's tailgate. "I'll work up an estimate."

"Good. I don't want anyone viewing a murder scene." Dad

slapped the truck's metal. "We're not running a little shop of horrors on Theodore Lane."

I squinted in the bright sunshine, watching Jay Kirby lug a tarpaulin-wrapped item out of the truck and set it on the ground. When he pressed a button on his jackknife, the blade shot out. Then he cut the thick twine in several places and removed the canvas covering. We all gasped in delight to see the darling brown carved bear, about four feet tall, standing on a metal mailbox. On either side of it—her, since it was a mother bear—two smaller bears cavorted on all fours. The box was far too large to have been placed inside the bear's mouth.

"I thought it was supposed to be a teddy bear, not a realistic bear," Mom said, "although at least the mama bear is smiling."

Jay glanced at me. "If you don't like it—"

"We love it," I said firmly. "The two baby bears are a perfect fit for our shop selling toys for children. Visiting kids will think it's adorable."

Uncle Ross examined the squared four- or five-foot stump of wood, the mailbox mounted on it, and the carved trio of bears atop that. He scratched his jaw. "How are you gonna stick that into the ground?"

"With this." He brought out a long metal pole. "Goes right up the stump's center. Keeps it stable and should last awhile."

"Then I'll set bricks all around that wooden mount. The next car that smashes into our mailbox will wrap around it like a taco shell!"

"I'd set it farther from the curb. Mailman could pull in the drive a bit, and deliver that way. Up to you, though," Jay said. "I sent out a post digger yesterday, but no one was around to get your okay. He went ahead with it over here."

"Let's get cracking then," Uncle Ross said.

Jay Kirby tugged a dusty bag from the truck bed, a bucket, and a stick crusted with old cement. Maddie, Mom, and I walked back to the house.

"I still wish it looked more like a teddy bear," Mom said.

"I bet if he'd done that, and stuck the box in the mouth, it would have scared all the little kids," I said with a laugh. "What a dumb idea. It wasn't Maddie's design, you ought to know she could do better. That was all mine."

"Everyone in Silver Hollow will love this mailbox," Maddie said. Mom went ahead of us into the house, but my sister hung back. "Jay Kirby is pretty hot. Isn't he your age? And single."

I knew exactly what she meant, given the rising tone in her voice. "I'm too busy to worry about anything but the shop. We've got to get started on the designs for the printed menus, the place cards, the tags on the table centerpieces—and our tea party is the first kickoff of the whole Oktobear Fest for the village. Summer's almost gone, you know. You've got less than a month to get everything done."

"Come on. Maybe he'll teach you how to hold a hammer the right way."

Since she was teasing, I ignored that. We'd be too busy for anything but putting our plans into action. No time for mayhem or murder. I crossed my fingers.

Things were getting back to normal, and we had no worries facing us. Aunt Eve would arrive soon, and that meant Maddie would be busy showing her how she'd been running the office and keeping the books. Uncle Ross was happier, with a bigger sewing staff. And I'd soon take back managing the shop from Dad. He needed to take it easy, since his cough lingered.

Life was good. Until Flynn Hanson's Mercedes screeched to a halt on the street. He pulled in around the group near the new mailbox, pushed up his shades, and then leaned out the open window.

"Hey, Sasha," Flynn called out, waving. "Got a minute?"

I groaned aloud.

A NOTE FROM THE AUTHOR

For those of you who are a little bit crafty, I would like to share a Coats & Clark crochet pattern for "Beach Bear Rita"★ with you via my Web site. Come visit me at

www.megmacy.com/crafts-of-bears

and take a look at this adorable little bear who is all decked out for the beach. I especially love the little blue bow on her head and the pail she's carrying with a goldfish in it . . . not to mention the yellow ducky float around her waist. Okay, basically I love everything about it! My sister made one of these in a weekend, so I know that it does not take long to make.

Enjoy!

Meg Macy

★Used with permission from Coats & Clark

Watch for the next

Shamelessly Adorable Teddy Bear Mystery

BEAR WITNESS TO MURDER

by
Meg Macy

Available in June 2018

Connect with U(s)

Visit us online at
KensingtonBooks.com
to read more from your favorite authors, see books
by series, view reading group guides, and more.

Join us on social media

for sneak peeks, chances to win books and prize packs,
and to share your thoughts with other readers.

facebook.com/kensingtonpublishing
twitter.com/kensingtonbooks

Tell us what you think!

To share your thoughts, submit a review,
or sign up for our eNewsletters, please visit:
KensingtonBooks.com/TellUs.